ENEMIES

ENEMIES

THE GIRL IN THE BOX
BOOK SEVEN

Robert J. Crane

ENEMIES
THE GIRL IN THE BOX
BOOK SEVEN

Copyright © 2013 Reikonos Press
All Rights Reserved.

1st Edition

AUTHOR'S NOTE
This book is a work of fiction. Names, characters, places and incidents are products of the author's imagination or are used fictitiously. Any resemblance to actual events or locales or persons, living or dead, is entirely coincidental.

Layout provided by Everything Indie
http://www.everything-indie.com

"I don't have a warm personal enemy left. They've all died off. I miss them terribly because they helped define me."

—Clare Boothe Luce

Dedicated to the memory of my aunt, Betty Jo McGuire, who never had an enemy in her life.

Acknowledgments

These people are not my enemies.

Kea Grace – Beta reader extraordinaire, this time around she scared the hell out of me by helping to put threats into the bad guy's mouth. Really, hanging someone from a meat hook? And they call me imaginative.

Carien Keevey – Kept a weather eye on my grammar, spelling, and other assorted parts of speech. Also gave some great story notes and feedback that helped me keep my eye on what I was trying to accomplish this round.

Julia Corrigan – Helped put the final polish on the work, keeping me out of the grammatical ditch, as it were. Many thanks.

Heather Rodefer – Fought me tooth and nail about the ending and ultimately helped me make it even better, in my opinion. Also helped put the polish on the manuscript and helped turn it into one of my best.

Karri Klawiter – Took the phrases, "Black and white," "Silhouette of a girl," and "London" and made a cover from them. Now that's talent.

Sarah Barbour – Edited, vetted, and generally made the whole book stick together. As usual. Also, she knew what kind of cat Ernst Stavro Blofeld had, so she is uber cool in my book (which is this one).

Nicholas J. Ambrose – Took the file and turned it into a book. Like magic. I'd say *Voila!* But he's English, not French.

The City of London, England – I started writing this book while I was there, and many of the experiences Sienna had were in fact my own experiences as an American traveling abroad for the first time. Though I didn't get my pocket picked by a handsy

Irishman on the tube. Luckily.

My family – Constantly supported me, kept me sane, and occasionally reminded me to take a day off. Love you all.

Chapter 1

I stared at him, he stared at me; he knew he was only centimeters from death. A gentle stroke of the trigger of my gun, and his loathsomee brain would be decorating the Coldplay posters on the wall behind him. It was a delicate air between us, him and me, as the world kept going somewhere outside the four walls of James Fries's house. There was a smell in the air, his cologne—heavy, overdone. It was just like everything else about him, from the leather jacket that looked like it would cost more than a third world country's GDP to the finely manicured nails, each smoother than the last, to the chiseled features that most girls would die for. More than a few had, actually.

"So …" he said casually, not meeting my heated glare. My gun never wavered off of him and he knew it. He was doing everything he could to try not to appear cowed by the subordinate position I had maneuvered him into. "We're just going to sit here until—"

"Yep." I maintained a level gaze at him, trying hard not to take my eyes off him even to blink. He was cagey, this bastard, overly clever, and I didn't want to provide him an opening. I didn't really think he was going to try something, but part of me really, really wanted him to, just so I could have an excuse to kill him. And I'd have to kill him, if it came to that, because I couldn't fight him, not right now. I was missing a hand from a battle I'd been in earlier in the evening. I had the stump carefully covered up, unwilling to let him see my weakness before the appendage had a chance to grow back. "The less you talk, the more likely you are to maintain the structural integrity of your skull all the way through to the end of our time together."

He gave a half-hearted laugh, but it was a thing of the wind, a subtle breath of air like a hiss rather than anything remotely jovial. "You're not going to kill me."

I didn't even blink as I fired. Twice. "No?"

Blood seeped across his clean white shirt and dribbled down his chin. A steady ooze of red radiated outward from both sides of his chest. "Bitch," he said, and a cloud of red and spittle was brought out by his speech, wet words tinged with the air and liquid seeping into his lungs from where I had shot him. "This won't kill me."

I watched as he slumped on the couch, the stains on either side of the buttons that demarcated the center of his chest growing worse by the second. It had been pretty decent aim, I thought, to put one in each lung, stopping him from calling out. He wheezed as he slid limply down the couch to a resting position on his side. I sat in my chair across the room, watching, never taking my eyes off him even as he registered the agony of what was happening to him. "You ..." he gasped, trying to force air into his lungs. It wasn't staying in, however, but draining out and filling his chest cavity. I was strangely unmoved, both emotionally and physically, as I watched.

"If you're going to call me a bitch again, you can save your breath," I said, keeping my pistol leveled at him. I aimed for the head this time. I really didn't think he was going to do anything threatening in his present state, but he was rapidly outliving any uses I had for him. The sting of phantom pain in my missing hand was making me ornery. Either that, or the recent rash of people I had killed had eliminated any desire on my part to be merciful to one of the most prolific serial killers I had ever encountered.

It was actually rather sad that I could say he wasn't even close to the most prolific. The man (beast) with that singular honor still resided in my own head.

"This won't ..." He spat up blood, even as his cheek pressed against the cloth of the couch he was now splayed on. He didn't look like he had much control over his limbs. The smell of gunpowder was thick in the air, finally blotting out his awful cologne. I was thankful for that little blessing. "This won't ... kill me ..." he gasped out then went silent, a torrent of red flooding out of his lips as his eyes glazed over, then closed.

"No," I said, relaxing in the chair, letting the gun slide out of my grasp to rest on my lap, "but it'll damned well shut you up." His muscles relaxed, and his body went limp on the sofa. I saw the soft up and down motion of his chest as he continued to breathe in spite of his injuries, his meta-human physiology already working to repair the damage I had done. "And frankly," I said, rubbing my eyes, which were burning, with my remaining hand, "that's all I need from you at present."

Chapter 2

"Was that truly necessary?" He sighed and shook his head almost paternally. I didn't buy it.

"Hello, Janus," I said. He had walked in without a word, seen Fries lying in a pool of his own blood, and cast me the look. You know the one—something between disappointment and resignation.

"Hello," he said, somewhat gruffly this time. He gave a wave of his hand at the mess of Fries on the couch. "Is this to be the omen on which we open the next chapter of our relationship?"

I tried to keep from curling my lip. "I saw the way Kat was all over your suit last time; I think I'd prefer something like this as an omen rather than something that might leave you open to any suggestion."

A wry smile, a little self-deprecating, made its way over his stony facade. "Fair enough." He stiffened, his tweed suit coat rustling as he went upright, as though someone had hit him in the back. "Good gods, he's still alive."

I shrugged. "Yeah. And ..." I frowned. "You just said, 'Good gods.'"

He stared at me in concentration, as though he were picking through his last statement. "Yes? What of it?"

"You self-reference in exclamation?" A deeply disturbing thought crossed my mind that caused me to grimace further. "Wait ... when you're with Kat, do you call out your own name?" My face soured, utterly beyond my control.

"If I may," Janus said sternly, "this man is still alive."

"Barely," Fries groaned, his eyes still closed. He was splayed out on the sofa, arm draped over the side.

"Oh, stop milking it, you big faker," I said. "You're fine."

"You shot me in both lungs."

"You're probably halfway healed by now," I said. "Besides, your boss and I have things to discuss."

"Do we, now?" Janus said with a cocked eyebrow. His beard was looking a little longer than when I had seen it a week or so ago. "Very well, then. You had James summon me from my business in Texas." He spread his arms expansively then nudged Fries's legs out of the way. The incubus groaned before moving them reluctantly, and Janus sat down, careful not to park himself in the puddle of blood. "What would you like to talk about?" He eyed the pistol in my hands. "And, before we begin, do you truly feel as though you need that?"

"Strictly for him," I said, gesturing to Fries.

"I don't think he'll be giving you any more problems," Janus said and gave Fries a sharp slap to the hip that caused the younger man to grunt in pain. "Isn't that right, James?"

"I will give you no difficulties," Fries said, gasping. "You, on the other hand, have given me—"

"A down payment on future pain," I said. "I could make another installment now, if you'd like."

Fries went quiet, and Janus gave a slight, almost imperceptible nod of agreement. "So," Janus said, "what shall we talk about? The state of the world? Employment opportunities?"

"Erich Winter," I said.

"Mmm." Janus gave me a slight nod. "Not one of my favorite subjects, I will admit. But very well. What about him?"

I watched the old god's eyes, and he watched me. "You know what he did?"

"Indeed I do," Janus said slowly. "Rumors percolate quickly through the meta world, especially when one spreads money around with recently unemployed persons who used to work for—"

"You paid some of the agents that used to work for the Directorate?"

Janus gave another easy shrug. "It would be foolish of us not to. We give them a little 'severance package' to compensate them for the fact that Erich Winter did not, and they are kind enough to send a few whispers our way." He grew more serious. "I was ... very sorry to hear about what he did to you, of course."

I didn't blink. "Your organization has done almost as bad or worse to me. Winter only metaphorically ripped my guts out. You remain the only ones who have done it literally."

Janus gave a slight grimace. "I have already apologized for this ... unkindness on the part of previous management, but if you'd like, I'd be more than willing to tell you how sorry I am again—"

"And I'd be no less likely to believe it now than I did then."

There was a faint settling of the lines at the crow's-feet around his eyes. "This is a problem, then," Janus said, his voice smooth. He rested his left hand on the wooden edge that was exposed at the end of the arm of the couch, relaxed. "Without trust, it will be difficult to have any sort of communication between us. I could tell you many things, but ..."

"Stow it," I said. "I'm not looking to trust you on anything other than a limited basis. But you want Winter dead, and I can deliver."

"Ah, but in point of fact I don't care whether Erich Winter lives or dies at present," Janus said, "so long as he continues to stay out of my way. Out of Omega's way."

I narrowed my eyes at him. "Are they one and the same— your way and Omega's?"

He shrugged again. "Not necessarily. I am hardly the Alpha of Omega, if you'll pardon the pun."

I rolled my eyes. "As I understand it, you have an entirely

different Alpha trying to batter down Omega at present."

His expression darkened though only briefly. "An unfortunate group of upstarts and malcontents who suffer from delusions of being a far greater danger than the nuisance they actually represent to us."

"That's not how I hear it."

"Yes, well," Janus said with a little bit of snap, "when you only hear one side of the story, you shouldn't be surprised when it turns out one-sided."

"Rather than two-faced, you mean?" I ignored the heavy sigh that Janus let out in response. "I'll give you credit, it was clever," I said. "Did you come up with that one all by your lonesome?"

He gave me a wary look. "We can't all be as witty as you. But … you want Winter, then? To fit him for a coffin, I expect, like you did with the others?"

I stared at him through narrowed eyes. "Which former Directorate employee told you about them?"

To his credit, he didn't blink away. "None of them. One of our cleverer technical fellows managed to get coroner reports for Clary and Parks, as well as a crime scene report for Kappler's condominium." His words came out slowly, almost as though he were chiding me. "That one was quite messy, as I understand it. Bullets in the walls, blood everywhere, two women missing."

"One's alive," I said coolly.

He cocked his eyebrow again. "Ah, the fabled Ariadne lives on to provide guidance to the next one to try and get out of the maze." He waited for me to respond, and when I didn't, he went on. "Because, you see, the original Ariadne, from myth—"

"I got it." I thought about it for a second. "But that wasn't her—"

"No," he agreed. "The original was quite a bit … huskier than you might have imagined." He shrugged. "Theseus did what he had to do, you know." His hands came to rest on his knees, and I watched his fingers knead them. "So, Winter. You want him dead, and you think I can help you in some way."

I let my gaze drift from Fries's inert body to Janus. "Can you?"

He stood. "I could, but I would only do it if you give me a compelling reason, not out of any need Omega has for him to be dead." He looked at me carefully. "If you want Winter, you must negotiate for him."

I let out an impatient sigh. "This isn't a negotiation."

"Everything in life is a negotiation," Janus said. "If we were to decide to go out for breakfast—" My stomach rumbled at his suggestion—"and you wanted Chinese but I wanted Greek, which would we decide on?"

"I generally don't think of egg drop soup when considering breakfast," I said warily. "I prefer real eggs."

He waved a hand at me dismissively. "You know what I am saying. We would discuss back and forth, have a bit of give and take, if we were reasonable people. I would try to persuade you to my way of thinking, you would try to persuade me to yours. The give and take, yes? I'd like this, you'd like that—"

"I'd like medical attention," Fries said in a low moan from the couch.

"You're about to get *my* attention again," I said and pointed the gun at him. "Will that suffice?"

"No," he croaked.

"No is a good word," I said, "You should learn what it means when a woman says it to you."

Fries looked up at me. "I—"

I pointed the gun at him, refining my aim to put the white dot of the center sight just below the middle of his forehead. "Choose your next words carefully, James." I waited, and he said nothing. "Good choice." I looked back to Janus. "What do you want from me?"

He smiled, his teeth showing only the slightest bit of yellowing. "I want you to come to London, to Omega headquarters. I want you to see how we work, the scale of what we're currently involved in fighting." His smile faded but only slightly. "I want you to join us."

I felt the slow grind of my molars. "No, thanks. I've already been part of one sham of a meta organization that nearly killed me. You know what they say about not learning from your own mistakes, right?"

He stared at me blankly. "I don't believe I've heard that one."

I ran the old phrase back in my head to make sure I had it right. "A wise person learns from the mistakes of others, a normal person learns from their own, and a fool learns nothing, ever."

"So does that make you a fool or normal?" Fries asked me with a pained cackle.

"I've shot you on several different occasions now," I said, "so what does it make you for continuing to get shot by me?"

"I'd avoid you if I could."

"Come on, James," I said with a little false enthusiasm, "you can do it. Try harder."

"If I may," Janus said, "might we come back to my offer? I could give you assurances that Omega means you no harm—"

"All of which are meaningless to me," I said, "because of Wolfe, Henderschott, Fries," I waved the gun at the mess of James still huddled on the couch, "Mormont, the vamps, Bjorn—hey, he's a real charmer, and now I'm stuck with him forever in my head—"

Janus's eyes twitched closed for a moment then reopened as he grimaced. "He is … with you, then? In your mind?"

"Usually at the moments of least convenience," I said. "He's blissfully quiet right now." A voice sounded in my head: *Just listening, Cookie.* "It would appear I spoke too soon."

A slight look of concern crossed his face but he waved it

away. "This is ultimately irrelevant."

"It's relevant to me; he's really annoying sometimes—"

Janus's expression darkened. "I meant to our discussion."

I rolled my eyes. "Try living with three former employees of Omega in your head. I swear, the only thing I have more of than former Omega employees is former Directorate ones." I went on, feeling a little like a gossip. "And Gavrikov! Do you know he never shuts up about your stupid girlfriend?"

"You want Winter," Janus said, his voice straining to get us back on topic even as he seemed to be trying to keep emotion off his face, "I can give you assistance in killing him. But there will be a price."

"Why don't you just tell me where he is and call it a ... present." I smiled. "Like a goodwill present to make up for all the shit you've put me through."

His expression turned to pitying. "Let us call him what he really is—leverage. A motivator for you to begin going through the actions it will take to convince you that Omega is the sole force fighting to preserve meta-humans from the impending calamity that Century is bringing."

I felt a tug at his words. "I don't care about Century. About any of that." *Liar, liar,* Zack said quietly in my head.

"No?" He stared coolly back at me, and let a hand go to one of his pockets, smoothing it shut. "I find it hard to believe that somewhere, beneath that ... hard-edged exterior you carry around you, that there is not a care present at all for your fellow man— and woman, I suppose they would say nowadays."

"I care about paying back Winter." I let the knife edge in my voice reflect the emotions I had beneath the surface. "I want him to die for what he did to me. You give me him, and I'll help fight your little war."

He hesitated, thinking over his next line, and I caught a hint of pity. "It is a war that belongs to all of us, I think. I hope in time you will see the truth of that."

"So long as I see Erich Winter's head on a pike first."

Janus gave me a low nod, but his shoulders seemed a little more slumped than when he had come in. "Very well. I will set our intelligence gathering in motion to track him down. But," he said wagging a finger at me, "it will be some time before we venture off to get him, even if we were to locate him tomorrow. That is the bargain—you will come with me, see our efforts. I tell you this so there is no misunderstanding. You see our work, what we do, and in three months, I will give you Erich Winter. Can you agree to that?"

"Will I find him without you?" I asked sarcastically.

He shook his head. "I think not. He has not survived for thousands of years through countless feuds among our fickle and murderous people by stupidly walking into danger." He waited in silence for a moment before speaking again, as though hoping I would leap into the conversation to answer before he had to ask the question. "Will you come with me to London?"

"Please do," Fries said with a low moan.

I gave it a long thought; there was a strong disagreement in my head. I don't just mean that I was internally at war; I mean that Wolfe, Gavrikov and Bjorn were enthusiastically supportive of the idea of me going to London—to meet with Omega, to pursue revenge—while the other voices, Kappler, Bastian and Zack, were somewhat more reluctant. It was like being in the middle of a shouting match, and I could barely make out all the different arguments being made in my head, just the general tone.

"Will you come with me?" Janus asked again, and the cacophony died down.

I stared at him for a long moment as I went through all the options. "Yes," I said, and there was a chorus of disharmony in my head at the decision. "I don't see any other way to get what I want, so yes." I listened in particular to one voice, one that I almost had to strain to hear behind the other, louder ones, but it was there. Zack. My love.

Watch your back.

Chapter 3

The flight was crowded, full to the brimming, actually, but it was direct from Minneapolis to London, and so I couldn't complain about that. The sterile air in the plane was dry, and I felt it cause my nose to dry out with it, as if I had inhaled a desert into my nostrils. The guy next to me was on the wrong side of thirty with earrings in both ears and sandals—sandals! In Minnesota. In winter. Try to figure that one out. He was dressed like the kind of guy who would go around calling everyone "bro" but probably let it slide into "brah." He also rudely hogged the entire armrest on that side in spite of my efforts to find a place to rest my elbow, thus pushing me into the overlarge woman in a black suit who sat to my right. She wore a sleeping mask, had five different pillows stationed about her body for comfort, and had been lightly snoring since takeoff.

It was my first flight, and I didn't know anything about flight etiquette, but as the person in the middle with no armrest and her hand (and stump) folded across her chest, I was about ready to unleash some of my fury by throwing my elbows outward. Unfortunately, that would kill my seatmates which, I sensed, would please no one but Wolfe. Perhaps it would please me. The pain that my hand was causing as it grew back was staggering, and a few times I bit back the urge to beat someone to death from both that as well as garden-variety annoyance with the whole situation.

The dull blue pleather seatback was stretched in front of me after I lowered the grey tray table to let my hand and half-hand rest on it for a change. I inhaled the dry air, taking a sip of the cup of water the flight attendant had brought me a few minutes earlier, trying to contain my annoyance at being mushed by the guy I called Brah and the Sleeper. Janus had wisely booked himself into first class using his corporate advantages. I hadn't complained at the time, but I certainly was prepared to give him an earful upon landing. I let the low thrum of the engines carry me off to sleep.

I stepped off the plane some nine hours after takeoff at Heathrow airport. In truth, it didn't look dramatically different from what I had left behind, save for the boring, by-the-numbers hallways that took me to customs with Janus trailing somewhere behind.

I had gone home before meeting Janus at the airport and packed clothes. I had a spare passport under the name Sienna Clarke that I flashed at the area of customs where there were signs referring to it as the UK Border. I wondered at that, since it seemed to me I was well within the country at this point, but it wasn't really my place to argue the semantics of national borders.

The clerk stared blandly at me for a few moments. "Purpose of visit?" he asked.

"Tourism," I answered, and he gave a sort of half-shrug and waved me on after handing back my passport.

I met Janus in the terminal near the baggage claim area. I had nothing to pick up, but he stood there in his tweed suit coat, waiting expectantly around a silver steel merry-go-round composed of segmented belts. He flashed me a sideways look. "This is where we part ways for a bit."

I looked back at him in disbelief. "Huh, what? I just got here."

"Indeed you did," Janus said. "And you are most welcome to go to our headquarters, if you'd like—"

I changed to a glare of annoyance. "I'd very much NOT like."

He gave a simple nod. "As I suspected. I am not presently going to our headquarters; I am going to take a taxi and visit Klementina before I return to working on Omega business tomorrow morning." He ignored my look of distaste. "Therefore, we part ways here. We have booked a hotel for you in the city, and I have a bit of pocket money for you to spend." He handed me a wad of twenty-pound notes. "I will meet you tomorrow morning for breakfast in your hotel lobby. Ah." He reached down and swept a small suitcase off the luggage conveyor in front of him.

"What am I supposed to do now?" I asked. "It's—" I looked at the clock hanging high above us from a wall, "—it's not even noon here yet."

He looked unworried as he began to roll his bag away, toward a sign that indicated taxi service. "Take the London Underground to the Russell Station stop." He indicated the wad of bills he'd handed me. "There are directions to your hotel on a paper note with the bills. Go on a sightseeing tour, see a film at the cinema, whatever you want." He shrugged. "You are here visiting, and thus in charge of your own time. Enjoy it." With that, he turned and began to walk away again.

I watched him go, feeling only the slightest edge, some irritation, but beneath it was the real driver of my present emotion. I looked to either side of me. There were crowds of people jockeying along the baggage carousels, while others breezed past me, bringing their own intoxicating mixture of smells and sight, their clothing ranging from the bright to the dim. The sound was loud, the chatter of a thousand voices. I watched Janus leave and felt the little tether between us that I hadn't even been aware of dissolve.

I was alone again—but this time in a land I knew nearly nothing about.

Chapter 4

I found the entrance to the London Underground without much difficulty. Signs were clearly posted, and helpful employees seemed to be stationed at the sticky points to help me through. I managed to procure a ticket for Russell Square's tube station from a finicky machine that didn't immediately want to accept the first note I fed into it. After it finally acceded and spat out a ticket, I made my way through the gates and waited in a big, open, tiled space that was like a cylinder laid on its side. Within the cylinder was another, this one cut into the ground in front of me and stretching off to my right and left, tracks running down the bottom of the channel. As I was looking from the edge of the platform, I felt a stir of air begin to blow from my right, out of the blackness that I knew would eventually spit out the train I was waiting for. I caught a whiff of that same filtered air that was so prevalent on the plane, but this was cooler somehow, less dry. It sent a tingle over my flesh as I took a step back from the edge of the platform.

A few seconds later, lights appeared in the dark and a train of red and silver burst forth, sliding at high speed along the tracks to come to rest in front of us. I lost count of how many cars were hooked end to end on it. A few people came out when the doors opened, more entering with me as I hesitantly walked inside. I carried my small duffel bag over my shoulder, my right hand clamped tightly on the strap.

It was hard not to feel out of place as I sat down on one of the vacant, padded, dark blue cloth-covered seats. The air was a little musty, and I heard a high-pitched whine as the train began to move. I looked around the car and saw that it was mostly couples traveling together on the train with me. A few serious looking passengers in business attire were sprinkled in as well, suitcases on rollers trailing behind them. I reached into my bag and popped a piece of mint chewing gum into my mouth to counteract the taste of bad breath I'd acquired after a nine-hour flight that included two in-flight meals.

Brightly colored ads were crammed above the windows, fighting for my attention with the flickering blackness outside that was broken whenever we passed a light. Part of me wanted to count the stops; another didn't care. I looked at the map across from me; I didn't even know how many stops on this line there were between me and Russell Square, but I knew it was a lot.

After just one more stop, the world opened up outside the windows as we came out into the light and the train began to run along a surface track. It was a sunny day in London. I recalled reading as a child that sunshine wasn't the most common state of weather in London, especially not in November. I knew from the weather warning upon landing that it wasn't terribly cold, either; in fact, it was somewhat unseasonably warm. I looked out the window and saw a sky tinged with scattered clouds, but a gorgeous blue was visible beyond them with the sun shining overhead.

After another stop, I stood, leaving my comfy padded blue seat behind and taking up position next to one of the overhead hanging rails near a door. I couldn't stand sitting anymore, not after the long flight, and based on the slow progress through the first few stations, I estimated it would take over an hour to get me to my station. When we reached the next stop, the doors opened and the stale train air was replaced with a smooth breeze from outside, with just a hint of warmth from the sun under the bite of the wind.

I looked out over the suburban cityscape. Houses with red-tiled roofs covered the land as far as I could see, broken only by the trees and occasional commercial buildings that filled these towns. I wondered how far off London itself was, how long it would be before the London Underground truly took me back under the ground, into the dark, and far away from the beauty of this moment that seemed frozen in time.

"You should have been here with me for this," I whispered as the train doors shut with a squeak and a hiss. "It should have been on our list."

Sorry, babe, Zack said. *I wish I was there, too. But I'm with you in ...* His voice in my head hesitated before finishing with enough amusement to cut through the graveness of the thought, *... spirit.*

"Not funny," I muttered. There was a weight on my heart as I stared out the window, the houses just past the station blurring as we began to move. Soon we were back underground again, the darkness around the train swallowing me up, the flickering of the lights overhead causing the whole compartment to go dark for a moment.

I felt a tug of something before the lights went back on, a person behind me, a hand in my bag, another in my back pocket. It was the lightest sort of touch, something expert, something I shouldn't have felt. But I did, as if a tingling feeling was coursing over my body in the places where I felt the abnormal pull on my jeans and the tightness of the bag's strap on my shoulder as it moved ever so slightly.

I whirled without thinking and slapped my newly regrown hand down on the one in my pocket, then put my other on the one that was in my bag. The lights came back on and I stared into wide eyes; a guy, a little older than me, a little taller, dark hair, and a mustache that was waxed at the ends. He was not terribly bad looking in a way that made me want to only drain him to within an inch of his life instead of taking it entirely. Looks used to count more for me, but my prior experience in relationships was going to cause me to cut him a lot less slack than he might have gotten a year earlier.

"Damn," he said mildly in a deep Irish lilt, an easy grin breaking across his face, though he still looked a little flummoxed, "never had that happen before." I maintained my firm grip on his wrists, and he didn't struggle. He gave me a wink. "Can't blame a lad for trying, though, can you?"

"I can not only blame you for trying," I said, clutching onto him, "I can make you suffer for it."

He cringed. "Ah, lass, not the forgiving type, are you?" The last word came out sounding like "ye" when he said it. "That's all right." His eyes flicked to his right. "This is my stop anyway."

The train began to slow and he snapped my grip around his wrists, much faster than a human could have done it. He reeled his arms back toward him and backed to the door a step. He looked at me a little warily and I saw him blink away a little lightheadedness as he looked at me, perplexed. His little move would have sent a human flying across the compartment. I didn't break eye contact with him, didn't take a step back; my balance and strength kept me in place, feet spread in a ready stance.

Adrenaline coursed through my veins and there was a little thrill of excitement within—whether from one of my ghostly accomplices or myself, I couldn't say—at the prospect of a fight. I tightened my hands into fists and watched the Irishman catch his balance, his pale skin, mustache, and two days of beard growth giving him a shadowed look as he snapped into a fighting stance of his own. It was looser, less martial arts, more boxing, and he gave me a little juke as though the mere threat of it could get me to back away. I caught a hint of sadness in his eyes and a dullness that told me he was still feeling the effects of my prolonged touch from holding his wrists only a moment earlier. I knew that he was a meta; I wondered if he had figured the same out about me.

"I don't think you know what you're getting into, little lady."

He raised his hands in front of his face like a boxer, as though he were going to throw a jab. His eyes flicked right again. The train was slowing; the station wasn't far off.

"Right back at you, Irish," I said and threw a jab that breezed past his defense, popping him in the nose. I heard the crack of the cartilage; I don't throw weak punches. His eyes crossed as he looked back at me and adjusted his defenses as he staggered from the force of my hit. For my part, I grinned and hit him again, this time in the cheek. His head crashed into the steel frame of the carriage door.

He tilted his head as he regarded me carefully, watching for my next move even as he tried to clear his head. "Canadian?"

"American."

"Shoulda known. So violent!" He bounced off the doors and took a swipe at me that I dodged. "Gah," his words slurred, "of all the times for luck to fail me."

I punched him in the jaw, holding back just a little. "It does not appear that fortune is with you today."

With that he sagged against the door, mouth open and dripping blood. "You noticed that too, eh? I'd always heard she was a finicky bitch, but I never had cause to believe it 'til now." He held up his hands in surrender. I hit him again, in the nose then the gut and let him drop to the ground. "I effing surrender, all right!" he said from the floor, slapping the ground as though he were tapping out of a wrestling match. "In case you didn't notice, I didn't actually get my hands on your wallet or any of your personal belongings—"

"You had your hand in my back pocket," I said. If he moved in any way I deemed dangerous, he'd be the recipient of one my kicks to the side of his head. It *might* not kill him, but luck would have to be on his side or I'd have to be feeling incredibly charitable. The jury was out on whether either of those would come to his aid. "That's a highly inappropriate way to touch a stranger."

"I assure you," he said, adjusting his nose back into place with a crack, "I did not actually touch you at all; not your posterior, not anything else. I was reaching for your wallet, but apparently you felt the little bit of pull on the outside of your pocket because most of the time I can keep from touching the person at all as I'm nicking their stuff." He adjusted himself on the floor of the car and leaned back against the doors as we surged to a stop in the station.

"You're not exactly selling me on why I shouldn't beat the ever loving crap outta you," I said.

"Miss," came a voice of a man from behind me, "could you please kick that thieving git in the head for all of us?" A man behind me said it, but a few others began to clap. "Can't even use the underground anymore without worrying some pickpocket's going to nick all our valuables."

I looked back at the fallen Irishman. "The people have spoken," I said to him with a shrug, as though I weren't in total control of the situation.

"Oh, for crying out loud ..." he said, staring up at me from where he rested against the doors, head back. They opened, and he tumbled out and past the crowd that had gathered at the door to get on at this stop. I watched him roll to his feet, but something held me back from following him onto the platform. "Welcome to London," he said with a kind of weary air, and he tipped an invisible hat to me as he gave me a slight smile, one that was shot through with sadness and relief in equal measure. I waited, and the doors slid shut. I saw him dust himself off, blood running down his face. I gave him a hard look as the train started to move. I saw fear and something else in his eyes as he stared back before breaking eye contact and shuffling off toward the staircases that led off the platform.

I retrieved my bag from where it had fallen, even as the

whispers swirled both inside my head and out of it, the car alive with chatter that hadn't been present a few minutes ago. Surprise, amazement, condemnation, and much worse.

And inside my head … the chorus and cry was loud. I shut my eyes and leaned my head back as it unfolded into a full-on conflagration, the argument blowing up as forcefully as if someone had pulled a grenade pin between my ears and let it drop where it may.

Chapter 5

You let him walk away, Bjorn said, his thick accent bleeding through over the train noise, making it recede in the background. I could almost see his face hovering in front of me, the flat monstrosity that he had been before I had drained the life out of him.

"I didn't let him walk away," I said, massaging the skin around my eyes and speaking low in the back of my throat, without moving my lips, "I made a decision not to kill him for picking my pocket while I'm in a new country for less than an hour."

Seems strategically sound to me, Bastian piped in, his tone clipped. *It's new territory, unfamiliar ground, and making a big splash out of the gate is a bad idea.*

As though she weren't just covering for her weakness, Eve Kappler chimed in, and I could almost see the snide, snarky look she would have been wearing.

"I killed you, didn't I?"

But didn't have the guts to finish the job on yourself, Eve taunted.

There was a triumphant silence for a moment before Wolfe spoke. *The Little Doll was just being cautious, careful not to stir the pot. She'll find him later, this little creature, track him, and then—*

"Do you even know me?" I asked, fingers digging into the sensitive flesh at my temples as though I could break my skull open and let the voices escape.

"Next stop, Russell Square." The voice spilled in through the fog that seeped in around my senses, dampening them and forcing me into a sort of cloud that covered me. My feelings of taste, of touch, of smell were all muted, and it was almost as if I could see the six people in my head hovering in the air around me, ghostly, like a wave of fog around me. I could still see the train car, but everything was darker, less clear, and the rattle and shake of the train was much less noticeable now.

She did what she had to do, Zack said, becoming clearer in my mind. His arms were folded; he was stern, my bulwark against all the other voices in my head. *Getting into legal trouble in England would be stupid, especially over such a trivial thing.*

If someone crosses you, Bjorn said, fury oozing out of his essence, *you must break them. Like she did with Winter's lap dogs.* I could sense Eve and Bastian bristle. *You crush your enemies, drive them before you—*

Enough, Conan, Zack said. *That's not how Sienna does things.*

Maybe she should, Bjorn said, and I caught the seeping sense of smug satisfaction. *If she did, you might not be dead—*

Because Old Man Winter would fear her enough to not try what he did? Zack seethed in my head, and even in his ghostly form, the tension wracking the body he no longer had was almost palpable.

There was a ripple of amusement from Bjorn. *If she had been strong enough to begin with, willing to do what was necessary, Winter would never have thought she needed the lesson he gave her.*

"And I'd be fortunate enough to not have you in my head," I said pointedly to Bjorn, stealing some of his joy, "because I'd have killed you deader than meatloaf in our last battle—which would mean you wouldn't be here now."

"Now arriving, Russell Square." The voice cut through the fog again, and I staggered out of my seat. I looked around through the dim and saw people watching me, wondering if I'd been talking out loud. I walked unsteadily to the doors as they slid open, and wondered how long I'd been on the train. I couldn't even remember the last stop or the one before it.

Losing your mind? Gavrikov whispered underneath everything.

"I'm not sure." I held my hands up to the sides of my head, as though I could clear it by doing what I'd been doing for the last few minutes, but I was failing miserably.

Makes sense, he said quietly. *It is the last thing you have to lose, isn't it?*

I staggered up the platform, large tiles covering the walls in a strange mosaic pattern. The platform was narrower than I expected, roughly the size of the train, and I followed the glaring sign that said, "Way Out," with an arrow pointing to the left.

Little Doll isn't feeling so well, Wolfe said in a voice almost like a chirp. I shook my head, trying to rid myself of the spin that had taken it over. I wondered if I was ill but only dimly, as though my brain weren't working at its full capacity.

Are you all right? Zack's voice was filled with concern. I could almost feel his hand on my wrist, trying to help me up.

"I'm fine," I said, taking the steps two and three at a time as I climbed to where a crowd waited in front of an elevator. Signage told me that the "Lifts"—the Brits and their damned word differences; it's an elevator—were on reduced capacity. The crowd filled the area, and my eyes veered to the right, where a sign announced that there were 179 steps to the surface. It also suggested not climbing them, making me wonder what the hell they were there for if not to climb.

I shook my head again, trying to ignore the swirl of conversation that was now happening behind eyes as they all talked, talked, talked. It was like I wasn't even there, that all the people currently occupying my brain were having a meeting and I, the one who actually owned the body, wasn't even in attendance.

Something is very wrong with her, Zack said in concern.

Under stress, Bjorn said, not concerned but wary. *She's—*

Weak, Kappler said. *She'll crack, just watch. I can't believe I was killed by this whelp, she is so pathetic—*

She's tough enough to kill you, Bastian said. *She'll get through this. It's a difficult time—*

All difficult times, Wolfe said, relishing my pain. The stairs thudded under my feet, but I barely noticed them. I started to run, my bag slapping at my sides. The walls of the spiral staircase were closing around me, the tiles a mosaic of dim colors, of darkness spinning around, as though they were lit up and not just some dull tiles from the 1980s or earlier. The world spun as I went up the staircase, and my reflexes allowed me to dodge around the one person in front of me, though I heard a gasp from someone.

I needed air, needed to breathe. The world was tight, and I hit my head on the ceiling as I took a high step. I didn't bother to check, but I knew a normal person wouldn't have done that. Even I wouldn't have done that, not unless I was jumping or doing something I shouldn't. My chest felt tight, my mouth felt dry, and I wondered what Omega had done to me, if anything. I hurried up the steps, and the taste of the meals I'd eaten on the airplane came back on me, acid reflux, in the back of my throat, gagging me. I kept on running until the stairs emptied into a hallway that I followed into the main station. I leapt over the gates that separated me from freedom, not worried about giving them my ticket, just trying to get away from the confining space, the world closing in around me.

I burst out into the cool, sunny day, autumn in full glory all around me, and caught a blustery breeze. It wasn't as bad as what I'd left behind, that much was certain, and it took me only a moment to get my bearings before I hurried down the street, hoping no one would follow me, or that if they did, I could lose them. There wasn't much of a crowd; it was the afternoon, and some stands were set up to my right to vend fruit and newspapers. I ignored the smell of citrus as I went by, though I realized I suddenly wanted a drink of it, of orange juice.

Can't handle the pressure, Bjorn said, and he shook that flat face of his.

Can't shoulder the weight of responsibility, Eve said.

Little Doll, Wolfe said with a wicked grin.

You're falling apart, Gavrikov whispered.

I hurried on, taking the turn when I saw the street I was looking for. Russell Square's greenery stared back at me from the opposite corner. I ran up a block as fast as I could, without thinking. I felt myself breaking into a sweat. I didn't know what was wrong with me but it was dire, urgent, and I needed to get away from public eyes. I heard the honk of a horn as I started to step out into the street and I saw a car coming toward me without stopping. I didn't even think, just pivoted into a spin and brought my leg around into the air, then down like an axe in a straight line. My heel landed on the hood of the car and I heard the bumper hit the pavement as I completely arrested the forward momentum of the vehicle. There was a sharp sound of the engine falling out, along with the transmission and several other vital parts, and I stood there in my ready fighting stance, breathing heavily, sweating uncontrollably. The driver stared at me from behind a deployed airbag with eyes as wide as any I'd ever seen.

Well done, Little Doll.

Not as weak as I thought—

Strong—

Run, Sienna.

She has a fire in her, Gavrikov said.

Run—

Getting better, Bjorn grudgingly admitted. *Like that—*

RUN, SIENNA! Zack's words lit an alarm in me, and I took

off down the way, hugging my bag to my side as I tore up a street, dodging down the next avenue at a speed I usually didn't exhibit in public. I saw the sign for my hotel and slowed, ducking into the entrance. I stalked across the lobby to the front desk, wiping the heavy perspiration off my face, off my hands.

The girl behind the front desk was young, maybe only a year or two younger than me. "May I help you?" she asked softly, in a thick Russian accent.

Like Klementina—

A Little Doll, she should be played with—

I shook the thoughts that weren't even mine out of my head. "I have room reserved for Sienna Clarke."

The Russian girl looked at me with her delicate features and bright blue eyes. "Can you spell that, please?" I did, and she fumbled with her computer. "I have you here for … indefinite stay?" She blinked and looked up at me as though to confirm.

"For now," I said, almost gasping. I needed to get out of sight. Needed to do something to cool down my overheating skin, to stop this panic attack or heart attack or whatever attack I was having.

"May I see your passport?" She reached out a hand out to take it from me and I offered it over to her. She took forever, typing things into the computer.

She'd be such a sweet taste, Bjorn cackled.

Could taste her for hours, Wolfe said.

You're disgusting, Eve pronounced.

"If you could hurry, that would be great," I said, catching the clerk's eye.

"You have free breakfast—" she started.

"Don't care," I said. "Room key?"

She blinked at me again and wordlessly handed me a little card that would unlock my door. "Room 7015." She handed me a small piece of paper. "Present this if you want the breakfast—"

"Thanks," I said, and snatched the key card and my passport

out of her hand. She pointed wordlessly to a hallway behind me and I walked toward it before she got another word out. I saw elevators as I rounded the corner.

She'd be a sweet meal, Bjorn said. *Could enjoy her for a day or so before she was all done.*

Little more than an appetizer, Wolfe said with a grin that made me ill(er). *You would need something heartier afterward, to get the taste off your tongue. Something like—*

"Oh, God, you people are appalling," I gasped as the elevator door dinged and opened to discharge a few people. I got in and hit the close button repeatedly before anyone else could get on.

Little Dolls are the sweetest meat of all, Wolfe seeped into my head. *Little girls, they're like—*

"Shut up, shut up, shut up, shut up—"

Don't be so crass, Wolfe, Bjorn said with a grin of his own. *The girls should feel special, privileged to be chosen out of the whole world of humans, to be consort to gods—*

"You're a special sort of disgusting, and I'd like you to shut up now."

This is pathetic—

So weak, can't even control her own mind—

Shut up—

I could use a taste of something Russian right now, maybe a French girl afterward as a chaser—

The little blond ones are the best, they're so smooth—

Just leave her alone—

You're all pigs—

Like Klementina—

"SHUT UP!" I screamed, pleading. "SHUT UP SHUT UP SHUT UP SHUT UP!" The elevator dinged and I staggered down the hall, the world pitching from side to side. The dull grey walls were closing in again. The elevator had been like the box, and the hallway wasn't any better. I heard movement behind the doors, and I hurried along, running now, watching the room numbers blur past, until I finally reached my own. I halted, slowed down, let myself breathe for a moment before I gently slid the key card in the reader and heard it beep then I forced the door open and shut it behind me. It still slammed, even though I was being gentle.

"Shut up," I whispered. "All of you, shut up. Just shut up. All of you—"

Can't stop us, Little Doll—

So weak—

No control—

She can't handle it—

There was a moment of fearful blackness, and there was a voice in my head that I hadn't actually heard in months, along with a face, one more reassuring than any other I could picture.

"Hold it together, Sienna."

I could see him behind the fog, but just barely—Quinton Zollers, a man I hadn't seen since he'd left me lying on the floor of his office. "Hold it together, just hold it together another minute—"

I passed out, slipping into the great dark void of nothingness, and I hoped I would be away from this chaos long enough that the others in my head would be gone when I got back.

Chapter 6

I knew her name was Adelaide when I saw her fight. It was inexplicable, but the knowledge simply appeared in my mind, just as I knew the fight I was watching was taking place several years before the time I was dreaming it. There were still ads on the walls of the train and the words carried a British accent, but everything else seemed older—or newer, as the case may be, as if it were the same trains, the same stations as they passed, but from an earlier time.

The 1980s.

The car was bobbing as the train went on, and Adelaide (how did I know her name?) had a mohawk. It wasn't a subtle one, either, but a full-blown spiked one, divided out into six good points, as if she could drive them into the heart of her foe and put a swift end to him. She whirled in a low kick and I saw her take his legs out from under him. He caught himself on a seat and bounced back up, even though I heard the crack of his back as he did so. People were backed away from the middle of the carriage, where the fight was going on, mashing themselves up against either wall of the compartment as though they could somehow push themselves through the walls and get away.

"You're not much of a fighter," Adelaide said, licking her lips, keeping her distance, her dark, ragged jeans and studded leather jacket giving her more the appearance of punk rocker than any kind of fighter. "You sure you don't want to just pack it in?" She moved fast—meta fast.

He was no slouch either, though. He was bigger than she was, well over six feet, bald, looked like he ate steroids for every meal and at snack times, too. He was in leather also but the more subtle kind, like a biker. He had an earring in one ear, and when he came at her with his hand knotted into a tight fist, he reminded me of Clary, only bigger.

She grabbed onto one of the anchor poles that was designed for passengers to hang on to, used it to whip herself around, and neatly evaded his attack while sweeping in from his own height with a brutal kick that laid open the side of his face from the force she put into it. She had a wicked grin the whole time, as if she was enjoying it. When he staggered, she followed up with a flurry of punches that pointed his nose in a new direction and made his lip over into a bloody Hitler mustache.

"I think I could do this all day," Adelaide said, taunting the man as he staggered. To her credit, she didn't slack off; she came at him from the side and pummeled him with a brutal strike to the back of the ear that sent him to one knee. He threw a backhand at her, but it was sloppily aimed and all it did was force her to take a step back. As soon as it was clear, she threw a roundhouse kick that snapped his head forward. He hit the wall of the train and the whole thing seemed to shake, as if it had been knocked off its tracks. I heard metal against metal, a grind as though the brakes being applied, and then the world seemed to slow down.

He whipped a hand around again in that moment and a blast of wind flung Adelaide through the air and sent her crashing into the window, splintering the glass where she hit. I heard the thud, could almost taste the blood from where she'd bitten her tongue, and I could feel the sharp pain in the back of her head. "Aeolus, huh?" she muttered from where she came to rest on the seats, lying across them as though she were splayed out on a couch.

Her foe rose to his feet, his considerable bulk showing in the flash of the overhead lights. "I prefer … *Fūjin*."

Adelaide squinted at him, blankly. "What?"

A flash of insecurity showed on the bald man's face. "It's …

Japanese. Wind god. You know, it's more … it has cachet."

She looked at him from where she lay. "Cachet?"

He stammered. "Y-you wouldn't understand, it's a … it's … I'm not like the others, okay?"

"Really?" Her head bobbed in slight disbelief, and she whirled her legs around to stand. "You're not like the other aioli?"

The man who had called himself Fūjin flushed. "I don't think the plural of Aeolus is aioli. That's a garlic sauce."

Adelaide got to her feet and squinted at him. "You're no garlic sauce, that's for sure."

The big man squinted back at her. "Are you gonna fight or what?"

She spread her arms wide. "You're the one with the range advantage, mate. Throw a vortex at me and we'll see what happens."

Fūjin shook his head. "You don't understand. I can wreck this car, this train, kill all these people and you with them."

Adelaide put her hands up in a defensive posture, as though she were ready to box again. "Then why don't you get to it and quit chatting shit?" She stayed out of his arm's reach. "You know why you don't? Same reason you're down here fighting me to begin with. You got a serious case of indecision, mate."

The big man looked down at her in pity. "You're calling me undecided. How old are you? Twelve?"

"I'm eighteen, but don't go changing the subject," Adelaide said. "You ran for the tube the minute you heard me coming for you, and when you couldn't get away in time, after taking a pounding, you finally decide to unleash your powers. You're undecided. You're not willing to let loose and do what you'd have to in order to stop me from taking you out."

"I don't see you coming at me right now," Fūjin said. "The minute you do, you might see me change my mind."

Adelaide smiled. "And won't that be an unfortunate thing for these poor gits." She waved at the back of the compartment, where people were stacked up three deep trying to melt their way through the wall. "You're not a proper villain, and I respect that. But you're not in control, either."

"I'm not coming with you," Fūjin told her, "not coming to … them." He stared back at her defiantly, his fingers outstretched. "I'd die before I went to them—and I'm in control of that."

Adelaide took a long, slow, deep breath in through her nose then shook her head slowly. "Not really." Her body was relaxed, from top to bottom, the points of her hair moving with the nod, like fists raised in solidarity. Without any warning she dived as though she were jumping for a Slip 'N Slide, and came in low, underneath Fūjin's raised hands. He fired off a burst of air, a tornado, but it went high over her head, dispersing in a blast of air when it hit the side of the compartment.

Adelaide slammed into his knees with her shoulders, managing to avoid ramming her head into his thighs. She hit with such force that I heard both legs break and Fūjin screamed in pain, which was made worse when she lifted her head and rammed her skull into his groin with bone-breaking force. "Mind the gap," she muttered, "as you've got one down there, now."

As he squirmed, his broken legs wrapped around her head, she stood, carrying him on her shoulders using her back, and brought him up, where his head slammed into the top of the train. She brought him over like a waterwheel and pivoted, slamming his head and neck down on the nearest bench. He hit with brutal force and the seat didn't yield. His face, however, did, Adelaide's meta strength smashing it to pieces against the hard object. She finished him with a booted kick to what was left of the back of his head, and his skull turned to a fine mush right there, splattering the grey plastic with a fine mist of red for several seats in every direction, coating the nearest ones with a thick spatter.

She stood there for a moment after, staring down at her

handiwork, her face covered in red, and then she looked up and saw herself reflected in the window. "You never had a choice, mate," she whispered, and her black leather sleeve came up and wiped her face, streaking the blood, smearing it in. "They didn't want you alive."

"Next stop, Piccadilly," a human voice came over the loudspeaker. "Piccadilly Circus."

Adelaide took one last look at herself in the reflected glass as the lights flickered on and off in the car briefly and shadows swallowed half her face, covering her, giving her the look of someone lost in the darkness. Her eyes were haunted when the lights were on then pools of blackness when they weren't. I saw them, and they looked familiar. Somehow I knew this was her first kill.

The train ground to a slow stop with a screech, and Adelaide looked to the people on either side of the compartment before stepping to the door. She didn't bother making a sign or any sort of gesture at them, just stepped up to the doors in the middle of the train and waited for them to open. "It'd be real smart if you lot were to wait for the next stop," she said, and there was nothing but menace in the way she said it. "Anyone who gets off here is likely to suffer from some ill health, if you catch my meaning." She pointed a long, thin finger at the mess she had left of Fūjin on the bench. "So, please, catch my meaning and stay on the bloody train." There was a squeal of unease and the people bunched at either end of the compartment backed away from the doors.

Adelaide looked at herself in the window one last time as the doors opened. She self-consciously wiped her face once more, but there were a few spots of blood still on her forehead and there were flecks of other matter in the spikes of her hair. She slid out before the doors were completely open then looked back from the platform at the train. No one got on at that compartment, and the platform was nearly empty. She waited until the train started to pull out of the station before she made her way toward the exit, toward the stairs, and somehow, I knew, the sunlight she hoped was somewhere far above her head.

Chapter 7

My head felt like someone had taken a hammer to it with righteous fury, over and over again with a staccato rhythm. The world tasted like dirt and smelled worse. After a minute I realized it was because my mouth was pressed against a solid, slightly fuzzy object—the floor. Sunlight was blazing into my vision and I blinked my bleary eyes then closed my dry mouth, which apparently was dry because I had been drooling in a puddle on the carpet of my hotel room. I didn't recognize the place at first, but after a moment I knew that's where I had to be.

There was still an insistent hammering coming not from inside my head but from behind me. "Sienna?" a thickly accented voice said, muffled, and I pulled myself to all fours in an effort to locate the source of the noise. I turned as I smacked my lips together and the thumps began again. It was the door, and someone was knocking. "If you don't answer the door by the count of three, I'm going to break it down."

"Hold on," I said, my voice scratchy and hoarse. I rolled to a seated position. I had lost consciousness in the narrow hallway of my room, just after getting inside and slamming the door behind me. My muscles ached, my tongue had a crust of filthiness on it that contained just about the worst flavor I'd ever tasted, something between foot odor and dumpster remains, and I felt nauseous. I looked to my side and saw the gaping opening to the bathroom. I rested a hand on the trim and used it to hoist up to my feet. I felt something drop off my shoulder and realized it was my duffle bag; I hadn't even laid it down before I passed out.

"Sienna?" the voice came again, and I reached for the handle and opened the door. Light streamed in from outside, too, where Janus stood expectantly, a pocket watch clutched in his hand, a particularly fine suit making him look like an aging banker. His grey hair was meticulously in place, and he peered at me through thin glasses as though he were concerned. "Are you all right?"

"I don't know," I said, blinking at him. A wave of nausea overcame me and I was forced to turn away, to dive for the bathroom where I hit my knees and heaved with no grace whatsoever. The smell of the toilet and what came out of my mouth only made it worse, doubling my nausea, and I retched again. The foul taste of the bile erased the disgusting aftertaste I'd woken up with and replaced it with the burning, acid flavor of what I was returning now. It came from the bottom of my stomach then from what felt like the bottom of my feet, I heaved so hard.

"So," Janus said in a mild voice from the doorway, "I take it you enjoyed your first night in England a bit too much?"

"What?" I said, taking a breath between heaving my lungs up. "How long have I been here?" I put my head back down in the toilet and threw up again.

"I left you at Heathrow yesterday," he said, somewhere between impatience and amusement. "You must have made fine use of the downstairs bar and the legal drinking age of eighteen."

"I …" I heaved my last and sat back on my haunches. "I …"

"I don't really understand such things," he admitted, "but then, I grew up in a time long before drinking ages, when everyone had wine for every meal, even as children."

I smacked my lips together as a milder wave of nausea passed through me. "How lovely for you."

"It was a simpler time," he said. "Are you quite finished?"

"For now, I think." I felt a pressure in the back of my throat. "Never mind." I bent my head down again.

"Good Lord," Janus said after another minute. "And now?"

"I hope so," I whispered. "Dear God, I hope so."

"We have business to attend to today," he said, and I heard the click of his pocket watch snapping shut. "Do you need a few minutes to ready yourself?"

"Ready myself for what?" I asked, rolling over to put my back against the wall. I stared up at him and caught a pitying look as he glanced back down at me.

"Ah …" He stepped into the bathroom, leaned over the bathtub, and grasped a small towel folded on the edge. He wet it under the tap and handed it to me from a distance, as though afraid to get too close. "You might wish to consider wiping your mouth."

"Thank you," I said acidly and did so. I slung the wet towel across the tub's edge when I was done. "What are we doing today?"

"I thought we could get breakfast," he said. "A working breakfast."

"Lovely," I said, resting my head against the tiles of the wall. They felt cool even through my matted hair.

"I suppose I could understand if you're not very hungry."

"I'm surprisingly ravenous," I said, "though I did just lose everything I've ever eaten and possibly things that my ancestors ate as well."

He gave a light chuckle. "I can wait if you need to clean up."

"Sure," I said, gingerly getting to my feet. My stomach seemed to have settled, at least for the moment. "Let me get my bag, and you can wait for me out there." I gestured vaguely toward the small room that lay beyond the hallway.

A few minutes later I emerged from the bathroom. Fortunately my ponytail had spared my hair from my gastrointestinal reversal, so I only had to rebind it. I showered quickly and dressed, avoiding the ordeal of washing my hair. I stepped out of the bathroom a few minutes later, fully clad in jeans and a sweatshirt, to find Janus standing at the window, which was open about three inches. He glanced back at me. "You didn't even make it to the bed, did you?"

"No," I said, laying my bag on one of the undisturbed single beds, the brown, ages-old comforter not leaving me with much confidence that it was clean in any way.

"You didn't drink last night, did you?" he asked, and I could hear an edge of suspicion.

"No," I replied.

"Perhaps … some illness from the travel," he said, staring at me carefully, his hands in the pockets of the vest beneath his suit coat. I realized it was the vest that made him look like a banker. Having the pocket watch anchored there was an interesting affectation; he looked every part the proper and distinguished gentleman.

"Let's hope," I said. It probably went without saying, but I did not want to talk to him about the voices in my head, not remotely, not in any way. They were a problem, a weakness, and the fact that they could drive me to blinding pain was hardly a new discovery to me. The fact that they could somehow render me unconscious was cause for concern, but it didn't need to be any concern of his.

Also, I was pretty sure I'd seen Dr. Zollers, the real one, invading my head, and speculating about what he was doing in there was probably a quick path to a whole tangle of mysteries that I didn't have answers to. Like, had he been the reason I'd had the vision of Adelaide?

"Ah, well, my girl," Janus said, and he was hesitant but reassuring. "Let us go, then." I knew he was an empath, and it didn't take much for me to immediately jump to the idea that he was reading me, knew I was reluctant to talk about any of it, and decided he was better off not asking. Part of me wanted to curse him for that; the other part wanted to know what he knew. I gave him a sidelong look that he ignored in favor of walking toward the door, leaving his back exposed to me. I ignored the opportunity;

he'd given me no reason to club him unconscious—yet—and despite what Omega had done, Janus hadn't wronged me. Again: yet. I was still watching for it.

The day was cool but not bitter, and he buttoned the bottom two buttons of his jacket as we hit the street outside the hotel. I supposed that with the couple of layers he had on, he was probably quite warm. I had brought a thin fall jacket, just in case, but honestly, the weather wasn't anything compared to Minnesota. This was merely brisk.

I followed him down the grey sidewalk as cars rushed by next to us on the road. I looked for a minute at the drivers, on the wrong side of the car to my Americanized mind.

Janus was shrewd enough not to say anything as we walked, and we crossed the street at the next corner. Every one of the buildings seemed to be about three stories high, except for the couple of hotels that jutted out of the middle and ends of the block; they were a few stories higher. The rest seemed to be of roughly uniform height, and I wondered how long they had been there. The fact that they all melded together in a similar style intrigued me. It was rather like housing developments with a complementary look that I had seen back in the U.S.

We came to a Greek restaurant and halted outside the glass facade. It had bold yellow letters across a faded blue canopy that extended over a half dozen tables scattered across the sidewalk. It was blustery enough today that no one was brave enough to eat out there, though, and Janus made a great show of staring at the menu in the window, while keeping his voice low. "Greek breakfast has never been to my taste."

"Is that because you were a Roman god?"

He gave a slight shrug of the shoulders. "It is true, I did miss the Hellenistic days, having not been born yet when so many of my contemporaries were milking the lands of Greece for all they were worth. It is possible that I did not learn to acquire a taste for some of the foods that were so popular to them, having grown up on more traditional Roman fare." He gave a short chuckle. "Which is nothing like that which you would consider Roman today. Food is one area where I am thankful for the advancements that technology has brought us. Others of our kind who lived in those days, and even those who didn't, they act as though it was some glorious time, halcyon days where wine was poured directly into our mouths by beautiful women, where every need, whim and desire was granted without thought or concern for those involved." He got a far-off look in his eyes. "I don't see it, though, the romanticism of it all. I lived in those times, and yes, we exercised the vital powers in ways that we no longer do, held sway in the courts of the world in a way that has faded, receded, but the way we lived ..." He let his voice trail off.

"I bet it was a real bitch living without flush toilets," I said, my voice hoarse from my morning's activities.

Janus gave me a slight smile. "You have no idea. The hygiene ... Humans had it easier than us, of course, with our superior sense of smell and taste. When we lived in palaces, I took baths every day, sometimes multiple times per day when it was hot, and the ones who didn't ..." He shuddered. "Bacchus was the worst. He would drink himself into a stupor, soil himself, then never bother to clean up, going back to the alcohol and letting the smell offend the rest of our nostrils, as though he weren't covered in his own feces." He gave a small noise of disgust. "I was not sorry the day that Zeus dashed his brains out, though there was more to it than that, of course—"

"What was his power?" I asked, half-listening to Janus and half-studying the menu. The food was beginning to appeal to me a little, the nausea receding. I read the description of the British breakfast, eggs, bacon, tomatoes and baked beans, and wondered a little about the inclusion of the beans. There was a blissful quiet in my mind, a kind of peace that I couldn't remember feeling in a long while. The peace of no one talking.

"Hm?" Janus looked up at me. "Oh, Bacchus? He was a Persephone-type, but he never wasted his talents for influencing life on mere humans, preferring instead to treat with vineyards, speeding the growth of their vines in exchange for wine. Quite the sot, as they say."

I squinted at the menu. "Persephones can grow plants?"

"Oh, yes," Janus said, "quite well. A Persephone can cultivate a field of thriving plants in the middle of a snowstorm." He frowned and turned to me. "Have you not seen Klementina do that before?"

"You mean Kat," I said, almost grinding my teeth. "I've seen plants respond to her touch, but I didn't know she was growing them."

"Indeed," he said. "A Persephone has a bond with life, influences it with the touch, can augment it, make it grow, guide it in the directions she so desires. I suppose if the Kat … personality, as it were," he said, almost sheepishly, "did not have much experience with the power, it would probably be somewhat limited. A Persephone with full command of her abilities," he clucked his tongue and shook his head slowly, "well, it is different from what you've seen, I suppose."

"Marvelous," I said, uncaring. "Are you going to eat?"

"Ah, yes," Janus said, "just one minute more." We waited, and I looked at him until the door opened to his right and a girl a little taller than myself stepped out. She looked just a hint younger too, dressed in black shirt and pants, with an apron tied across her waist. She wore a broad, feigned smile as she stepped out to greet us.

Her hands were neatly clasped in front of her. "Good morning," she said with an accent. "Can I help you?"

"We were considering breakfast, my dear," Janus said with a condescending sort of sweetness.

"We have the best Greek breakfast in town," she said, her accent only faintly noticeable; she showed no sign of knowing Janus, and I wondered what his game was.

"Of that I have little doubt," Janus said, pouring it on thick with his own brand of sweetness. It reminded me of seeing an old man flirt with a waitress. I thought about Kat and Janus and realized that I might in fact be witnessing just that. I started to feel nauseous again and wondered if I was about to be involved in a thousand-year-old man making an effort at picking up a teenager.

"Why don't we go inside and take a seat?" he said to me, jarring me out of my reverie. Personally, at that moment I wanted to be about a thousand miles away or, barring that, at least in a different restaurant with the man, preferably someplace with guys as waiters. That might be more palatable.

"Come right in," the girl said and held the door open for us. Janus made a great show of stepping inside, gesturing for me to follow. I passed the waitress with a little reluctance; part of me wanted to tell her to get out while she could. "My name is Athena," she said, and that part came out sharply accented, "and I'll be your server."

"Excellent," Janus said as she led us to the table. "Do you know where your name comes from, Athena?" I realized somewhat belatedly that Athena was in fact, Greek, and working at a Greek restaurant. Coincidence? Doubtful.

"I was named after the Greek goddess," Athena said, a little off balance, "of wisdom, inspiration, law, justice, strength—"

"Let us call her what she truly was," Janus said somewhat broadly, "a woman who encompassed the ability to speak to the betterangels of our nature, to borrow a fitting phrase."

Athena cocked her head at him. "Ah ... all right. What can I get you to drink?" she stepped aside at the table she had led us to while Janus and I took our seats. We were near the front window, and behind us was a long counter. To either side of us were unoccupied tables set up with seats for twos and fours but no larger groups. They were all unoccupied, and I wondered what time of day it actually was. I was guessing I had missed traditional breakfast hours and we were about to shift to lunchtime.

"I will take a glass of wine, whatever the house white is," Janus said with a wave. He glanced at me. "My friend will take water."

I blinked at him in confusion. "I will?"

"It might be best for your stomach," he said. "And you, Athena?" he asked, turning his head to look at her. "What would you like?"

Athena blinked at him in confusion. "I … uh …" She seemed to strain the very boundaries of her English, looking for what to say. "I'll get you your drinks—"

"Why don't you sit with us for a few minutes?" Janus asked, and he said it gently. It was strange, but the way he did it compelled even me. I wanted her to sit even though a moment earlier I didn't care what she did.

"All right," Athena said hesitantly and pulled up a chair from a nearby table to sit between the two of us. I stared at her, and she stared at me from behind her thick-framed glasses. On a man, they would have been hipster glasses. Hers were older, I guessed, and probably all she could afford.

"Athena," Janus said, "I want to tell you something. Something you already know, really. You are not a human being." She blinked back at him and started to speak. "Now, now, let us not play games. You were raised in a cloister, I would guess, around other metas, yes?" He tilted his head to look at her with a piercing gaze, and I saw her burn beneath it like an ant under a magnifying glass. "You need not answer. I can tell that it is so. You ran away, yes? From home? To the big city of London?"

She nodded, hesitant. "I found … passage … a job … from a man in a nearby town, to work in his brother's restaurant here in

London."

"Ah, so you came from Greece itself," Janus said with a smile that was cool, a little distant, something beneath the surface. "And your family? They remained in the cloister?"

It was her turn to be cool; her eyes shifted downward. "Yes."

There was a moment of quiet, and Janus seemed to take stock of the situation before speaking again. When he did, it was lower, wearier, and infused with candor. "You know, don't you?" She looked up at him, and he looked back. "That something is coming?"

She gave a slow shake of her head. "I heard rumors. Before I left." Her raven hair hung loose around her shoulders, straight and perfect, in a way that I only wished mine would. "That something was coming. Something bad. Cloisters were disappearing, ones where the village elders had known each other for hundreds or even thousands of years, just going quiet in eastern Asia, Turkey, eastern Europe."

"Ah," Janus said, and there was no mirth or light in his expression, only a sad understanding. "Yes, something is coming."

"Death," Athena whispered then seemed to catch herself. She looked for a moment as though she wanted to stuff her hands over her mouth, as though she could crowd the thought back into her, as if she'd never spoken.

Janus cocked his head. "It certainly brings death. But what do you know of what is coming? Have you seen—"

Athena began to shake and placed her palms flat on the table. After a minute of silence she removed them, and there were wet spots of moisture in the shape of handprints left on the table where she had rested them. Her eyes came up, and I realized they were a dark brown, the irises shadowed in the low light of the restaurant. "The village elders talk of a darkness that spreads from the lands of old, of enemies coming back from a bygone time." She leaned forward and whispered. "They talk of whole villages being wiped out, villages of metas strong and powerful being erased from the land." She looked left and right, as though someone might hear her. "I left so they wouldn't find me."

Janus leaned back in his chair, crossing his legs and adopting a thoughtful posture. "Have you heard more than rumors?"

She was quiet then, looking down. "My father was an elder. He traveled to Cappadocia, to a cloister there, one that had been there for thousands of years. The elder there was powerful, had been a local deity in his youth in the days of the Romans." It took me only a moment to realize that she was speaking of the days of the Roman Empire. "The village was dead."

Janus stirred, only a little. "Dead?"

Athena nodded, meek as a mouse. "As though he had come upon them himself."

"He?" I interjected, looking to Janus, who shook his head subtly, as though trying to warn me off.

"Athena," Janus said, causing her to look back to him before she could answer me. "What was the state of the village? What did your father say he saw?"

"Bodies," Athena said quietly. "Bodies everywhere, in their homes, in their places, lying on the floors and in beds, as though *he* had come for them."

Janus held out a hand to stay my questions, putting it up as though he could ward me off by a simple wave of his hand. "Athena, dear," Janus said, "it is not him. It may, perhaps, be someone with powers like his, but I assure you that it is not him destroying villages. Indeed, I can assure you that it is not even the same meta every time—"

"No, it is him," she said, swallowing, her throat making an unnatural motion. "My father was there for the last time he spread his fingers across the lands, and he said it was exactly the same, the same thing happening, the same darkness." She shook her head in disbelief. "You can tell me a thousand times I am wrong, but a thousand times I will tell you I am right, that he has returned to cover the land in his darkness again."

No hand was going to stop me this time. "Who?" I asked, and I said it loudly enough, insistently enough, that she broke out of her focus on him and looked to me, her dark eyes shining. "Who are you talking about?"

She looked at me with a hint of confusion, then let her gaze stray back to Janus, who seemed to shake his head in resignation. With that little permission given, Athena turned back to me. "Death, of course. Him. The one who would destroy the world and claim all the souls for his own."

My mouth was dry, and the air had gone still in the restaurant. The sun shining in from outside felt like it had been captured behind a cloud, and I was left to stare at her, probably open-mouthed at the words she had used.

"You know," she said to me, waiting for a reply that I couldn't give. "Him. Death.

She gave a small shudder, and the name came out in a fearful whisper.

"Hades."

Chapter 8

"Hades?" I asked Janus after we were done in the Greek restaurant. "She thinks death is coming for us all, the literal one, the guy himself."

"I assure you he is not," Janus said stiffly as we walked down the sidewalk, not in the direction of my hotel but the opposite way. He kept himself upright, not deigning to look back, and I was left to follow along.

"Is he still alive?" I asked, trying to match his speedier pace.

"No," Janus said simply as I came alongside him, our reflections catching my eye as we passed by glass shop fronts. "He is long dead."

"Was he an incubus?" I watched for his reaction, and he semi-cringed.

"No," Janus said finally. "He was not."

"But there's more to the story than that?"

"There always is," Janus said, eyeing me with something approaching annoyance. "The important thing is that we have convinced Athena to come in from the cold, to get her under Omega's protection."

"Speak for yourself," I said, "I didn't convince her of anything. I'm still not sure that being under Omega protection is any better than being left to die under the gentle auspices of Century."

He gave me a wary eye. "You think death is preferable?"

"Death is preferable to a great many fates I can think of," I said with only a hint of bitterness.

He didn't speak for a moment, but his pace slowed. He kept

his eyes focused straight ahead, then placed his wrinkled hands in the pockets of his suit coat as the wind whipped between us. "I suppose I would see that way as well, if I had experienced what you have of late."

"Yeah, well," I said feelingly, "you haven't, so—"

"You think I have not experienced great tragedy in my life?" He gave me an almost amused look, one eyebrow raised. "You think I have not been horribly betrayed before?"

I narrowed my gaze and looked at him. "I doubt you've ever had the people you trust most force you to kill the person you love."

He stopped dead on the sidewalk. "I watched my parents killed before my very eyes by Zeus himself, in a fit of pique. I was ten. You see, Artemis, my mother, dared to resist his charms, his advances," he took a step closer to me, "and when my father, Apollo, intervened to save her, he too was killed by Zeus's rage. I watched him, powerless to do anything to stop it, until there was nothing left but ashes when the fire from the electricity subsided. I have lived in the presence of monsters my entire life and tried to never become one myself. Years later, I got to see a human mob kill a god. Of course, they did not know she was a god. She was only six, after all." His expression grew darker. "Still, they killed her—witchcraft, devilry, something of that sort—before I could intervene. This was after I left Zeus's court and tried to live among the humans to avoid the games of power and politics. The girl was my daughter, and to see them kill her with a sword before I could cross the hundred feet between us ..." The air went out of him. "Well. It was the last regret they ever had, their hasty action, because I was not hasty in my revenge at all. Thorough, but not hasty.

"There are monsters everywhere, and that was my lesson that day. Human, meta-human, it matters little. The entire race is compromised, shot through with weakness of emotion, of the heart. To glorify people in spite of their flaws is the trick I had to learn." He looked jaded. "Most of the time it works. So, yes, I have seen people I trust, admire and respect butcher those whom I loved, and I have also seen it done by total strangers. Neither one feels much worse than the other." He turned back down the street, looking, as though he could see a destination in the far distance. "But I suspect you know that. All the rest is merely something that you are clinging to in time of great sorrow."

I followed his gaze but didn't see anything in particular he could be looking at. "Some days ... lately ... I don't feel like I know anything at all."

A wan smile spread across Janus's face as he looked back at me. "I think that also is a uniquely human—both meta and standard—feeling."

"So Hades is dead?" I asked, staring at Janus.

"He is," came the reply. "He died before the Roman Empire even fell from the height of its glory. And he was no incubus, as I said."

"Why do I get the feeling there's more to this story than you're telling me?"

"Because," he said, and he sounded weary, "there always is." He gave me a look. "Do you know why we want you—you, specifically? Why we've been after you since day one?"

"Not really," I said, quiet. "Are you going to tell me?"

"I can't tell you everything," he said, and his words were shot through with a deep-seated tiredness that I felt in my bones as well. He gave a smile that reflected it. "So much of what you are as a succubus—and one of only three whom we know of that currently live—is ... clouded." He seemed to give a moment of consideration. "Succubi and incubi have lived on the margins of the meta-human world for ages. As a type of meta, yours is the most feared, most hated. Cloisters do not accept incubi and succubi among their number, fearing—perhaps rightly—that your powers lend themselves toward a casual application. If you've ever met one of your own kind who has embraced their power fully, you know why."

"Fries," I said with a whisper. "Charlie."

"Yes," Janus said with a solemn nod. "To fully use all the ability at your fingertips—literally—in many cases results in a sort of addiction to using said powers. Much like your aunt, the incubus or succubus becomes obsessed with drawing souls, feeding this ever-increasing emptiness within. It is very much like drug addiction, save that people become a disposable commodity, something to be drunk like wine." He cocked an eyebrow. "And much like wine, it can become required rather than occasional, a constant need, a desperate desire to be fueled in every possible instance." He cast a look across the street, where a tour group of students lingered next to a bus stop, backpacks on their backs. They didn't look much younger than I was. "A succubus on the prowl looks at a city street and sees nothing but targets, souls to be absorbed, a rush to be felt."

I looked at them, so young, and I didn't feel that—maybe a hint of it, a desire to walk through the middle of them and brush against them with ungloved hands. But not the desire to wade in, to drag the screams from them as I had with Wolfe or Kappler. "My mother wasn't like that."

"Indeed not," Janus said. "Your mother is probably the most disciplined of all of your kind. She can take a single memory from a person's mind with the skill of someone opening a filing cabinet, sliding out a single piece of paper and leaving the rest untouched. That takes a great deal of practice and considerably more than just raw ability, I assure you. She is the most powerful of your kind presently walking the planet." He held up a hand to forestall my response. "Not in terms of raw power. I understand that you have her outmatched in that way, but she has decades of practice that have refined her abilities into something unmatched in the world."

"She is strong," I conceded. "I've seen her take a person's memories. I think I leave a little more of a mess when I do it, though I have done it."

"Ah, yes, I read about that last night," he said with a subtle nod. "Ariadne, was it?"

I gave him a wary look. "I let her live."

"I heard," Janus said. "Turned her loose in the parking lot of a mall with no shoes."

"I gave her a coat."

He let out a small sound of amusement. "Well, then, that must absolve you of any responsibility for her well-being. I'm certain it was of great consolation to her when she lost those toes to frostbite."

My jaw fell open. "She lost toes?"

Janus let out a small laugh. "I kid. But it is nice to know that you still care, at least a little."

My face straightened. "Your group employed Wolfe. I doubt that it matters to you how much I care."

Janus gave a slight shrug. "To them, perhaps not. To me, it is all the difference in the world. This is why you are here now, and were not on any of the occasions they previously tried to capture you. I told them, when I took over, that they were going about it all wrong. They are used to dealing with monsters like Wolfe, like … others," he said carefully. "I told them you are dealing with a girl—woman—who has a heart, who has a soul, but you try to entrap her as if she were an animal or perhaps a beast that needs to be caged." He made a tsking sound. "They would use you to help save the world of metas from destruction and the world of humans from slavery. A noble cause, I think, which is why I have remained with Omega through … some ups and downs, let us say. As a decent person, I think this would be an aim that you would agree with. Yet they went about it by trying to capture you by force, to make you come with them." He shook his head. "Foolish,

I said. Directed at the wrong audience." He shoved his hands deeper in his pockets. "I think after dealing with monsters for so long—including some who are very much within our own organization," his face tightened, "you become accustomed to approaching all situations by immediately leaping to the same conclusions, and theirs usually involve applying force."

"You make them seem innocuous," I said, "as though they had no culpability in sending all the fiends that they did after me. Wolfe was just the start, remember? Henderschott was no peach, either. And trying to get Fries in bed with me—"

"I don't think that having Fries sleep with you was part of any plan," Janus said stiffly, "I believe that was a concession made to get him to try and recruit you."

"Nice," I said. "It's good to know that your organization would have no problem with a man using me for sexual gratification without thought or regard for what were to happen afterward. That certainly strengthens my opinion of you."

Janus let out a sigh. "I am not condoning the actions they've taken."

"I don't hear you condemning them, either."

"I have a hard time mustering much anger for condemnation given what's presently on its way toward us," Janus said. "Yes, I would not have done it that way myself, but I understand the fear—the raw fear—that Century breeds. Look at her," he waved back toward the Greek restaurant a hundred yards behind us. "She's convinced that we're returning to the darkest age of our history, a time when Hades was annihilating entire populations—"

"You don't think that sounds like what's happening now?" I looked him over.

"Oh, I'm very certain that Century is taking some pages out of Hades's book," Janus said calmly. "But Hades is dead. Very dead. Very certainly dead. I watched him die, and it was in a manner that left no ambiguity as to whether he might rise up again or not."

"You're being vague."

Janus gave a slight nod, made a sound of acknowledgment. "Some ground is best left untrod. There are things I cannot tell you, things about why we need you, specific things about yourself that I am simply not allowed to get into."

"Sounds like we're back to the same issue as with Fries—you people don't care how you use me so long as you get to use me, huh?"

"It is neither as simple nor as vulgar as you put it," he said, sounding a little exasperated. "What would you be willing to do to save the world? To save your people?"

"Very little at present," I lied. "Remember, I'm here for revenge, not because of the gallantry of your quest."

He let out a mild exhalation of annoyance then shook his head. I was sure it was feigned, though, that he could see through my lie. "Very well. We'll have to work on rekindling your concern for others as we go on. We have things to do now, anyway."

"Oh?" I asked. "We've just swayed some girl into coming into your fold, so what else is on the agenda? More recruitment?"

"Heavens," Janus said, "if only. If only there were more to recruit, more to protect. Unfortunately, there are few, which is part of the problem with our little subspecies. Too few and far too dispersed to be of great use. This is why Century is such a threat. They have banded more of the powerful metas of the world together than Omega has ever been able to."

"Whatever," I said. "I want Winter, and I still don't care about all this other stuff, these hoops I have to jump through to get him. What's next?"

"Yet still I notice you continue to absorb the background and the history I give you on all these events," Janus said. "It is almost as though you are learning, saving them up for a time when you will need them."

"Look at it however you want," I said. "But don't forget the agreement under which I came here. You can try and recruit me for the next three months, but if you don't deliver on the promise of getting me to Erich Winter and allowing me to kill him, all your recruitment efforts will be for naught."

Janus gave me a slow nod. "Very well, then. Let us move on." He turned and started to walk back down the street as the wind came howling through again.

"Wait," I said, and he paused to look back at me. "Where are we going?"

A small smile lit his aged features. "Why, to Omega headquarters of course." The light faded from his eyes. "I believe it is time that you came into the den of those you have so long despised so that you can see for yourself exactly what you are up against."

Chapter 9

Janus's car was a black Mercedes that slid through the light morning traffic as I stared out the window at the bright, sunlit London day. The blocks passed one by one, though it was disconcerting to find myself sitting in the place where the driver would be were I in America and that we were driving on the opposite side of the road from what I was used to. Janus had the window slightly down, and a soft breeze ruffled my hair as we waited at a traffic light.

There was a stir in my mind, a chorus of voices in the back, having a conversation that I was trying my best to ignore. It was a mild squall, though it didn't feel like it. A vein throbbed in the space behind my eyes, a solid twitch that pulsed with every beat of my heart, a little shooting pain that made me wonder what sort of discussion was going on in my brain. I listened for a moment, caught a heated dustup between Bjorn and Wolfe about Hades, and then got distracted.

"You can hear them in your head, yes?" Janus looked sideways at me from the driver's seat, an almost-touching look of concern etched on his features. I say "almost" because I wasn't inclined to believe it was real. He did have a specific purpose, after all, and it wasn't to make sure that I felt loved and cared for. Or if he did have that purpose, it was a means to the end of getting what he wanted.

"Yes." I rubbed the bridge of my nose with my fingers, hoping that massaging the tension would relieve the pain. It didn't.

"What are they speaking about?" The car accelerated away from the light when it turned green, down the street ahead of us.

"Bjorn and Wolfe are arguing about Hades," I said. "I'm not paying much attention right now." There was a moment of quiet in my mind. "Wolfe worked for Hades, along with his brothers, right?" I heard Bjorn howl something at Wolfe about murdering children, which got a swift and visual reply that almost made me retch, something on the order of not bothering to deny but instead glorying in that fact.

"It takes a toll on you, yes?" I saw him start with the concern again, and I remembered the last time someone had come at me with that sort of fatherly interest; it had come to a rather abrupt end when he orchestrated the murder of my boyfriend.

"That obvious, huh?" I let my fingertips lightly dance over my forehead, soothing the skin there with just the barest touch, light over the top of it, the sensation distracting me from the throbbing pain.

Janus let out a low chuckle. "Perhaps not to all, but I am an empath, and your emotional states are as obvious to me as a physiological defect would be to a physician."

"I'm deformed," I said, "I've got seven souls in one body. It's like I'm Siamese twins but only in my brain." I blanched as Bjorn shot a withering reply at Wolfe, something about working for a pure evil—which I thought was ironic, coming from the source. "Or like having an internal hydra in my mind. I'd gladly cut off some of their heads," I growled, causing them to quiet for a moment, "but I expect the only thing that would get the job done would be doing it to mine."

"That seems a bit of an overreaction." Janus guided the car into a left hand turn at an intersection, and far up ahead over a hill I caught a view of downtown. A building that looked like an elongated version of a Faberge egg with glass windows shone in the morning sun. "You will learn to control them, given time."

"Oh, yeah?" I asked, looking up at him. "Seems like most succubi I've talked to already have a firm grasp of how to control their souls pretty much out of the gate. Even my aunt Charlie couldn't understand how I had so much trouble with them."

"Because they're metas," Janus said tightly. He hesitated, leaving something unsaid.

I cocked my head to the side and looked at him, tight-lipped, his hands on the steering wheel. "You mean the souls I've taken." He looked sidelong at me, only briefly, then nodded his head once, sharply. "Why does that matter?"

"It matters," Janus said. "Using the powers we metas have requires a certain amount of will. Think for a moment on the minds you have absorbed—Wolfe was a force of nature, a beast of his own sort. Gavrikov was one of the most destructive beings to ever walk the planet. Bjorn was the son of a man who proclaimed himself the God-King of the Norse. These are not your normal souls, and your introduction to your powers was not done as it usually would be, by accidentally and partially absorbing someone close to you before awakening to your abilities. You had no such warning, and the first minds you took in were ones that had more willpower than you did yourself."

I frowned at him. "Would it matter if I absorbed someone with less will?"

"I don't think you are getting the point," Janus said, and shot me a cautious look. "You had two strikes against you, as they say. You absorbed metas, who are naturally somewhat more predisposed toward stronger will because of their abilities, and you absorbed them wholesale. That is not usual for a newly manifested incubus or succubus. Typically they would take a piece of someone first, stopping before the task is complete, giving them the ability to acclimate themselves to the … shadows, I believe your people call them—the results of a partial absorption—rather than dealing with a full and complete personality embedded within you from the start." His expression darkened. "And not just any personality, but Wolfe's."

"'Shadows'?" I thought for a moment then concentrated hard within me, searching for something inside, a faint wisp of Ariadne's memories. They were there, a small echo of the woman herself, a few thoughts, some sights and sounds, smells, sensory memories that I was able to peek through just as I had a few days earlier when I had absorbed them from her. There was very little there—a few memories of Eve, of Old Man Winter, a few highly personal. "You mean the part of a person that remains even if I don't take their whole soul."

"Yes," Janus said with a nod. "By absorbing just that portion, there is no battle of wills with the newly absorbed, because there is very little will that comes along with small fragments such as those. They are a mere shadow of the full person, you see? A typical succubus would learn who they are after perhaps taking a shadow or two through accidental contact with a human being in most cases. In the case of your mother and her sister, I am told they were raised to know in advance what they would likely be and were prepared. It is how your mother learned to become disciplined with her power. She had no fearsome Wolfe to face right out of the gate, she learned to control a shadow, then accumulated another and another before taking in her first soul, and by then she was fully ready for it. Charlie too, though I have only suspicions to go on there."

"How do you know about how my mother learned?"

"Two ways," he said. "One, we have her old Agency personnel file, which includes the account of her upbringing in her own words." He gave a slight smirk. "And second, we have access to a source that complements this."

I let the phrase hang out there for a minute. "You mean she's told you herself."

Janus let out a long laugh. "Good heavens, no. Your mother hates Omega. We clashed with her when she was at the Agency, and there is so much blood between us now that she would not voluntarily give us a drop of her spit if we told her it would save the entire world." He shook his head. "No, the source I speak of is *her* mother."

There was a long pause, and I realized I was holding my breath. "You know my grandmother?" I hadn't even hoped to ponder the idea of my mother's mother; I had never been allowed to discuss the outside world when my mother had me in confinement, and thus the topic never—not even once—came up. She didn't even acknowledge she had parents, never referenced them, and I had always wondered if they even still lived.

"No," he said quickly. "She is no longer alive. Before she passed, however, which … is quite another story … she did make record of your mother's upbringing, which was … shall we say … untraditional for a meta."

"How did she die?" I whispered, and turned my head to look out the window.

"Another time, perhaps," Janus said softly. "This falls under the domain of things I am not allowed to tell you."

"Way to build trust," I said, but the words lacked feeling. I had become used to being given only the minimums in my life— the minimum level of information, of trust, of love from the people who supposedly cared for me. I felt a swell of umbrage from Zack at this thought, but I quelled it with the truth of how we began—that he had been intended to spy on me for Old Man Winter, to seduce me to keep me in the Directorate's reach. I felt fresh pain from him, as if I had stuck my finger in a wound and twirled it around—beneath the continued argument between Bjorn and Wolfe, which had settled into low level bickering. I knew I'd hurt him, but I felt fairly resigned about the whole thing.

"I apologize," Janus said, and there was a scratch in his voice. "If it were up to me, I would tell you everything, lay it all out on the table, let you sift through the entire mess at will. And it is a mess, make no mistake," he said, scratching his chin, which was smoothly shaven in spite of the wrinkles, "filled with the requisite errors of judgment on all sides, anger and fighting, threats and escalation, ambitions and squabbling. Yet all of it has led us to the point where we stand today."

"You make it sound like an episode of a soap opera," I said, massaging my temples with my forefingers. "Or a little like the bickering in my head."

"It is probably not so far off," Janus admitted, "and every side has its secrets, things that they think will be the end of their cause should they creep out."

"What about you?" I asked. "What's your secret, Janus?"

He thought about it for a moment. "I have none that would ruin me. I know a few that would cause my employer considerable difficulty should they come out, but none that would cause me so much as a moment's discomfort."

"Oh?" I asked, feeling a nasty little desire to prove him wrong. "How about the fact that you're sleeping with Kat?" There was a surge of anger behind my eyes from Gavrikov at the mere mention of that, and Bjorn and Wolfe instantly settled down to watch the fireworks.

"Hardly a secret," Janus said with a shrug. "Not exactly controversial, either. As old as I am, do keep in mind she is over a hundred now herself. It is not as though she were actually eighteen—though I suppose it appears unseemly, given my age. Still," he said darkly, "behavior much, much worse than that would not even be frowned upon by Omega, which I suppose lends credence to any argument you might care to mount about the type of people we are."

I stared at him, watching with undisguised curiosity. "You freely admit it?"

"Certainly," he said with a shrug. "I am not forbidden to, and I have already told you I associate with monsters in the course of my duties. It is not as though this is some news to you."

ROBERT J. CRANE   63

"No," I said quietly. "Just surprised you admit it, is all."

"There is very little I would not do to save our people—and the humans—from whatever is coming at the hands of Century," Janus said. "That means working with people of power who are very long-lived and who have allowed immortality to sweep away much of their decency. Where they might have started out as good people, in their centuries of life, they have accumulated power and traded away a great deal of that decency in exchange." He shrugged again. "This is simply the way it is with the powerful and long-lived. You give a person absolute power, and few can withstand the corrupting influence it presents." He cracked his neck by turning it to each side, and I cringed. "If you need any further proof of that, merely think about how you felt about killing only a month ago—and imagine the moral drift that could occur over the course of lifetimes, even to a person who had a strong center once upon a time."

"We're not all monsters," I said in barely a whisper.

"No," Janus agreed, "but given enough time and exposure to power—of the world-ruling variety—we all have to capacity to do at least one terrible thing. The difference with a monster is that it never even occurs to them that it is a terrible thing."

He kept quiet after that, steering us down the streets in silence. I watched the buildings pass one after another until we reached a neighborhood just on the cusp of downtown. The massive skyscrapers were just above the horizon and I wondered which we would be going to when Janus turned, taking us down an old alleyway lined in red brick. I watched the lines of mortar between them streak by as we went, until we came out in another alley, turning right. We went for about a hundred feet before he turned into what looked like a loading dock. He pulled the car through a garage door that opened when he touched a button mounted on his visor, and we entered a parking lot with about thirty vehicles dispersed around it. I realized it must have been under the building, and the loading dock was there to cover the fact that it was a clandestine entrance.

We pulled into a parking space and when the car stopped, I got out. The smell of oil and metal was heavy, along with the pervasive feeling that this place had been here for a long time, decades at least. Janus gave me a reassuring smile and started toward a heavy steel door at the far side of the lot. I followed, my quiet footsteps lost in the sound of his shoes clicking against the pavement. He thumbed a button on his key fob and I heard a lock click behind the painted steel door, which he held it open for me, like a gentleman.

I stepped inside a short hallway, and there was a security guard behind a plastic window to my right. I stared at him and he continued to read the paper his face was buried behind. "Sir," he said with a thick British accent as Janus went by, not looking up from the newspaper.

"Shane," Janus said in acknowledgment, looking at the man. "How is the family?"

"All well, sir," Shane said, looking up and giving Janus a smile with his nod. "Thank you." His accent was so thick it took my brain a moment to realize what he'd said.

"This way, my dear," Janus said, holding out his arm to indicate heavy elevator doors at the end of the passage. When we arrived, the elevator dinged as though it had been summoned just for us. When the doors opened, there was a thin black woman waiting inside. I knew who she was before she said anything, from a memory I had seen. Even if I hadn't already been familiar with her, I would have realized she was graceful just by the way she was standing. She wore a tan skirt, white blouse and a jacket that matched the skirt. Her necklace was a series of beads with a claw hanging down at the center of it, and her smile could only be described as catlike. It was directed at me, and I tried to decide if she was attempting to be disconcerting.

"Bastet," I said, stepping onto the elevator before she could acknowledge me. Her knowing smile evaporated, but I could feel one of my own straining to break loose on seeing this presumably imperturbable woman caught off balance within three seconds of our first meeting. "How goes it?"

"Sienna Nealon," she said, recovering quickly. "Of course you would know me because others in your service have known me."

"If by 'in my service,' you mean rattling around in my head," I said with a sharp smile, "then yes, that's right."

"Bast," Janus said, stepping onto the elevator. He wore a smile of his own, but it was pure, deep amusement that wrinkled his brow. "You seem to have been taken a bit off your guard."

Bast gave a smile, but it was shallow and insincere. "I'm used to knowing strangers but not being known."

"Kind of a funny attitude for a goddess to have," I said. "Weren't you the object of worship once upon a time?"

Her nostrils flared in subtle irritation. "That was long ago. I prefer to work behind the scenes nowadays."

"Sure," I said with a nod. "It's probably something you just get over after a while, being worshipped by thousands of people. It's all, 'We love you,' 'We adore you,' 'You're beautiful'—" I pretended to look her up and down. "Well, you know, at least, you probably were once upon a time. After a couple thousand years, it's understandable—"

"You really are quite adept at getting under a person's skin, aren't you?" Bastet said, looking at me sideways.

"I believe you're a fan of doing the same," I said coolly.

"So, how do you know me?" she asked, arms folded. "From Bjorn?" Her smile grew nasty. "Or that passing introduction I had to your boyfriend before—"

"Bast," Janus said quietly, "Sienna is our guest here. It would be nice if you were to treat her as such."

Bast seemed to consider this a moment, never taking her eyes off of me. "She has claws, Janus."

"And you don't?" he asked with more good humor than I would have had if it had been me with a potential recruit I was trying to impress.

She gave a catlike smile. "My claws are reserved for when I really need them."

I smiled back at her. "So, they put a scratching post in your office, huh?" Her smile faded. "Litter box?"

"She's not funny," Bast said. "I thought she would be funnier."

"I save my best quips for when I'm punching someone in the face."

The elevator dinged and opened on an office floor, rows of cubicles with workers manning them, quietly tapping away at keyboards or having quiet conversations. The whole place was unremarkable, just like the fourth floor of the Directorate, really, with offices around the perimeter behind glass, sunlight shining in from behind. As the elevator doors opened, no one from the cubicles seemed to take any notice of us.

A face appeared at the edge of the elevator door, sliding around. Curled blond hair followed it, falling around the thin shoulders of a small-framed girl I knew all too well. Her hair shone in the sunlight that flooded the room, and she wore a sweet, mischievous smile that she shot at Janus. "Hey, sweetie," she said to him, making my stomach turn. She looked to Bast, and her smile dimmed. "Bast," she said, then turned her head to look at me, and her face went vaguely malicious. "Sienn—"

I took pride in the fact that she didn't see my punch coming, that it shot out in a flash, that it crumpled her nose as if I had smashed a paper cup filled with liquid. I was even prouder and oddly emotionally gratified when blood squirted out and she fell back onto her flat ass, stunned, like she was a kid on a playground who had just been knocked down unexpectedly and was about to let out one hell of a cry. Her face was crumpled in pain, and it brought a malicious smile of my own to the fore. "Kat." I shot a look at Bast. "Declawed."

Bast shrugged indifferently. "Still not funny."

Chapter 10

"Are you quite able to control yourself?" Janus asked, standing in his office with me in one chair and Kat in the other. It was a smallish room, about ten feet by ten feet, with glass windows surrounding us and giving us a view into the offices next door. It reminded me a little of a newspaper office in an old movie. The blinds were open, affording us a view of the bullpen of cubicles outside, which had been even quieter as Janus had helped Kat into the office, his disappointed gaze bidding me to follow.

"I controlled myself just fine," I said, leaning back in my chair. "I saw her, I punched her in the face, and I kept myself from beating her to death afterward." I shrugged. "I could have done a lot worse."

Janus let out a loud sigh that I was fairly certain wasn't exaggerated at all. "You could have restrained yourself entirely."

Kat was sitting next to me, looking resentful as she held a tissue against her face. "Sweetie, she broke my nose."

"Call him that around me again and your jaw is next." I smiled bitterly and Kat's visage turned horrified, then looked to Janus as if expecting him to referee our tête-à-tête.

"Is this really necessary?" Janus asked.

I started to answer. "She betrayed—"

"Your organization," Janus interrupted. "An organization which betrayed you less than half an hour after you found out she had done so. Was it really so terrible, what she did to them—to them, not you?"

"I don't know," I said, cracking my knuckles, "why don't you have her lean a little closer and we'll see how I feel about it?"

Janus made a noise of despair and waved for Kat to leave, which she did, a sullen look on her cheerleader face. "Is this how it is going to be?"

"You work with monsters," I said, "a little face-punching shouldn't be that hard to cope with."

"I expect it from monsters," Janus said. "Not from you."

"You don't know me."

"I do, actually." He calmly came around his desk and sat down, easing into the brown, leather padded chair. It squeaked as his frame hit it. "I can sense your emotion, you know, on a minute-by-minute basis—"

"Which didn't seem to help you stop me from obliterating your girlfriend's nose."

"Because it was too fast," he said with a shrug. "You spun from enjoying a subtle needling of Bastet to rather extreme violence at the sight of Klementina within a second, second and a half perhaps." He watched me as he raised a leg and rested it on the edge of his desk, leaning back in his chair to match my uncaring posture. "She betrayed the Directorate. Are you truly that upset about it?"

I stared back at him with some sullen of my own. "She betrayed *me*," I said, but I felt a dash of unease. In the moment, I had felt like she'd betrayed me, but some things that happened after that pissed me off even worse. The thought of her touching Janus, calling him "Sweetie" made me ill. As I watched him, I knew he was sifting my emotions at the same time I was. A face popped into my head as I saw her in my mind's eye on the night of the Directorate explosion, of how she touched Janus and my vision turned red—

"Oh," I said quietly.

"Oh, indeed," he replied with a quiet all his own. "It would appear that you are truly not that upset with Klementina on the basis of her betrayal of the Directorate."

"It annoys me," I said. "That's plenty enough for me to punch her in the face."

"Perhaps," Janus replied. "But I think we both know that is not why you did it. Feeling ... angry and avenging for another's sake are somewhat noble emotions—"

"Don't get too far up on that high horse," I said, standing abruptly and causing my wooden chair to squeal as I pushed the legs against the floor. "You're not Dr. Zollers and I don't need a therapist, anyhow."

He watched me from where he sat at his desk, judging carefully. "Perhaps not. But I think ... a friend ... might not go amiss right now."

I laughed. "Let's keep it professional, Janus. I know who my friends are."

"Do you?" There was genuine curiosity in his voice, as though he were studying something particularly peculiar.

"It's easy enough to keep track of," I said, stepping behind my chair, as if interposing it between the two of us was enough to protect me from him, from anything he said. "There are so few left. Enemies, on the other hand, those I seem to have plenty of."

"Probably not as many as you think," Janus said, pushing back and standing up himself. "But then again, how would you know?"

"If it's less than I think," I said, watching him, "it's only because they're dying at a vastly accelerated rate, so quickly I can't keep track of all of them kicking off."

He shrugged. "If that's the way you feel—"

"It is."

"All right, then," he said, wary again. "I do ask you to try and refrain from making more enemies while you are here. I don't think Klementina bears you any ill will—"

"Even after I punched her in the face?" I asked, amused. "Are you sure you can read emotions?"

"But I do ask that you try and keep yourself from doing any more damage to your image," he said with another sigh. "Is it not enough that you already have to combat the negative reputation that being a succubus gives you in the meta-human world? Need you add more difficulty on top of that?"

I reached for the door, realizing that if I waited, I would be continuing to let him dictate to me where I went and when, just as I had been since I got here. I opened it, then wheeled around. "Well, you know, when you're surrounded by enemies—or monsters, if you prefer," he gave a slight roll of his eyes as his expression sank, "it's probably not a bad thing if they end up hating and fearing you."

"Yes, well," Janus said as I closed the door behind me, "you seem very adept at finding out, no matter where you go."

Kat was waiting just outside the glass door, and looked at me warily over the red-stained tissue she held over her nose. "That hurt, you know."

"I know."

"Did he talk you through it?" she asked, eyeing me as she dabbed at the blood on her upper lip. "Are you over it now?"

"He walked me through it," I said coolly. "Turns out, when I punched you before, it wasn't because I was upset about you betraying the Directorate, and by extension, me. It was because I was super pissed that you betrayed Scott by sleeping with Janus." I gave her a broad, faux smile, and she gave me an uneasy one of her own. Lulled. Perfect.

I punched her in the nose again, and once more, she didn't see it coming. This punch wasn't as hard, but it didn't have to be since her nose was already broken. She let out a pained gasp, landed flat on her ass once more, her eyes already shut and welling with tears. "That one was for me," I said, strolling back toward the elevator. "The good news is, I think we can call it done; I'll let you off the hook for betraying the Directorate seeing how things turned out later."

"Thank you," I heard her mumble before she slumped to the ground, holding the already-stained tissue to her nose and letting out a pitiful sob as I walked away.

Chapter 11

I wasn't sure what to expect when I made it back to the elevator. It seemed like the direction to head, since I didn't really feel a compelling need to walk around the bullpen to tour the Omega operation. The sound of paper being shuffled produced a feeling of boredom in me, and as the sun made its way across the floors from the windows, I realized that if I were a cat—like Bast, maybe—I would probably curl up in one of the shafts of sunlight and nap the day away. Something about the knowledge that it would be months yet before I got my shot at Winter was producing a complete lack of urgency or desire in me to do much of anything.

Also, I was genuinely tired. More tired than I could recall being at noon on a weekday, ever. Especially since I'd slept for something like fifteen hours. Being a meta usually meant I was over-the-top filled with energy. The two punches I had just delivered to Kat notwithstanding, right now I felt like a kitten could win a wrestling match with me. Before I had a chance to ponder that energy drain, there was a stir behind me. I turned and heard the whispers from the cube-dwellers. I'd heard them before, just after I punched Kat, but this was different, something else, a reckless energy running through the room. I stopped to listen, but the urgent whispers were buried under the ambient noise to a degree that made it impossible for me to tell what was being said, just that it was important.

I stretched to my tiptoes to look back at Janus's office. He was there, the door pulled to, with Bast inside with him. I was surprised it wasn't Kat, since I had just given her another drubbing in full sight of him, but she was nowhere to be seen, presumably still on the floor in a heap, and he was totally focused on whatever Bast was telling him. He glanced away from her to look across the room and caught me watching. He didn't offer a gesture to the effect, but I knew he was bidding me to stay where I was. Something was happening.

I felt anchored to the spot, and I wondered if it was his doing. The two of them finished their conversation and then he was out the door with so much urgency that I feared he would break the glass. He cut a path through the middle of the cubicles, as dour and serious as I had seen him. "Come with me," he said when he reached me but didn't stop, heading instead for the elevator that I had been going for only a minute earlier.

"Why?" I asked as I fell in behind him. "Was two punches too much?"

"One punch was too much," he said as the elevator dinged and we stepped inside. "Two was excessive."

"Ooh," I said, not entirely feigning a frightened reaction but burying it under my bravado. "Is three going to be the end of me?"

He raised an eyebrow at me. "Doubtful. Even if I were personally upset by your behavior, it is hardly my decision to cut you loose." He stared at me for a moment. "Not literally but from this operation."

"Why not? Seems like you've done more to bring me here than anyone else has been able to."

"True enough," he said tensely as the elevator made its way up—to my surprise. "But now that you are here, I doubt they would blink if you were to slit Klementina's throat in the middle of the office during lunch hour, in full view of everyone." He turned to glare at me. "I don't think this needs to be said, but I would take a very dim view of such an activity, and outside my capacity as your contact with Omega, I can assure you that you would regret it for the rest of your life."

"Did you just threaten me?" I looked at him with more than a little amusement. "If I'm as important as you people seem to think I am, couldn't I just negotiate with your boss and have him throw in Kat's death as a sweetener to the deal I've already worked out with you?"

"Undoubtedly," Janus said, and his voice was hard as iron. "And if that is the type of person you truly are, a murderer, then please, make that request and do it swiftly." He averted his eyes from me, turning them toward the elevator bank. "Let me know who I'm dealing with. I would prefer to see you for what you are from the outset."

"I've killed a lot of people, Janus," I said, staring him down even as he didn't look at me. "I was merciless about it, wiping M-Squad off the map. When we talked on the night you destroyed the Directorate, you seemed so sure I wouldn't kill any of you. You even explained away how I killed Wolfe and Gavrikov. You justified them for me."

"They were eminently reasonable killings." He stood facing the elevator panel, as though it was something fascinating he could read, like a literary classic.

"Then please," I said, and I realized I was actually pleading, "explain away how I killed Glen Parks." Janus shot me a sidelong glance filled with a little alarm in his blue eyes. "I shot him in the face, you know. Or Clary? I drowned him after pinning him under a ton of machinery in a swimming pool, did you know that?" I saw the subtle nod. "Eve and Bastian, well, I would have shot them both to death, but it got a little dicey and I ended up draining them both dry." I held a bare hand up in front of my face as I spoke just above a whisper. "I think with the last two, I finally got a taste for it. My power, I mean. You know, like you talked about with the others. I felt it, and it felt good." He turned to face me, but he was calm, unconcerned save for just a hint of unease in his eyes. "I would have done the same to Erich Winter, and I came to you so you could help me find him so I could kill him. So let me ask you:

what's the justification for what I've done? Hm? How do you explain these away, Janus? How do you presume to tell me I'm not a monster now? I have left a trail of bodies behind me." I waved around, as though indicating the direction I'd come from. "How do you spin that as reasonable? How do you think of those as anything but the acts of a monster?"

"I think I would explain them as what they are," he said quietly. "Vengeance. The righteous fury of an angry woman." He moved his hand back to the elevator console and thumbed the emergency stop button, filling the air with a klaxon that honked at us like an angry goose, digitized. "Do you know much about Athena-types? Like the girl we met this morning?" He smiled. "Odd that she was actually named Athena, but do you know anything about them?"

"Just what you said." I ticked them off on my fingers. "Goddess of Wisdom, Law, Courage—"

"The original Athena was goddess of many things," he agreed. "She was like a mother to me after my own was killed, but let me tell you that her powers are mostly rooted in the better nature of men. And women," he hastened to add after I shot him a cockeyed look. "She can stir creativity, a desire for justice, a yearning for truth, and if she is truly strong, can almost catapult these emotional states into a level of genius in those she works upon like nothing you have ever seen. If you look upon any great work in mankind's history, at least half of them were probably inspired by the efforts of an Athena-type."

"So she can toy with emotions," I said sullenly. "Like you."

"Not at all like me," he said. "I can affect your direction, can alter your emotions. A strong Athena can direct an entire society toward a program of space exploration or get it to embrace the arts with a fervor nearly bordering on religious zeal. They are inspiration and can drive the mind of man to new heights. I can only direct people at the level they are currently at, toward anger, fear, contentment, whatever. Athena could inflame the emotions of entire societies but only in a positive direction." His eyes bored into mine. "One of those things she was goddess of—one of her powers—was to make righteous warfare. Do you know what righteous warfare is?" I shook my head. "Perhaps an outdated concept in the modern world, but it was—in the original Athena's words—the most difficult state to induce, especially for one used to directing the arts, the law, and all these other emotions, because it involved taking a person, or a society, and dipping them into a realm usually reserved for truly horrible things. Making war, on the surface, would seem like a wholly unrighteous endeavor, and it often can be. But there is justification, at times, for harsh action, and this is the area that Athena specialized in."

Janus took his hand and put it on my upper arm, grasping me. I could feel his grip through my shirt and it was strong, reassuring. "Simple vengeance is not just warfare. I do not want you to think that. What you have done so far, with your M-Squad, and what you mean to do with Winter, these things are not righteous. Your anger is righteous. The desire for vengeance is human, entirely human. But there are greater purposes, things that justify doing what you have done. There are justifications for killing a man. Not in the way you have done it, I think, save for with Wolfe and Gavrikov, but they do exist."

"You think I made a mistake," I said, but I didn't pull away from him.

"I think you let your emotions carry you into thinking you were righteous, and now you realize the folly of that." He leaned closer toward me. "But you and I have talked about monsters, and you know that this is the first step to becoming one, to kill easily, indiscriminately."

"They wronged me," I said, and felt the anger boil over in emphasis as I said it. "They—"

"Oh, yes, they did," Janus agreed. "And so will the next, and the next, until at last you look at the grievance for which you just killed a man and realize that it was because he was standing in your way as you tried to pass." He thought about it for a moment. "Actually, that seems to happen a lot nowadays, often in the automobiles with the road rage." He became serious again. "But the path from where you are to thinking that any killing is justified because you will it—because they stand between you and what you want—this is not a one-step process, and you decide what your next step is. I would suggest to you that you find something else to fill the emptiness that you are currently staring into within yourself."

"I'm not ..." I felt sullen again. "I'm not empty."

"Oh, no? Then what would you do with yourself if I turned you loose right now and asked you to fill the next five days on your own, without any plan or other ideas?"

I swore under my breath. "I ... I don't know. Be a tourist," I said, but I didn't believe it.

"Oh, no, you're not empty at all," Janus said. "This is the dark side of obsession, the empty feeling you get when you're not doing what you're intended. What will you do when Winter is dead? Hang out about your house? Study the snowfalls of Minnesota while the world of metas burns around you?" He smiled but he looked grim. "You are no monster."

"How do you know?" I asked trying not to sound as small as I felt.

"Because a monster," Janus said, "wouldn't care how many people Wolfe killed in the mad rush to get to them. They would only care that it wasn't them." With that, he stepped back and let go of my arm and pressed the emergency stop button again. The horn ceased, the lift shuddered, and we started up again.

"That was a long time ago," I said.

"Yes, well," Janus said, and I could tell something was weighing on him heavily. "I suppose we'll see how you feel about it shortly." My ears perked up and I gave him a quizzical look. "There was a cloister of metas in an English village not far from here. We were not associated with them, but we knew of them. They are … quiet, now, shall we say."

"They're dead, you mean." A dull, steeping sense of dread filled me at his words. "They're dead, you mean."

"Not necessarily," Janus said. "We were not associated with them, so they could have fled the country in advance of what has been happening. The attacks have spread to Europe, after all, but have been quiet here."

"But you think they're dead," I said.

"I think they are dead, yes," Janus said with a slow nod and a quiet finality about his words. He met my gaze. "But I think it would be best for all our sakes … if we were to go and find out for certain."

Chapter 12

It was hardly my first time in a helicopter, but the chop of this model was particularly distracting, the bump of it in marked contrast to the Black Hawks that I had become used to riding in. This one was an old civilian model that looked like it was used for tourists, and I sat in the small compartment in the back with three others—Bastet, Janus, and a man I hadn't met yet but whose entire bearing told me he was annoyingly earnest, even though he tried to play it a little cool. He didn't pull it off very well. "Karthik," he said, as he extended a hand to shake mine. I looked at it with pity, and he nodded and withdrew it with a chagrined look. I wondered if he'd ever met a succubus before; plainly he knew what I was all about if he took his hand back so quickly.

Unless he just figured I was unfriendly. I was all right with that too, though.

We experienced some turbulence off and on as we flew relatively low over the English countryside. I watched London fall away behind us, a bit at a time, and reflected on how different it was from Minneapolis. My city was dingy in places, but the buildings had a newer, boxier feel to them. I had caught another glimpse of London's skyscrapers as we took off. They were no doubt impressive, and in truth newer in a lot of ways than what Minneapolis had. But the rest of the buildings were where the difference lay. Most of London felt old, riddled with history spanning back hundreds of years. It carried an aura of age, of being preserved. It was the old world, a place where history was everything. Minneapolis was the new world, nothing older than fifty or a hundred years, and most of it far newer than that.

I watched the buildings thin as we headed north, and I realized that a part of me missed the new world. As much as I appreciated it, the truth was I had no more connection to the old than anything else transitory in my life. It was just another place, with no more significance than anything else I'd read about in those old books that had piled up on the shelf in my room over time.

Green fields and freeways (I'd heard them called motorways here) passed underneath. The chopper was quiet as we flew, and I wondered why they weren't at least talking to each other. Janus looked quiet, his face slack as he stared at the steel floor. Bastet was tense, I could see, and she had changed into a flight jumpsuit that looked to be made of heavy cloth. Her hands were exposed and she wore sandals, which I thought was odd before realizing that as a cat goddess she probably had literal claws. Karthik, on the other hand, was dressed in something only a few degrees off from what M-Squad had worn when we'd been on missions.

After about an hour, I felt the chopper shift and begin to descend. I looked out the window and saw a village that could only be described as quaint. Everything was brick, rows and rows of brick homes, with flat roofs that came around the edges of the buildings like helmeted tops. For some reason I thought of Oliver Cromwell. Hell if I know why.

The pilot took us down to a gentle landing, and I slid the door open before Karthik could do it for me. Janus showed no reaction as I glanced back at him, but I could see both him and Bast queuing up behind me to make sure that they didn't waste an unnecessary moment on the helicopter after I'd gotten off. I felt my shoes slip into the long grass patch we'd landed on, could feel but not hear the crunch of the grass underfoot over the wash of the rotors. The green waved and blew from the air that our helo was disturbing, and I got clear of it with a slow, determined stride. No point in acting like I was in a desperate hurry or anything.

Karthik passed me just beyond the perimeter of the helicopter blade, and I noticed a single pistol on his belt. I thought about asking for a weapon, but we were fast approaching a half dozen police officers blocking the main road into town, their subcompact cars the sort of thing one would find in the smallest of parking spaces in the U.S. Here they appeared to be standard issue.

They were wearing vests, fluorescent yellow with silver reflective strips. Their hats were tall, too, ridiculously tall to my mind. I followed behind Karthik and exchanged a glance with Janus, whose steely look told me everything I needed to know: *be quiet and let us do the talking.*

"Hello," Karthik said with a smile as he flipped a badge out. "What have we got here?"

The cops all looked at each other, exchanging sidelong glances, until the one out front, a short balding fellow with reddish-blond hair spoke. "About time you lot showed up. It's been ages since we called it in. The whole village has gone quiet, like all the phone lines are out or something. People called in from Wales, said they were trying to reach their cousins but couldn't." He shrugged. "So we sent over—"

"You should tell 'em what we found," a stocky cop next to him said, a guy with short dark hair and way too many extra pounds.

The reddish-haired officer turned and rolled his eyes at the second. "Well, we didn't find anything now, did we?" He turned back to Karthik. "We did a brief search, by the book. The place is empty. Like they all picked up and moved off in the middle of the night."

No, Little Doll. My eyes widened involuntarily; I still wasn't used to hearing disembodied voices in my head, even after all this time. Especially not in the middle of a conversation. My first instinct was to act like not a damned thing was happening. I didn't really care about any of the Omega operatives' opinions of me, since they knew what was going on in my head (sort of) but I had some reticence with having random strangers think I was insane. *Smell that?*

The police officer continued to talk to Karthik, but I tuned him out and took a deep breath, trying to sift it through, savor it. It was cold air, which always held its own smell. I caught a little of the scent of the grass and some nearby flowers that were pleasantly pungent. There was a faint aroma of exhaust from the helicopter, even as it throttled down. Finally, I caught it, barely, underneath it all, as the wind began to turn toward us from the east.

"What is it?" Janus asked me quietly, so quietly that none of the humans would have heard him. It took me only a moment to realize he'd picked up on the flow of my emotions, tripping him to the fact that something was amiss.

"A scent in the air," I breathed back, and I saw Bastet close her eyes and take a deep breath through her nose as it flared to take in the smells around us. "This way," I said and veered to the right, away from the line of officers.

"Where's she going?" the short, dark-haired one called out.

"Investigating a lead," Karthik called back. "We'll be a few minutes. Maintain your perimeter."

I heard a few muttered utterances from the officers before the red-haired one spoke up again. "Did you bring a psychic out here?"

We trod down a sloped hill, walking over the green fields that were dry, the cold air surrounding me a brisk counterpoint to what I was used to from winter back home. I wondered if it would snow here, and if so, how soon it would come. The village was spread out in front of us, both down the hill and up the next, a near-endless collection of houses and other assorted buildings. The one I was drawn inexorably towards was a church. It had a gothic facade but wasn't particularly large. It had one tower with a pointed tip that reached far above a second, squared one. The main part of the building stretched back from the impressive entrance. I knew as I looked upon the massive white doors that whatever I was smelling would be found inside.

I ascended the steps slowly, carefully, as though afraid that the doors would burst open and something would come clawing out at me. What that would be, I had no idea, but I thought surely it must just be a figment of my imagination. I also thought it curious that I didn't fear it would be a squad of men with guns, because that would kill me just as surely as some beast ripping my throat out. Actually, it was more likely to. I felt a flash of irritation that I'd had to stow my guns before I got on the plane to come over here. What was the likelihood Omega would give me one?

"I need a gun," I whispered to Janus, who was only a pace or two behind me. Karthik was edging up on my shoulder and I exchanged a look between the two of them as Janus looked to Karthik. Karthik, in turn, reached to his belt and handed me a small, boxy thing with a handle and a trigger that looked like a gun, but only if I squinted really hard. And was stupid. It was lighter and felt like it was made of plastic. I held it up and noticed some yellow crosshatching on the "barrel" as I waved it. "What the hell is this?"

"Taser," Karthik replied.

"Well, this will certainly help me if we run into a meta that can kill an entire village."

"Sorry," Karthik said, and I could hear the notes of genuine contrition in his tone. "Guns aren't quite as easy to procure here as in America."

I stared at the flimsy little shock gun in my hand and shook my head. "More's the pity; I doubt this nine-volt battery is going to do a hell of a lot to something like Wolfe."

"And a pistol would?" Janus asked with a smile.

I shrugged as I reached the top of the church steps. I

continued to lead, even though Karthik had a perfectly good 9mm clenched in his hand. I let my thumb click the little handle to release the door, and I started to swing it open slowly, listening for noise from within over the sound of squeaking hinges.

"Excellent work," Bast hissed from behind me. "I'm certain they didn't hear that door open in Surrey."

"Is that far?" I asked, not moving my eyes off the darkness within the church as a wave of air pushed out from inside. The smell was stronger now, turned loose by the opening of the door, a hint of rot and worse. I had a feeling I knew what we were going to find inside, so it came as a surprise to me when I looked down the main aisle of the church to find the entire place empty, the marble floors shining from the dim light being let in by the stained glass windows.

"Looks clear," Karthik said quietly, and I felt him relax, heard him reholster his pistol.

I took another sniff, and behind me, Bast did the same. "Hardly." The smell was thick; faint, but much stronger than it had been outside. I shot a look at her. "What do you think? Basement?" She nodded, and we veered off, opening doors to see if there was an entrance underneath either of the towers that lay to our right and left. After we found that there wasn't, we advanced slowly down the center aisle of the church, my shoes clicking against the floor. Janus's did as well, his leather wingtips squeaking with each step. I shot him a look; the suit and tie was hardly the right approach for what we were doing here. "Are you sensing anything?" I asked.

He gave a slight shake of the head. "Not really. Other than the three of you, and the rather bored sensation of most of those officers outside."

"I have a feeling things are about to get considerably more interesting for them," I said as we reached the far end of the church. There was a door for the pastor to enter through into the back chambers, and we headed toward it. This time, Karthik dodged ahead of me and I let him.

We entered a small set of rooms like a dressing chamber, and sure enough, there was a stone staircase against the far wall. The rich, velvety red carpet gave with considerable softness as we crossed it. A chill crept into me as I wondered what we'd find next. The idle thought came to me that I'd actually never been inside a church, and I wondered in a detached way if my life would have been different if I had. I shrugged it off, thinking about how I lived in a world where people who used to be called gods were standing within easy reach of me right at this very moment and I tried to not give it any more thought.

The air grew damper as we descended, the colorful carpets and rich woods of the back rooms giving way to the musty smell of basement air. I kept quiet as I followed Karthik down, his black hair vanishing in the dim light. I squinted my eyes to see if it might improve my vision, but I realized that there were few light sources visible from where I was standing. Egress windows were sunk down the sides of the basement, which was a massive space spanning the entire footprint of the church. I looked down the concrete pillars and realized that there were shapes huddled on the floor, unmoving.

Karthik stopped and I bumped into him; a clumsy move for me. His strength was enough to stop us both from tumbling down, however, and I managed to keep my balance after our collision. I stopped on the bottom step, looking out over the vast concrete basement.

"Well," Bastet said behind me, her voice a choked sound, like she had swallowed ash, "I suppose that answers the question of where the villagers went."

The smell was heavy here, the first stages of decomposition hanging in the air, along with the other odors that presented themselves when someone died. The floor was covered with them, corpses, all packed tightly together—women, children, men and old folks. I could see them with my waking eyes, but it was almost as though it were a dream. There were easily fifty of them, and I wondered if they were all metas, or if there were humans mixed in with them as well. Not one of them moved.

Chapter 13

"Water?" Karthik asked me as I sat on the ledge of the chopper, watching Janus and Bast talk to the cops who were still holding their perimeter around the village. I looked up to Karthik's warm features, and he offered me a bottle that I immediately accepted, taking a long drink that reinvigorated the dry mouth I didn't even know I had. I finished it in two long gulps and he smiled at me. "I had a feeling you might be thirsty after our flight." His face fell a degree. "And … everything else, of course."

"I could stand to eat, too," I said, looking at the empty village ahead. "Is that strange? That I could see a spectacle like that," I waved my hand at the church in the distance, "and still be hungry afterward?"

Karthik gave me a light shrug as he sat down beside me. "I suppose it just means you've seen enough death that it doesn't bother you like it used to."

"It should," I said. "I've never seen anything like that. Those people were innocent. There were children in there." A shudder ran through me.

"Our enemy is a merciless one," he said, and drank from his own bottle of water. "They don't spare a thought to who they might kill in their mad quest to wipe us all out."

"So you're a meta too, huh?" I gave him the sidelong look. "What's your power?"

"Rather mundane, actually," he said with a smile. "I'm very low level for my specialty, but I match up well on physical strength and dexterity, so I've managed to prove myself useful."

I eyed him carefully. "And your power is …"

He shrugged. "I'm a Rakshasa."

"I don't know what that is," I admitted.

"No one ever does," he said with a smile. "There are very few of us left. I can, uh … well. Perhaps I'll show you at some point, when there's an actual need for what I do."

"Sure," I said with an almost dismissive nod. "This isn't the first of these sites you've been to?"

"Not at all," he admitted. "I've been to the ones in Greece and Turkey, and more recently Germany and France. It's getting bad out there. Almost all the metas in Europe live in cloisters. It's making it all the easier to wipe us out."

"What's Omega doing to stop it?" I asked, genuinely wondering.

"Everything we can," Karthik said, clenching his fist at his side. "The problem is that while we've always wielded considerable power, it's not total power by any means."

"You mean you don't normally go dropping into these cloisters and tell people how to run things?" I wore a faint smile as I asked.

Karthik smiled back. "We really don't. These are independent cloisters. Omega recruits from them, trying to find young and disaffected metas looking for something outside their quiet village life but as a rule, we focus our efforts on things that matter to us— exerting power in the places it most benefits us."

"So you don't spend all your time hunting down metas like me?" I let my bare palms rest on the edge of the chopper floor, felt the cool metal against them along with the pressure of the edge.

"Very little of it," Karthik said. "The thing you have to understand is that in the 'old world,' as it were—not the Americas—cloisters are everything. They're tightly knit communities, they police themselves, they mostly retain their own offspring and keep them in the same villages. You don't see as many of these wildfire metas here as you do in America. You know, the ones who don't know what they are, that manifest and then suddenly get crazed with power and go on a crime spree?"

I felt my lips curl. "Met a few of those, yeah."

Karthik shrugged. "They happen here sometimes too, usually from a meta father impregnating a human woman and not sticking around. The child has no idea what to expect when they come into their own abilities. We deal with those occasionally, on contract and under the table for the EU, but generally we're focused on our own activities. Growing our influence, our power." He didn't blush but looked almost ashamed for a moment. "Our wealth."

"So you're telling me that Omega is just a moneymaking organization?" If I had baked any more skepticism into that question, it would have exploded over everything.

"Not only but primarily," Karthik said. "It's why I joined. They promise wealth, and they've consistently delivered. It's how they recruit disaffected kids out of villages. You do your term of service, and a portion of your pay goes into Omega's investment portfolio. By the time you retire, you're bloody wealthy."

"Uh huh," I said. "How exactly does Omega make that money?"

Karthik laughed under his breath. "By using our powers to gain unfair advantages in the world of commerce, of course."

I rolled my eyes. "Specifically?"

"Oh, think about it. You place a telepath in a position to be around very powerful men and women, and then make investments in companies based on the information they bring back to you." His smile crinkled lines around his eyes. "I know it sounds nefarious, and it's certainly illegal in some jurisdictions, but it's hardly the most odious scheme going."

I shook my head at him. "Sorry, no. Don't buy it."

He raised his hands to either side as if to absolve himself of having to prove it to me. "I know you'd like to believe we're some shadowy, dark organization—"

"Because you are."

"—but it's never as simple as it appears on the surface." He met my gaze and didn't look away. "Most of us are here for the money. It's honest work and good pay."

"Which part of the 'honest work' involves sending guys like Wolfe after girls like me?" I asked with a wicked grin. I probably shouldn't have delighted in taking the air out of him like that, but … I did.

Karthik deflated. "I'm sorry, what?"

"I think our business is concluded here," Janus said, returning to us with Bast a step behind him.

"Really?" I asked coldly. "What fortuitous timing."

"Don't flatter yourself," Bast said with narrowed eyes. "We don't worry ourselves about your conversations."

"Except to have Janus tell you that we're having one that might be concerning?" I asked as Janus cringed and cast an accusatory glance at Bast.

"Not concerning," Janus said with aplomb. "Barely worthy of counterargument."

"I see," I said. "So, Karthik … did they tell you about the time they set loose a couple vampires on me?" I watched his expression fade as mine grew immensely satisfied. "They shot down a helicopter and ate the throats out of the pilots."

"I'm sorry, what?" Karthik asked, almost confused.

"Or how about the time they had one of their operatives—an incubus—try to seduce me?" Janus clenched his jaw slightly. "He almost gutted me." I took a deep breath. "Which reminds me of Wolfe." I caught a momentary exchange between Janus and Bast, one in which he looked mildly annoyed. "What's the matter? This listing of sins past isn't bothering you, is it?"

"I would have done all that and more to bring you back to us if the Primus asked it of me," Bastet said with an edge to her voice that left me in no doubt that she meant every word of it. "What we are playing at is the entire future of our race—"

"What was your excuse for what you did to Andromeda?" I asked, and watched her expression deteriorate into mild surprise. "Locking a girl away, doing some sort of experiments on her? This … Sovereign guy, this Century group, they weren't on the warpath when you did … whatever it is you did to her, were they?"

"I don't have the faintest idea what anyone is talking about here," Karthik said quietly.

"It's above your pay grade," Bastet snapped.

I looked to Janus and he was quiet, still, concentrating on me. "Don't go trying to implant any suggestions in my head right now. Just because you don't want your lower levels to smell your dirty laundry doesn't mean I have any problem bringing it right out front and center—"

Janus made a motion with his hand as if to wave me off. "All of this is information he would eventually learn anyway, should Karthik continue to advance." He gave Karthik a reassuring look. "And I have no doubt he will. However, you must understand why it is not widely advertised."

"Because it's dirty laundry, not clean laundry," I replied. "If you had the whitest sheets, you wouldn't care if everyone saw them hanging on the line."

"What interesting imagery," Bast said, "since you're the one who is presently soiling our linens."

"I'm sorry," I said with mock apology, "is all this truth just a little too much for you?"

"This is quite enough," Janus said. "Yes, you have been wronged by us. I have admitted it. In one of her more charitable moments, perhaps under the influence of alcohol, Bast would admit it as well—" There was a look of pure, silent, unadulterated fury from her that told me differently. "No one is disputing that." He cast a look sideways at Bast. "Well, no one but Bastet is disputing that. But we have our reasons, for you, for …" he paused, " ... Andromeda, for all that we do. You may choose to believe that, or you may remain skeptical and continue to build the case in your head that we are an all-consuming evil that is merely trying to hoodwink you. Whichever you choose, at the end of our tenure here, I will give you the location of Erich Winter, and you will be able to decide whether you wish to go murder him at that point, in cold blood—no pun intended—or continue to help us advance the cause of protecting our people from extermination." He shrugged. "Either way, it is on you, and no amount of past sins—yours, mine, ours—will stop me from doing all that I can to ensure the survival of our race." He pointed to himself. "That is my aim. What is yours?"

Without another word, he calmly stepped past me and into the helicopter. Bast gave me a self-satisfied smile as she boarded. I exchanged a last look with Karthik, one marked by embarrassment from him, before I stood to get into my seat. The helicopter's blades were already spinning as I fastened myself in. I didn't look in at the three of them as we began to take off, as though by looking away, I could forget that I was in a foreign land, with people I couldn't trust, whose aims I didn't truly know.

As we lifted off, it occurred to me that that was exactly where I stood with the entire rest of the world as well. I didn't know whether to be upset at the thought or not, so I just ignored it and held on, letting the rattle of the flight settle into my uneasy bones, and I tried to remember that, if I were to be honest about it, this was as close to feeling normal as I could expect at this point in my life.

Chapter 14

There was someone waiting on the roof of Omega's headquarters as we touched down, a familiar figure in a suit. For the briefest of moments I wondered if they'd somehow dragged Ariadne in to work with them, but as we began to descend I realized the woman's hair was shorter and not red. The door swung open after we touched down and I recognized her as she gestured for me to get out. "Eleanor Madigan," I said with a nod as I walked past her. "I almost didn't recognize you without lightning spitting from your hands."

"Based on what I've heard of your visit thus far, I'm certain you'll be seeing that side of me before we're all done," she said in even tones, her light British accent reminding me of a flying nanny I'd seen in a movie a long time ago. "Sir," she said to Janus with utmost respect.

"Eleanor," Janus said as he stepped out of the helicopter. "We missed you on our excursion."

"Ah," Madigan said with a curt nod. "I'm afraid I was handling some business south of the Thames this morning and couldn't get it concluded in time to reach you before you left. I do have a message from the Primus, however."

"Oh?" Janus said, a thick, grey eyebrow raised in slight surprise. "Go on."

"He requests the presence of your company immediately," Madigan said, nodding sharply, almost as if she was bowing in deference to him. "He says the local police at the incident site have already had a preliminary finding from a local pathologist."

"Indeed?" Janus said. "Well, then, without further ado, I

suppose." He turned to me. "Sienna, if you'd care to wait, you may, or if you'd prefer to go back to your hotel—"

"No, sir," Madigan said. "The Primus requests her presence as well."

"Requests it, does he?" I asked, feeling cheeky, as they'd say locally. "Well, in that case, let's not disappoint your King Douche by keeping him waiting."

Janus sighed audibly over the sound of the rotors finishing their last few turns. "I would ask you to try to be polite, but I know that would be fruitless, so I merely ask you try to restrain your desire to do violence until you may visit it upon someone who is fully deserving of your wrath—such as, say, Erich Winter."

"You don't want me getting into a rumble with your Big Cheese?" I asked, watching Janus register extreme discomfort and Bast's face lock into irritation. "Fair enough. I'll try not to needle him if he doesn't needle me."

"Dear God," Janus said in seriousness as he turned away from me, "this will be the shortest meeting in the history of Omega."

I didn't ask what he meant as we descended back to the main floor, emerging from the same elevator bank as last time. There was a door on the wood-paneled far wall, the only one that wasn't open to a glass-windowed room. I followed Janus through the quiet of the work floor, the cubicle dwellers keeping to themselves, heads down.

Janus paused and opened one of the double doors for me. With a last look that suggested something along the lines of *Play nice*, I stepped inside. Part of me wanted to ask Wolfe, Bjorn and Gavrikov what I should be expecting, but I didn't want to have a conversation with myself as I was walking in to meet the man. Or woman. Not like I hadn't met women who were totally psychotic beasts who ran over people with nary a thought. One of them was even in my head.

I was disabused of the notion that the Primus was a woman as soon as I walked in the door. The office was in a state of renovation. Half of it was covered in wood paneling reminiscent of everything I've ever imagined a country club would look like in the olden days. There were blank spaces on the walls where paintings had until recently been hanging, dirty outlines marking their removal. There were countless bookshelves as well, some of them emptied. From the accumulation of dust, I guessed that the cleanup had been recent.

The man behind the desk was younger than I expected. He didn't stand to greet us but watched, his posture lazy as he sat there, impeccably dressed in a suit that probably cost more than I made in a month when I was working for the Directorate. He had a leg up on the desk, resting it, and was tilted back in his chair. His hair was brown, his eyes were dark, and his features were sharp. I felt coldness radiate off him in waves. Not literally, like Winter, just a chill eye, like I was being surveyed by someone without any emotion. It decreased his attractiveness by a considerable margin, making him ugly to look at. He wore a little smile, and I would have sworn it was there just for me, but I got the feeling he'd been wearing it since before the door had opened.

As we walked in, heading toward the two aged wooden chairs sitting in front of the desk, he gave me the slightest incline of his head as he watched me. It made me feel a little dirty. He made a motion toward one of the chairs in front of him, and I sat, adopting a posture just as lazy as his. I realized with only mild surprise that Kat was sitting in the other chair, her nose still a little swollen but looking far better than when I'd last left her.

"Sienna," Kat said reluctantly.

"Gutterslut," I replied with a cordial nod.

There was a moment's pause then Kat cracked a nervous smile. "Just like old times, huh? Sitting in front of Old Man Winter's desk? Or Ariadne's?"

"Do you even remember those days?" I didn't look at her.

Bast and Madigan took a seat on a couch about ten feet behind us, against one of the walls.

Kat paused, as though taken aback by the question. "Of course I remember those days. I haven't forgotten everything, just—"

"Just the last guy you were sleeping with," I said, looking back to see the Primus favoring me with a sly, almost malicious smile. I cast a look back at Janus and grinned. "I'm taking wagers—who do you think will forget the other first—you or her?"

Janus looked wary again. "I don't have the power to forget things the way a Persephone-type would—"

"I meant from old age," I said, twisting the knife and noticing the flash of irritation in Janus's eyes, "but if you'd like to forget her sooner, I have some expertise in that area—"

"This is all so cute," the Primus said in a high voice, his accent unmistakably American. "I may not even need to watch TV tonight. Not like the BBC has anything interesting on it anyway," he said, an ugly tone undercutting the lightness in his voice. "All the sniping, backbiting, the repartee. It's like a reality TV show airing right here in my office. You know, minus the reality part of it."

"You're not from England," I said, tracing a look back to the Primus.

He gave a slight shrug of the shoulders to go with his grin. "Born and raised in Los Angeles. What can I say? I'm of the new world, not the old." He waved his hand around the room, indicating all the construction. "That's why all this stuff, these remnants … they gotta go. This is the twenty-first century, not the eighteenth. I'm here to bring Omega into the next age, not keep it cowering in the last one."

I looked at him carefully, putting things together. "You're new."

"I've been around for a while," he came back at me.

"I meant as Primus," I said. I looked back at Janus and he gave me a subtle nod. *Rick,* Wolfe's voice came to me. *Son of the last one.* "Your name is Rick."

Rick brought his hands together and clapped them twice in approval. "Very good. Who told you? Wolfe?"

It was my turn to shrug. "Could have been Bjorn or Gavrikov."

"Wow," Rick said. "You got both of them, too, huh?"

"Yeah. Isn't it in my file?" I shot him a mean-spirited look.

"Your file's pretty incomplete, especially regarding our own agents and how they died." Rick turned his gaze to Kat. "After all, we haven't really had someone who's gotten close to you until recently."

"What about Mormont?" I asked.

Rick shrugged. "What about him? He went mercenary, tried to make a big play to bring you in and failed. I read about that op and felt sad for the idiots who backed it." Rick looked pointedly past my shoulder to where Bast was sitting. "Why would you trust some sad-sack human who's banking for a big payout to deliver the most powerful succubus of our time? Dumb. Just dumb. Typical of the kind of backwards, non-visionary thinking that used to fill this office." He looked around, and I realized he was waiting for someone to speak up and defend his father. I felt bristling behind me, but whether it was from Madigan, Janus or Bast, I didn't know. I just knew it was present and contained. Barely. "We're working on remedying that, though," he said with a smug grin.

"Oh, yes," I said with some smugness of my own. "Visionary thinking. That's what you've been lacking around here. I'm sure that'll fix everything."

"It'll help," Rick said without any trace of humility or worry. "But enough of that. Let's hear about this village." He shifted his attention to Janus. "What's the word?"

"All dead," Janus said. "But I suspect you already know that."

"I'd heard," Rick confirmed then shifted in his chair to put his other foot up on the desk. "Did you see how?"

Janus shook his head. "The bodies appeared unmarked to me, though I didn't get particularly close."

Rick smiled. "Feeling a little squeamish at the sight of the dead, J?"

Janus didn't bite at the goad that was tossed his way. "I have seen my fair share, and that of several hundred others. No, I'm afraid that my problem was more oriented to a lack of experience with forensic pathology. We saw no signs of physical violence, but that doesn't rule out poison, cardiac arrest—"

"Removal of souls," Rick said with a pointed smile toward me. "So, you don't want to speculate? Afraid to bet your ass that you might get it wrong and I'll be pissed? Fair enough." He slid a page off the desk and toward him. "Toxicology reports aren't the fastest thing in the world, but the preliminaries for one of the victims came back pretty quick." He looked around between all of us. "Anyone wanna guess?"

"Ooh, ooh," I said, raising my hand, "I'm guessing they were bored to death, and that it originated from London, probably right here in this office, in your chair." I looked around and caught Janus's face fall. "Did I win a prize?"

"Nice," Rick said, the smug not even dented. "Nope, you do not win." He thought for a moment. "Although, technically, I guess, they could have been bored to death." He threw the paper down. "The point is, it doesn't look like poison, at least not from the preliminaries. It looks like they just up and died, keeled over while clinging to each other."

"Are there actually poison-spewing metas that could do something like this?" I asked as a quiet settled over the office.

"Not that I know of, no," Janus said, his hand covering his

face, as though he could use it to wipe the expression off. He was distracted, unfocused, lost in his own head.

"What is it, then?" I asked. "What killed them?"

"In some of the previous cases, it has been bullets," Bast said from behind us. "Or obvious meta powers, like a massive fire burning them to death."

"But he's saying there's no obvious cause of death," I said, pointing to Rick. "Who could just kill a room full of people like that, and not leave a sign of any sort that they've been murdered?"

"I don't know," Rick said casually, and the way he said it made me suck in a deep breath of air, the stale scent of old cigar smoke hanging in it and coloring my taste buds. He dropped his feet off the desk and leaned forward toward me, seeming to savor the very air I wanted to choke on. "No marks, no poisons, no signs of beating or bullets." He smiled. "It's almost like someone just touched them," he said pointedly, with that wicked smile, "and they died."

Chapter 15

"So it was succubus?" I asked. "Or an incubus?"

Rick shrugged, still wearing a maddening smile. "I don't know. Could you have done that?"

"Drain an entire room of metas without having any of them fight back or leave any sign?" I gave a quick look around the room. "I dunno. Want to try it right now?"

Bast stood suddenly behind me, and I could feel Karthik tense where he stood near the wall. "I think she's kidding," Rick said to both of them, with a slight wave of his hand. "Unless you can devour souls from a distance now."

"That escapes me at present," I said. "But there's that old saying about looks being able to kill? Maybe I'll work on it."

"Perhaps something associated with fear," Janus said. "They might have died of heart attacks or something of the kind—"

"So we're back to theories and conjecture," Rick said, flattening his hand and laying it along the top of the desk. "I prefer to work with hard facts." He looked us all over. "Go figure it out, then let me know what you come up with."

"How many meta cloisters are there in the United Kingdom?" I asked. "There can't be that many."

"There are not," Janus said. "There is another in the north of Scotland and two in Ireland."

"We don't have the manpower to stage some kind of bodyguard force around every cloister in the isles," Rick said. "I want our people protecting our own, here at headquarters. If you want to send out an envoy to convince these cloisters to huddle up with us, that's fine, but we're not gonna go running out to northern

Scotland for anything other than a burial detail to see what's up with those people."

"What about the non-cloistered metas?" I asked, looking to Janus, who watched me with a flat stare. "Like that Athena we talked to this morning? Why aren't more metas running like her, if this kind of calamity is falling on the cloisters?"

"Oh, but they are," Bast said from behind me. "We're finding them as well, in ones and twos." She let out a cruel smile. "Well, we're finding pieces of them, anyway."

"I'm sorry, wait," I said as I tried to process that thought. "You're saying that they're being killed, too?"

"Quite violently, in fact," Janus added. "Very much at odds with what we have just seen. Whoever Century has set out to track these spares, they are not doing it nearly as quietly as they have been with the cloisters that have been falling. Those metas have been dying after being torn to pieces or shot to death." He shuddered, so subtly it was almost unnoticeable. "It is not a pleasant way to go. I think I would prefer to go out quietly, in a church basement."

"So, multiple metas, multiple teams," I said, thinking out loud.

"Yeah, yeah," Rick said, and I caught the first hint of annoyance from him. "Like I said, enough speculation here. Go brainstorm if you have to, and bring me back some hard facts and solutions to our problems. Keep in mind our priority is still protecting our own, not people who haven't signed on with us."

"You're a real wellspring of humanity," I said.

His look darkened. "I'm in charge of Omega, not the whole damned world and all its puppies and kitties, too."

"You're not in charge of the kitties?" I said, mockingly. "That's odd, because you seem like a p—"

"That's quite enough," Janus said quietly. "We need to focus on the problem at hand. There are indeed people who need our help, and we should reach out to them as quickly as possible, to all the additional cloisters in the isles. After that, we can look to gathering up some more of the strays before the tracker teams—or whoever is killing them singly—manage to make it to London."

"You have your orders," Rick said to Janus, forcing a wide smile after spending a good long while leering at me. "The rest of you can get out; I need to talk to Sienna for a minute."

"Ooh," I said, "looks like I have to stay after class. Bet I'm in wicked trouble now."

I watched the others file out one by one, Janus the last, holding the door and hesitating before leaving and closing it behind him.

I turned back to Rick and stared at him over the desk. "Aren't you worried?"

Rick gave a slight bob of his shoulder. "About what? I'll weather this extinction just fine, and so will Omega."

I cocked my head at him. "I actually meant about being left alone in your office with a woman who's probably killed more of your operatives than anyone else on the planet, but thanks for the helpful insight into your megalomaniacal personality. I haven't heard any rampant ego for the better part of a day, so it's nice to get in a dose now and again to remind me of what it sounds like."

He made a slow sound of, "Pfffffft," as he blew air out the side of his lips. "No, I'm not worried about being in an office alone with you." He didn't deign to look at me. "Do you know why that is?"

"I hope for your sake it's because you're the most uber-powerful meta this side of that Sovereign guy," I said with only barely concealed amusement.

"Wouldn't you like to know?" he said, dripping sarcasm and looking at me sideways as he leaned his chair back and I saw him in profile. The guy was such a prick, he didn't even bother to look at me head-on. "It's because you're not stupid. You know where the power rests here. I'm the Primus of Omega, and that makes me the most powerful man on the planet."

"What is he, Wolfe?" I whispered in the back of my throat. "Bjorn? Gavrikov?"

His power was as closely guarded a secret as any I've ever seen in Omega, Bjorn said, and I could feel Gavrikov agreeing with him. *His father kept him far from our operations, far from London, for almost his entire life.*

I have only met him once, Gavrikov said, *and it was when he was still a child. He is young, only a little older than you.*

" … power rests with me," Rick said, "because when the day came that my old man died, the Ministers of Omega—some of the most powerful metas in the world—knew who the natural successor was. I'm the Primus because I'm the most powerful man on the planet; I'm not the most powerful man on the planet because I'm the Primus. You see how that works?" He finally looked over at me. "Of course you do. You know how it works because when you were at the Directorate, you were never the one with the power. It was always Winter, and he jerked you around like a dog on a chain."

I felt myself bristle in sheer rage. "Wolfe?" I whispered in the back of my throat, my mouth closed. "Do you know what he is?"

I heard Rick let out a little giggle. "You know what I'm saying is true, don't you? That it's always been about power, and you've never been in the driver's seat. It's always been about who's yanking your strings, whether it's through a paycheck, through threats and coercion, fear and intimidation—these are the things that drive people. See, what you have to decide is who's going to have power over you. Because it's going to be someone. You're a pawn, after all, and there's no practical way for you to exert agency over your own dealings. You tried the Directorate for a little while, saw what they're all about. But now you're with the big boys. And as long as you know your place, we're not going to have a problem. All right?"

I felt the streak of fury run through me right to my core. "You think you ... what? Own me?"

He laughed, a long, cackling one that pissed me off even more. "I don't own you. I don't have to own you. I have power over you. That means you'll sell yourself out anytime I need you to, just like everyone else—to survive, to get what you want, whatever that might be."

"You think so?" I stared at him coldly.

"If you're smart," Rick said, and he pursed his lips in an infuriating smile, "you've already figured out who has the power here. If it takes a while to accept it, that's fine. But you *will* accept it. Once you do, you'll find that being a loyal servant of Omega doesn't go unrewarded. A hell of a lot more rewarded than you were at the Directorate, I can promise you that, anyway. But the converse of that is punishment—"

"Wolfe," I whispered again, "what is he?"

Don't know, came the rasp finally, *but let's find out.* I blinked at the response, trying to figure out what he meant until the follow-up came a moment later.

Kill him.

I was out of my seat a second later, already flying over the desk. I don't know if you could say I was proud that he didn't have a chance to register surprise, but he didn't even respond facially before my fist connected with his cheek and sent him flipping out of his chair. I followed right after him, landing on his belly with my knee. I heard all the air rush out of him as I did so, and I didn't waste a moment of time in punching him twice more. I heard the shattering of his face as I smashed his jaw and broke the bones around his eye.

"Who has the power now?" I shouted as I slammed his head to the marble floor, cracking the tiles and his skull. I heard the door open behind me and I stood suddenly, grabbing the chair that he'd been sitting on from where it had fallen when I had knocked him out of it. I stood and held it above my head, the rollers above me and the leather back in my hands. It weighed a hundred pounds, easy, and it felt light in my grasp as I let it hang there.

I saw the others rushing back in now—Bast, Janus, Karthik— he was already going for his gun, but he'd never make it in time— Madigan, and Kat. Madigan was the only one I had to worry about, and she was the last coming into the room. Everything was in slow motion, and I saw Janus reaching out a hand to me, shouting at me to stop, to not do it, and I suspected he'd be toying with my mind any second.

I brought the chair down with all my meta strength and it dashed Rick's—I never did catch his last name, did I?—brains out all over his pretty marble floors, a spray of red and grey matter splattering as the frame of the chair shattered from the impact.

There was a collective gasp around me as I took a step back from what I'd done and surveyed the room. They'd assembled in a little half-circle centered on me and I could tell they were all about a second from action. Karthik was raising his pistol and Madigan's hands were already up. I had held onto the arms of the chair as a weapon, and I flung them at Eleanor and Karthik, catching each of them in the torso and sending them flying back, impaled. I wanted to feel bad about it, but I wasn't going to do it now.

There was movement outside the office; probably security details coming as I could hear the sound of feet on the floors, of people speaking outside in the cubicle farm. Bast was limp, slumped, staring over the desk at me in sharp disbelief. Janus's eyes were closed, and Kat was openmouthed as she knelt next to Karthik, preparing to heal him with her touch. "You've changed, Sienna," she said into the rushing void that was the office, the desperate quiet.

"No shit," I shot back. "In case you haven't noticed, even without your new necrophiliac habit, you're pretty different yourself." I reached down and grabbed the remains of the back of the leather chair and threw it, hard, out the window behind me, shattering it.

"Where will you go?" Janus asked, watching me as I eased closer to the window. "What will you do now?"

"I don't know," I said, letting my foot rest on the sill of the window. I looked down below into a busy street, and saw traffic passing by on the road. It was a long way down; I was on the fourth floor. "Guess I'll find Winter myself."

"It doesn't have to be that way," Janus said quietly.

I laughed. "I just killed your leader." I gestured to the splattered remains of Rick. "I kinda doubt his meta healing or even Kat's touch is going to put him back together again."

"Probably not," Bastet said with quiet rage, "since he was human."

I looked at Rick's head; there wasn't much left. "Excuse me?"

"He was a human," Janus said quietly. "His father's only remaining son, but born a human to a human woman. He was only in the position of Primus because we needed to maintain continuity during this time of transition. He was just a man."

"A really arrogant, blustering man," I said, and felt the heat on my cheeks. Had I really just beaten a defenseless man to death? "He just spent the last few minutes trying to convince me I was utterly under his power and that I should be ready to basically whore myself out to whatever purpose he had in mind for me."

Janus gave a slight nod. "Young and foolish. You understand, I suppose?"

I looked at the mess at my feet. "I suppose." I glanced back to them. "So long, Janus."

"You don't have to leave," he said, and I caught the urgency from him.

I swallowed heavily. "I think I kinda do."

Without another word, I turned and stepped over the edge. I

heard swearing as I did it, the voices of Bast and Janus, already arguing. I fell about fifty feet and landed perfectly—right in the center aisle of an open-topped, double decker bus. It was a long drop, and I felt it in my ankles as I landed, but I managed to avoid any injury to myself or the bus. I dodged past the surprised people around me, marveling at my sudden drop out of nowhere, and I took a seat in one of the black plastic chairs and took a breath.

I looked back over my shoulder as the air from the bus's passage whipped my hair around. Janus was up in the window, watching me, his eyes tinged with disappointment that I could see even from this distance. His eyes never left me, following me even as the bus turned around the corner and out of his sight.

Chapter 16

I hopped off the bus after it turned the corner and sprinted full out for the underground station sign I saw up ahead. I popped inside and bought a ticket to take me back to the Russell Square station and rode in silence through the first three stops. The air was heavy but cool, and it felt almost a little stuffy inside the train itself. It was busy, and I had to change trains at Holborn station. I walked through the crowd, oblivious to anything but my own problems. I jostled and brushed against pedestrians, never long enough to feel my powers work but enough to feel the presence of others just on the outer perimeter of my own sense of self.

Did you just kill the Primus of Omega? Zack asked me, his tentativeness coming through in the way he said it. *Did that really just happen?*

It was beautiful, Wolfe rasped. *Glorious. The pampered scion of a dying family brought to a bloody end, his head splashed all over the floor just as marvelously as if Wolfe had done it himself. He's not so arrogant now, is he?* The sound of a chortle echoed in my mind.

"Oh, God," I whispered as the crowds moved around me while I walked to the Piccadilly line platform over a series of escalators and moving walkways.

Killing the Primus of Omega is a big deal, Bastian said with something that sounded like grudging respect.

Yes, Eve tossed in, *I'd be dancing if it weren't for the fact that I'm dead.*

Sienna ... Zack said quietly, *what were you thinking?*

"I don't know," I said and it came out choked. I realized in that moment that I truly had no idea why I'd done what I'd done, other than the fact that Rick had seriously pissed me off in his attempt to assert verbal control over me.

I got on my train, watching the area around me with care. I didn't know what Omega's next move would be. Part of me couldn't believe that I'd killed their leader. The other part felt disgusted at the realization that he'd been just a man, not even the one who'd sent all of their clowns after me. Somehow his speech had twisted me up inside, listening to him go on and on about power, about how he and Winter had it and how I didn't. Something snapped with just the slightest provocation by Wolfe. It hadn't taken much, I knew that. I wouldn't have been asking Wolfe about what he was if I hadn't already been thinking about attacking the man, after all.

The walls of the underground blurred together outside the windows, and the clack of the tracks beneath us grew to a maddening pitch as I heard the screech of the train, jarring me out of my thoughts. I didn't know where to go, didn't know what to do. Janus had seemed surprisingly pragmatic about Rick's death when I left, but I didn't know if that was mere show or if he really meant it. For all I knew, they were absolutely fine with me slaughtering everyone in the building. On the flip side, they might have been placating me just long enough to throw me into a storage tank like they had with Andromeda. It was hard to say without a mind reader at my disposal.

I thumped my head against the window behind me. How was I supposed to know who to trust? I was surrounded by people who—according to them—had nothing but the purest motives, but every time I looked at them, their acts didn't quite seem to match their rhetoric. Omega had done incredibly underhanded and nasty things to me in the past; I had a real problem believing that they were any kind of a force for good.

Then again, had you asked me a month ago if the Directorate

was a force for good, my answer would have been yes.

The train screeched to a stop in Russell Square and I disembarked, taking the stairs five at a time on the spiral up and scaring the hell out of several people as I passed them, bouncing off the wall in a few places and leaping over them like I was some sort of expert in parkour—which I was, though not through practice.

I hit the hotel lobby and found it packed, students from every corner of Europe filling the place to the gills. They all had laptops and wireless devices out, and a smell of slightly unwashed humanity filled the space. When I made it to the elevator, I pushed the button for my floor and waited with a dozen other people. I forced myself against the back of the elevator as others crowded on. An overweight man who spoke in a brogue pushed himself against me, unintentionally pinning me into a corner next to a thin woman who spoke with an Eastern European accent.

I felt trapped, and for a moment, it was hard to breathe. I resisted the temptation to reach out and grasp the two people closest to me by their bare necks and wait until my power started to work. A trickle of sweat ran down my temple and my mouth felt dry. My hand shook, and I kept it firmly against my side, though the urge to just do it was screaming in every synapse of my brain, as if I hadn't had a drink of water in forever and there was a full glass in front of me, waiting for me to reach out and take it. After all, why not? I had just murdered one man in cold blood, why not a couple more, but this time in a way I could truly feel and enjoy it.

The elevator dinged, the door opened, and fortunately three people got off. The fat man stepped away with the newfound space that the sudden reduction in passengers had given us, and the skinny woman worked her way out the door at the next floor.

When we arrived at my floor, there were only a couple people left on the elevator, and I dodged past them and went up the hall quickly to my room. I thrust the key card into the lock and waited for the familiar beep that acknowledged it before I pushed down on the handle and threw it open. I scooped up everything I owned and tossed it into my bag before going out the door again less than sixty seconds later.

Sienna, Zack's voice came to me, *we need to talk about this.*

"We will," I said, almost breathless as I pressed the button to summon the elevator, over and over, "but first I have to get somewhere else. Somewhere safe."

The elevator dinged and opened and I thrust myself inside to find the box empty, thankfully. I put my back against the wall and took a deep breath. As the doors started to close I heard a ding and the elevator across the hall opened. I caught a glimpse of Karthik, Bast and Janus just as the doors clinked shut. The last thing I saw was Bast's eyes widening in surprise as she saw me.

"Dammit!" I cried out and hit the button for the second floor instead of the lobby. If the three of them were coming up to see me, the odds were good that they'd have others with them, perhaps stationed around the entrance. Chances were I could take them out, but with the lobby as packed as it was, I might need to break some heads—possibly the heads of innocent people—if I wanted to make it out. As bloodthirsty as I had been of late, that thought still stopped me cold.

The doors opened on the second floor and as soon as they did I was out into the hall. The hotel was two buildings, and if I could manage to get across to the second building via the hallways, I could sneak out on the back street and run for the underground station. As for where I was going after that, I hadn't the faintest. I'd have to figure it out on the train. One step at a time.

I tore down the hallway and took a right as it came to an end. Just as I was turning I heard the elevator ding a hundred yards behind me. I paused and looked back; stupid mistake, as I saw Bast and Karthik shoot out of the elevator doors. Karthik caught sight of me and was running as I turned the corner, my eyes on the elevator at the far end. It occurred to me a moment later that Janus must have stayed to let them know which floor my lift had stopped on via cell phone or walkie-talkie. It didn't matter now, but it was a clever thing to do given that they could have lost me if they'd just left it to whoever was in the lobby to catch me.

I saw another bank of elevators at the end of this hallway, and I knew I'd reached the other hotel. The problem now was knowing just how prepared they were for me. I didn't really want to go out a window for the second time today, at least not if I didn't have to. I saw a sign for the stairs and I didn't even think twice about it, just burst through and started jumping them a landing at a time.

I was three down when I heard the door above open, and I knew either Karthik or Bast was closing in. "Stop!" I heard Karthik from above, "We just want to talk to you!"

"I'm not in a chatty mood!" I shot back and leapt the last few steps down to the exit. I took one look at the only door and realized it was a fire door that opened to who knew where. It had a bold warning telling me that in order to properly operate it I had to push down the metal bar and wait fifteen seconds to open it.

I slammed my shoulder into the metal framing and ripped it off in one second, sending it spiraling into someone just outside. I felt bad about it until the person standing next to him shouted, "There she is!" and I realized it was an Omega agent in a suit. I recoiled as he reached for me then kicked him in the chest so hard he took flight and hit the concrete wall behind him with enough force to break a few things.

"Sienna, stop!" Karthik yelled from behind me as I took off to the left. I was in a courtyard that led into the lobby of the hotel, and I knew the exit from here. I ran toward it through a cobblestone tunnel that led out onto a main street. I was a block and a half from the Russell Square station and I was fairly certain I could beat them to the underground. I was less sure where I could go from there, but I had a reasonable idea where I could lose them from having glanced at the underground map earlier.

"We need to talk to you!" Karthik shouted again. "It's important! This is bigger than you and your problems with Omega!"

I gave him points for persistence, but I wasn't about to stop and engage him in a quiet debate on why he was wrong. If I stopped, I'd have to kick the hell out of him, and I really didn't want to. I'd already impaled him once today.

I turned south and ran with all my meta speed, dodging pedestrian foot traffic, running up walls and bouncing off as necessary to increase my speed. People were shouting in surprise as I shot past them, jumping here and there. I set off the car alarm of a vehicle parked on the street as I used it for a springboard to cross. I nailed the landing and kept running, chancing a look back to see Karthik right behind me, surprisingly closing the gap.

I puffed as I slid into the entrance to Russell Square station and jumped right over the turnstiles without buying a ticket. I heard someone shout for me to stop, but the next sound I heard was Karthik knocking the hell out of them as he did the same, so I figured I didn't need to worry about it.

The green tiles in the stairwell were a blur as I shot down. I avoided colliding with others on their way down by doing the same thing I'd done earlier, leaping from surface to surface on the walls judiciously as I descended, ending with a landing that would have made an Olympic gymnast proud. I would have considered it more impressive if not for the fact that I heard Karthik only steps behind me, knocking people over as needed to try and catch me.

I tore off down the tunnel that led to the northbound Piccadilly line and hoped like hell that the train would be here shortly. As I reached the platform the sign above said it would be arriving in one minute. I cursed and threw down my bag, sliding into position next to the opening of the tunnel. I waited there and heard Karthik coming a moment later. His breathing was what gave him away; I was holding my breath so as to avoid a similar fate.

He slowed as he exited the tunnel but not nearly enough. I hit him with a clothesline that I'm sure he felt came out of nowhere. It caused his legs to fly out from under him. I caught him and slammed his head and shoulders into the concrete and tile floor. He looked up at me with shock, and I knew I'd broken something significant, possibly his skull and spine. His mouth opened and shut, and he made almost no noise.

"I'm sorry," I said, on my knees, next to his fallen body. Blood dripped out onto the floor and onto my hand where I held him in place. "I'm sorry. I hope this heals. But I'm not going with you." I stood and withdrew, leaving him there. He gasped and reached out for me again, but I searched the platform with my eyes and found his gun lying next to the train. I picked it up and put it into my bag as I retrieved it. "Tell them to leave me alone." There was a subtle movement of air, like someone had turned on a fan as the wind blew out of the tunnel where the approaching train was coming. I looked back at him, his sad eyes watching me. "Tell Janus … I'm sorry." Not that he'd believe me.

The train roared into the station and I stepped on in a crowd of people. I watched Karthik through the open doors as he rolled to his side, then his chest, and started to crawl across the platform to the train. I sighed and hoped that time was not on his side.

It wasn't. He was still five feet away and moving with desperate slowness, one arm over the next when the train doors closed. I watched him, but not his eyes, as the train started to move. The lights flashed out as we pulled out of the station, and I was left with darkness as I watched the fallen figure still on the platform—just the most recent in the long line of people I'd hurt.

Chapter 17

The train pulled into King's Cross St. Pancras station a few minutes later and I was the first out the doors, shoving people out of my way as I got the hell out. I followed the signs that led me up toward the surface, not exactly sure where I was going but certain of a few things. One, I didn't really want to try to leave the country yet. That would require an airline ticket, which I could afford, but I was concerned it would flag Omega's attention. Two, I wasn't sure I could safely stay in London. I had some cash but not enough to be able to afford more than a night or two of a hotel stay. I had credit cards, but if Omega was anything like the Directorate, they had a tech nerd like J.J. who could use that to track me down, and I'd be getting a knock on my door just a few minutes after check-in.

I didn't like the way Omega was pursuing me, but I understood it. I definitely didn't trust that all they wanted was to talk, though that certainly fit better with Janus's style than anything else that had been tried. All this ran through my mind as I took escalator after escalator toward the surface.

One thing I did know was that King's Cross station could probably get me anywhere in the country I wanted to go. The question now was, where did I want to go? Where *could* I go?

I thought about the cloisters they'd mentioned back at Omega headquarters, about the one in Scotland. I wondered where it was, and after a few minutes of thinking, I could not recall them mentioning. My odds of finding that became very low, since it's hard to go somewhere when you don't have a name for it.

I pushed off to the side and felt the swell of voices in my head as I leaned against a grey wall and smelled the scent of the musty underground. I lay my head against the hard brick and tried to think through my next move.

We should go back and make peace with Janus, Bjorn said. *This is not the end of things with Omega. They can forgive murder—*

"Why not?" I said to myself. "After all, they've done enough of it themselves. It's probably as casual as flossing to them."

We need to get out of the country, Bastian opined. *Maximum damage is done, now it's time to flee. Unless you want to really take it to Omega—*

"I didn't come here to wage a war. I came here to find Winter."

Janus will still give you Winter, if you give him what he wants, Bjorn said.

"But what the hell does he want?" I asked, and realized my voice had gotten loud enough to draw stares from the commuters walking past. "No one will even tell me what these assholes want from me, which is maybe the most frustrating thing about this whole deal."

"Excuse me, miss," came a voice with a strong Irish accent from off to my side. I rolled my eyes and turned, ready to unload on him, but I realized after just a beat he was terribly familiar. Waxed mustache, sparkling eyes—annoyingly so, like they knew something you didn't. It was the guy who had tried to steal from me on the train only yesterday. "Are you lost? Looking for Platform 9 and 3/4, perhaps?"

I blinked at him. "You're awfully chipper for someone who got his ass so handily kicked just yesterday."

He shrugged. "I bounce back from injury pretty quickly. Something I expect you know a thing or two about. Besides, I try not to hold a grudge. You did catch me trying to steal from you and all."

"I did indeed. I'd kick the hell out of you again, but I'm a tad busy at the moment." I waved him off. "Wait. Are you here thieving again?"

He gave a light, shameless smile. "I have to make a living, you know."

"Have you tried an honest day's work for an honest day's pay?"

He pretended to give that serious thought. "You know, I did once, but then I found out nicking wallets and jewelry on the tube is a more lucrative business than fetching coffee for eight hours a day." He stared at me flatly. "I do have to ask you, though … I don't run into our kind all that often. Are you with them?"

"Them who? Omega?"

He looked at me with open eyes and a smile like it was the most obvious thing in the world. "Well, yeah. Who else would I be talking about?"

"I don't know," I said. "No, I'm not with Omega."

"Eh, I figured an American girl like you, far from home, you must be with them," he said with a loose shrug. "Not like you run into a lot of independents 'round these parts—especially lately."

"What about Alpha?" I asked. "Aren't they a presence around here?"

"Alpha?" He asked, confused. "Oh, right, them. Made a big noise a few years back, tried to muscle in on Omega. I think they're mostly in southern Europe. Can't say I've heard much about them, but then, all's I hear are rumblings."

"From whom?" There was a slight breeze in the tunnel we stood in as I watched him.

"I tend to run with a crowd that's in the know, if you catch my meaning, and especially about Omega—with their business activities and proclivities and whatnot."

I heard a train in the distance and it blotted out everything else I heard. "What's that supposed to mean?"

The Irishman blushed. "I'd uh … I'd prefer not to discuss it in public. Sensitive topic and whatnot." He looked around, then leaned in and lowered his voice. "You just never know who's listening, after all."

I resisted the temptation to punch him in the face until he spilled what I wanted to know like a broken piñata let loose candy. "I need to know about Omega. Where can we go that you can talk about it?"

He raised an eyebrow, and I caught a hint of something perplexed on his face, though it was hard to tell under the mustache. "I … um … you're not propositioning me, are you? This is genuine request for information?"

"I'm a succubus," I said quietly. "You don't want me to proposition you."

"Right you are," he said with a nod, realization spreading slowly over his features. "Well, uh … look, I'll tell you what I know, but … um … it could take a bit, depending on how much detail you'd care to get into, and whatnot—"

"I need a place to stay," I said, causing him to take a step back.

"I thought you said you weren't propositioning me," he said.

"I'm not." I ignored the looks that the crowd of passersby was giving us; his voice had risen on the last bit. "I'm just putting that out there because I'm going to need to ask eventually and I figured I'd get it out all at once. Someplace cheap, because I don't have a ton of cash and I can't use my ATM or credit cards right now."

"I look the sort to know how to skirt by on the cheap, do I?" He sounded mildly offended.

"Yes," I said flatly. "Did you not know that?"

"I … well, I never," he said, his voice high. "Like I'm some sort of petty thief or something."

"You are," I reminded him.

"Oh, right," he said, and the mischievous smile was back, the act of being offended evaporated in a second. "Yeah, I know some cheap places 'cross the river. Some flats that might be … questionable. Not really safe, as it were, not to a normal person, anyhow …"

"I'm not normal."

"That's what I was getting at, yeah," he said with a nod. "I just wouldn't want you to be surprised when someone comes at you with a knife."

I watched him with jaded eyes. "I'm never surprised anymore when someone comes at me with a knife."

He blew air out through his lips and made a frightened and contrite face. "Oh, my. You are a feisty one, aren't you?" He extended a hand then yanked it back away. "Sorry. Forgot for a second what you were. Name's Breandan. Breandan Duffy."

I extended my hand then took it back in a smooth motion that went right to my hair, like I'd seen Zack do once when he was trying to be funny. I did it with a smile on my face until I got to my hair and found it a tangled mess that caught my fingers. I looked up and knew that whatever expression I was wearing at that point wasn't conveying the coolness I had shot for. "Sienna," I said at last. "Sienna Nealon."

"'Tis nice to meet you, Sienna Nealon," Breandan said with a gesture back toward the way I'd come. "We'll be needing to take a train this way. Would you care to follow me?"

"Sure." I nodded. "Lay on, McDuff-y."

He smiled and even laughed just a little bit. "Clever, but I'm Irish, not Scottish." We crossed the stream of people heading in the opposite direction and joined the queue heading back down to the underground platforms. "I have to ask you, though—something's been bothering me. How'd you do it?" His face was all sincerity, with just the slightest tinge of nervousness as we got on the down escalator. The de-escalator, they should call it.

"Do what?" My hand rested on the black plasti-rubber grip

that moved down along with the escalator. De-escalator. That thing.

He looked around as though he expected someone to be eavesdropping, but there was no one close to us save for a couple making out two steps above us. He watched them for a few seconds before shaking his head in disgust. "Please, save it." He looked back at me. "You know. You made luck betray me."

"I did huh-what?" I made my best confused face. It didn't take much, since what he said wasn't making any sense.

"My ability," he said in a hushed voice. "You know, where I can spin the wheels of luck, keep her on my side."

"I didn't know that was your ability," I said. "How's it work?"

He looked embarrassed. "Well, I just sorta … use it … and people don't pay attention or notice when I nick things from their pocket, for instance. People all look a different direction at the moment when I'm perpetrating a crime. That sort of thing. You're the first one who's ever caught me." He shook his head, lightly amused. "I was a little worried, you know, that my luck had run out. But it turns out you're like me, so you musta just broke through it somehow. Thought maybe it was something your kind could do."

"Are you sure you didn't just have a malfunction?" I asked. "Maybe you got nervous and couldn't pull it off without—"

"Hey hey hey!" he said, mildly outraged. "What are you trying to say? That I had some sort of performance anxiety?"

"They make a pill for that, I've heard."

He frowned. "I was not nervous. It was just another day, another pocket, another bag to lift from. No big deal, nothing to get flummoxed over, and even if I were—which I wasn't," he said emphatically, "that has no bearing on my abilities. I can twist luck for myself however I want and twist it the opposite way for others." We had reached the platform and waited with a crowd of people. "Here, watch this."

He pointed his finger nonchalantly toward a man who stood a few paces away, a cup of hot coffee steaming in his hand. As if on cue, a woman walked by in high heels, each step clapping smartly against the floor of the platform. As she passed him there was a crack like a gunshot and her heel broke, sending her ankle sideways. She cried out and fell, her long blond hair swaying as she did. The man with the coffee dropped it and it spilled all down his front as he reached out and caught the woman, bracing himself to keep from being knocked over by the impact.

I looked back at Breandan and he frowned. "That was supposed to be good luck. Well, okay, it works a bit oddly for others sometimes, but not for me."

I watched as the woman pulled herself up off him, still leaning against him and apologizing profusely. Their eyes met as she pushed her hair out of her eyes and they both stopped speaking.

"Looks like you just set in motion the plot to a romantic comedy," I said, not quite scowling but unmistakably irritated for no good reason. "What are you, a Cupid-type?"

"Well, it normally doesn't work quite like that," Breandan said with a frown of his own. He studied the woman whose heel he had contributed to breaking, and his eyes lingered just a little too long on her lengthy legs, so I snapped my fingers in front of his face and he broke off and turned back to me. "Shoulda kept that bit of luck for myself, honestly. Anyway, normally it'd do something like … someone would drop a wallet as they went by, or if I hit 'em with it as they're buying a lottery ticket, they'd win the little prize, you know? Actually, I do that for myself sometimes," he said without an ounce of contrition. He looked back at the blond woman, who was gently running her hand across the man's wet shirt in a way that suggested that he was indeed going to get lucky, and frowned again. "Bugger." He glanced back at me. "Anyway, no, I'm not a Cupid, and I doubt that's love so much as lust." He lowered his voice to an almost unhearable level. "I'm a … leprechaun."

I looked up at him; he was almost six feet tall. "You're not as short as I would have pictured you." I gave him the once-over. "Also, you should wear more green."

"If you make a Lucky Charms joke, I'm leaving you right here on the platform." He laughed, and I stared at him while he did it. Not coldly, just … uncertain. The voices in my head were quiet, surprisingly, as I watched Breandan. The train came through with a screeching of the tracks, and I waited there, eyes flitting between it and him. He was someone I'd only met once, in passing, while he was stealing from me. Now I was going to go with him? I was going to trust him? My head buzzed as a riot of conversation suddenly swept through it, six voices in argument.

One I heard louder than the others, though, and for once it was Aleksandr Gavrikov, quiet, reserved, and yet at the forefront: *Why not? It's not like you have anything to lose other than your life.*

"When you put it that way …" I said, out loud.

Breandan cocked his head at me, eyes squinted. "What?"

"Nothing."

"You coming along?" he asked, waiting for my reply.

"Yeah," I said, and we stepped onto the train. I watched it pull out of the station, and wondered where it would take me. After a moment's thought, I realized that at this stage in my life, did it really matter where it went? It's not like I knew where I was going.

Chapter 18

When we got off the train and back above ground, it took me a few minutes to realize I was not in the best of neighborhoods. The brick on the buildings around us was crumbling from disrepair, and the streets didn't look like they were in particularly good condition, either. Cars were banged up, older models, and seemed to match the general state of the neighborhood. Tall apartment buildings were peppered around us, and I wondered what sort of digs I had gotten myself into by asking Breandan for help.

"This way," he said casually as he opened the door for me into a multi-story apartment block. It was a boxy looking building, with something on the order of a courtyard in the middle of it. "We can talk for a few and I'll see what I can find in terms of empty apartments here."

"Here?" I asked, looking around the faded walls.

"Don't care for the area?" he asked with wry humor. "I thought you were fine with whatever you could get."

"It'll do," I said, feeling the tiredness creep in again. It wasn't even four in the afternoon, and I'd slept half the day away. But I was already ready for bed, though—if I could find one.

We rode up in a small elevator that reeked of body odor. Breandan gave me an apologetic look. "It's cheap, though."

"What?"

"The place is cheap," he said, gesturing to the inside of the box. "It smells, it's tiny, cramped rooms, but it's cheap. You know, if you need to scrape by on the margins, unnoticed for a bit."

I shrugged. "I should probably just go home. I don't think

there's much reason to stay here. Maybe wait a few days until the heat is off, buy a ticket out of Gatwick or Heathrow, and clear the hell out."

"That's the spirit," he said. "One place is as good as another, so long as it's temporary."

"It's all temporary," I replied as the doors opened and we stepped out into a long, narrow, windowless hallway. Besides, it's not like it could ever be worse than the box.

We went about twenty doors down and he opened a lock on an old, dark brown door that looked as if it had stood the test of time. For centuries. I tried not to sneer as he opened it and led me into his humble abode. It took me about three seconds to realize that when he'd said, "scraping by on the margins," he meant it.

There was a couch in front of a TV, but it was brown and beige, and looked like it had been made in the seventies or eighties and had never been reupholstered. The TV was one of the older, standard-def models, and it sat atop a battered old table. There was something of a kitchenette just behind the main living room but it was small and cramped, and I could see dishes piled high in the sink from where I stood. A door led off into what I presumed was a bedroom, but the floor in front of it was covered in dirty laundry.

I wrinkled my nose at the smell; it was plain no one had been cooking, but something had been smoked in the room, and recently. Breandan shot me an embarrassed look. "Me mates and I have a tendency to light one up every now and again." I gave him a nod and turned my attention back to the couch. "So … you want to know about Omega first, or do you want to go about the business of finding a flat of your own to let?"

"To let?" I asked, as my head started to spin. I was so weary, it took me a minute to realize that let meant rent. British English was confusing. "Never mind. Honestly, I am so tired right now."

—*should ask about Omega first,* Zack said.

—*don't need to worry about Omega. We should head back to*

the States now, Bastian chipped in.

—none of it matters anyway. I'm dead, why do I care? Eve asked.

—need to go back to Omega, Bjorn said. *They'll help—*

—can't be trusted, Gavrikov said. *Janus is the only one—*

Kill him, Wolfe whispered.

"I need to go to bed," I said, clenching my hands tight and keeping them at my side. "How long will it take for you to get me a … flat?"

Breandan looked at me slightly wide-eyed, one wider than the other, his eyebrow at an odd angle. "Uhh, hours, in all likelihood. I have to talk to a friend who won't even be awake for a bit yet."

"Night owl?" I asked.

"Drug dealer," Breandan said. "But tends to have the run of the building. She'll know which units are vacant, which ones can be moved into on short notice, if you catch my meaning."

"What a charming crowd you must run with," I said, not really feeling judgmental but probably sounding like it. "I need to sleep *now.*" The world was tilting around me, the voices in my head a cacophony of argument.

—trust Omega—

—don't trust Omega—

—don't trust anyone—

—who cares—

—kill them all—

There was a throbbing in my temples that blotted out all else. I clenched my eyes shut and stuck my index fingers against the sides of my head and rubbed, hard.

"Uh, you look like you're about to collapse," Breandan's voice cut through all the others.

"Yes," I agreed.

"You can use my room," he said. "Uh … it has a lock. I'll sleep on the couch tonight."

"A perfect gentleman," I said with a smile, my eyes still shut. "Thank you kindly."

"Oh, yeah, no problem." I opened my eyes and he stood there, watching me uncomfortably, as though I were about to explode all over his floor. Which was a possibility.

I made my way past him and through the open door, kicking his laundry as I went. I shut the door and had only a moment's thought of my own to spare for what he must be thinking about me right then before the chorus in my head grew so loud I couldn't contain it any longer, and the last thing I saw was the bed rising up to greet me before I fell into blackness.

Chapter 19

"You made a terrible mess." Janus's voice rang with extra emphasis, and I knew it was him before the scene came into focus. It took me a minute to realize he wasn't talking to me, that he was talking to someone else, someone just as reluctant to be sitting in front of him as I would have been were I actually there.

Adelaide was sitting across the desk from the man himself. Janus's grey hair and impeccable suit were only slightly different than the one I'd seen him in that very morning. It looked older somehow, less modern and fashionable, and I remembered again that Adelaide, for some reason, was living in the 1980s, and that I, for some other reason, far beyond my ability to adequately explain, was along for the ride with her.

"I did what I had to," Adelaide said, but her manner was surly and snappish. "I couldn't very well let this Aeolus go wandering about when I'd been handed a kill order, could I?"

"That's not correct," Janus said. "But let us leave that aside for a moment. You splattered the man's brains all over the compartment of a passenger train, in full view of countless people. We are not talking about some minor, trifling problem. You have exposed yourself to considerable trouble. They will make posters with your face on them—"

"They will have posters with my mohawk on them, you mean," she said, her legs crossed and her black leather jeans squeaking when she moved. "Lucky for us I can change up my look with ease."

"That is not the point," Janus said. "The point is that you made a mess, and you failed to clean it up. There were other ways to go about it, other ways to limit the damage, and you failed to employ even one of them." Janus turned and stood with his back to her, facing the window that afforded him a view of London. "What we have to ask is whether at this point you will be a good operative for Omega or not. And it is an open concern at the moment."

"I did the best I could," she said, and I caught the hint of exasperation. "Time came to put him down, I did it. Just like I was taught."

Janus turned to face her and there was a ripple of emotion across his face. "I would not consider your teacher to be the most reliable guide for how to conduct yourself in civilized society. We do not go about slaughtering anyone the minute they get in our way. That is savagery. That is bestial. That is—"

"The way of the Wolfe," came a voice as the office door opened. It was thick and raspy, and the room was filled with a sudden musk of something primal. It was Wolfe, all right, standing taller than most men when he wasn't crouched over like a dog ready to attack. Which, in this case, he wasn't. He looked at Janus like the predator that he was, and Janus looked right back at him. "The way of pain, of fear—"

"Of shameless bloodletting, copious destruction and pointless death," Janus said, keeping watch on Wolfe's slithering entrance to the room. "You have certainly trained her well."

"Wolfe taught her what she needs to know. How to avoid that pesky hesitation that costs you so many field agents right off the bat." Wolfe wore a feral grin, and his black eyes burned into Janus.

I watched Janus concentrate on Wolfe, on the black eyes, and I sensed a shift in the room. "You taught her to kill first, ask questions later. Unfortunately, I was rather hoping to question this target. He did, after all, get a look at—"

"Sovereign," Wolfe hissed. "Wolfe told you what he looks

like."

"Five hundred years ago," Janus said. "He's likely changed since then."

"Still the same smell," Wolfe rasped, his eyebrows arched down in a fearsome expression. "Janus didn't say what he was sending the Little Doll out to do or Wolfe would have warned her to be gentle."

"You are not her supervisor," Janus said tightly. "You were to train her, and her training is over."

Wolfe let a lazy smile come across his face. "The Wolfe leaves his mark, a mark that goes deeper than any command you can give the Little Doll, a mark that will outlast any order. Best Janus gives the Wolfe marching orders. That way they won't get …" he looked sidelong at Adelaide and I sensed a deeply unsettling connection between the two of them, "… misinterpreted."

Janus stared down Wolfe. "They had best not get misinterpreted anymore, else we will have to consider other possibilities for your … employment here."

Wolfe let out a full-blooded hiss, as though he were thinking about coming across the desk at Janus. "Wolfe is not to be trifled with. Wolfe is not to be threatened—"

"By me?" Janus asked with amusement creasing the lines of his face. "Would you prefer the Primus or the ministers threaten you?" He leaned over the desk toward Wolfe and Adelaide. "I am not a man who tends to pass off his duties to others or hands tasks back up the chain undone. When the Primus tells me to do something, I do it, regardless of what is asked. If that involves handing a girl," Janus gestured to Adelaide, who sat silent, watching Janus with narrowed, angry eyes, "innocent, sweet, pure, over to a monster to have him turn her into a killing machine, then I swallow my objections and do so. My personal morality may scream in outrage. It may tell me that to hand over such a girl to a beast who has shown no respect for life is wrong, that it is appalling, that it is not something I want to associate with. It may even tell me," and Janus's face twisted into something worse, something beyond fury, "that it would be better to take this beast, and use all my power … to neuter him. To turn him into a helpless puppy that will do no more than chase his own tail for the rest of his near-infinite days."

Janus's knuckles were flat against the desk, his jaw was squared and set, and if he was lying, he damned sure didn't look like it. "But I don't do what I want to do. I do what I'm ordered. My question for you, Wolfe … will you do the same? Because if not … you become rather more … expendable."

Wolfe let out a growl and leaned forward onto the desk, his fingernails like claws, digging into the surface. "Is that how Janus sees it?"

Janus didn't speak for a long minute, and Adelaide and I watched this contest of wills with no small amount of alarm; she, because it seemed destined to erupt only inches from her face, and me because … well, because it was just that gripping.

"No," Janus said. "That is not how I see it. That is how the Primus sees it. Now … will you be a good dog and respect your leash? Or do you wish to spend the rest of your life licking your own genitals in a corner of the office?"

Wolfe recoiled in fury, leaving five long scrapes along the surface of Janus's desk. "Wolfe will not forget this."

"Good," Janus said. "Never forget. Never forget what I can do to you, what I *will* do to you, should you slip the leash." He waved at the door. "Now get out, and close the door behind you."

Wolfe stalked off, making me wonder if he'd stop to open the door before plunging through. He opened it, stepped through, and was about to turn it loose in a slam that would break the glass when Janus spoke up again:

"Ah, ah, ah," Janus said. "Gently.

Wolfe seethed so loudly I thought he'd spit blood, but the door was shut without being broken, and Janus turned his attention back to Adelaide. "I'm sorry you had to see that, my dear," Janus began. "But unfortunately, you are a part of a bigger whole, and as part of Omega, you must realize that the mission is of critical importance. Nothing else matters, nothing but winning. Succeeding. Beating the odds. What you have done today has compromised an important source of information."

"I thought he was a definite kill," Adelaide said, and there was a little shake in her voice. Whether it was from the confrontation she'd just witnessed or the realization that she'd blown her mission, I didn't know.

"No, he was supposed to be capture only," Janus said. "We did not want him dead until after we could question him."

"I'm sorry I failed you," Adelaide said, and I saw her cheek twitch underneath the heavy black eyeliner that coated her eye.

"It is not me who you have failed," Janus said carefully, sticking a hand in the pocket of his vest. "It is the Primus."

Adelaide's face went blank with the sort of horror that can't truly be expressed. "Please. I'm sorry."

Janus clicked his tongue. "I trust you will try harder on your next assignment?"

"Yes, yes," Adelaide said with a fervent nod. "I won't fail you again."

"Temper your enthusiasm for Wolfe's approach," Janus said. "He can get away with the things he does; you cannot. Even more than most of our operatives, you come into this with a handicap of your own—"

"I know," Adelaide said, her head bowed, the points of her mohawk shaking as she did. "I'm … thankful for the opportunity. I was merely trying to do what I had been told."

"Recall that you report to me, not Wolfe," Janus said, "and you will not make an error such as this again. Now, go—report to the stylists downstairs, have them give you a once-over to transform your appearance. We can't have the police hounding you every step of the way, after all." He let a light smile grace his stern features. "Go on."

"Thank you," Adelaide said and stood, opening the door and excusing herself. She didn't exactly fold before Janus but close. It reminded me of a similar conversation I'd had with Ariadne.

"And Adelaide?" Janus said, catching her just before she walked out.

"Yes?" she paused, her hand on the wooden door. The glass in the middle of it was streaked with fingerprints, a greasy mess that made it look like it had been smeared with oil.

"You did not use your power in the encounter, correct?"

"No," she shook her head quickly.

Janus studied her for a moment, inscrutable. "Very good. Go on."

"Thank you, sir." She tucked the door shut behind her.

Wolfe was waiting just outside, down on all fours, watching Adelaide as she came out of the office. His scrutiny made even me uncomfortable, and I lived with him in my head. I couldn't imagine how Adelaide felt about it.

"Don't look at me like that," she said with more starch than I would have given her credit for. "You set me up for failure."

"Wolfe only told the Little Doll what she needed to hear." His fingernails clinked on the tile, like a lion stalking slowly toward its prey.

"Horseshit," Adelaide threw back at him. "I killed him. Like you wanted. You basically set me up for it; you taught me to kill fast, urged me on to it, got me all riled up to get out there and prove myself, and then it turns out I've bollocksed it up. I killed the man for no good reason." She didn't seem that bothered by the killing, more by the deception.

"Little Doll killed him for a very good reason. Little Doll

needed to get her first kill in, oh yes she did." He smiled wide, his sharp teeth looking ready to sink into a vein. "So much training, all … theoretical," Wolfe said, surprising me with a big word. "Little Doll needed practical experience. To be a killer. To be like Wolfe. Like they want you to be." His grin grew wider.

"I think they want me on a bit more of a leash than they have you," Adelaide shot back. "I'm coming in at a disadvantage and you're pushing me to break all the rules. They hand me a plum assignment, an important one that requires subtlety and finesse, and rather than get a chance to prove myself, you decided to make a mess of it for me by giving me the wrong idea."

Wolfe shrugged. "The Little Doll is angry and fearful of the wrong people. Little Doll should be thankful that the Wolfe managed to get her over the first obstacle cleanly. Now the Doll is ready for anything."

"Oh, I'm ready for anything, all right," Adelaide said coldly. "But whatever comes next, I won't be hearing it from you."

Wolfe bristled. "Wolfe trained the Doll, taught her everything—"

"Oh, yes," she interrupted, "you've just taught me a brilliant lesson."

"And now the Doll throws it back in the Wolfe's face?" He sneered. "Ingratitude brings a penalty of its own, Little Doll."

"Try me," Adelaide fired back hotly, her face red with emotion. "We both know that if it comes down to it, I won't hesitate now."

Wolfe hissed. "Little Doll had best watch herself."

"Wolfe had best stay clear of me," Adelaide replied. "I'm not your Little Doll anymore." She brushed past him without another word, without fear of his response, and he seethed as she did it. Seethed, but did nothing else.

She made her way to the elevator, pushed the button, and waited for the door to open. Once it did, she stepped inside the familiar box, and looked out over the main floor of Omega's headquarters. Across the distance, Wolfe still watched her, following her all the way with slitted eyes, saying nothing, and holding his place until after the doors had closed on Adelaide.

Chapter 20

I awoke to light streaming in, the feel of nausea infecting me, and a kind of grinding fatigue that seemed to have settled in my bones. I couldn't decide which I wanted to do more—lie there and feel sick or roll over and go back to sleep. The choice was made for me a moment later as the nausea swelled and I gagged, running for the little bathroom in the corner of the room. I dodged inside to find a small toilet, sink, and a shower, all of which looked like they hadn't been cleaned in quite some time.

I found I didn't much care as I fell to my knees and heaved, my stomach draining its contents and making me wonder what I had done to so wrong it for the second morning in a row. I lay there stretched out next to the bowl once I was done, and I heard the door to the bedroom open. A moment later there was a knock at the doorframe.

"Everything all right in here?" Breandan's voice came around the frame from the bedroom.

"No," I croaked. "I just had a digestive hemorrhage that cost me everything I was going to eat for the next month."

"That's a lovely image," Breandan said, poking his head around the doorframe to see me lying on the tile. "Can I get you some tea?"

"God, no." I cradled my head. "Two days in a row of this, and I haven't even been drinking."

"Oh, yeah? What's wrong, are you in the family way?" He looked down at me sympathetically.

"In the family way?" I looked at him in pity. "What is this, the eighteenth century? No, I'm not preg …" My voice trailed off as a tingle crept over my scalp. "No. It's not possible."

He raised an eyebrow at me and leaned against the wall. "I assure you, that from a purely physiological standpoint, it is entirely possible for women to become pregnant. I'm told it's how we propagate the species, in fact."

I rubbed the back of my hand against my forehead and found it drenched with sweat. "Why am I not surprised you wouldn't know firsthand?"

"Well, that was a pointed little dig, now wasn't it?" Breandan said with a little smirk, but his voice was hollow, his face ashen. "You sure I can't fetch you some tea while you try and decide whether you've been fertilized or not?"

"I can't see how I could—" I stopped and rolled back to my knees to heave again. When I finished, I spit the last foul taste out of my mouth. "How can this be?"

"I'm not describing it for you if you don't already know. Seems like that'd cross a line, since I just met you and all— notwithstanding the fact that you did sleep in my bed last night."

"Thanks," I said, and used a bit of paper to wipe my mouth. "Okay, so, yes, it's possible. I just don't think it's probable, let's put it that way. We were …" I looked at him with slight embarrassment, " … safe."

"Oh, I'm certain you were," he said with a formal nod, "because it never, ever happens that being safe could go wrong. In fact, they don't even have a word for that circumstance because it never, ever happens." He pretended to have a thought dawn on him. "Oh, wait, yes they do—it's called an accident. But surely it doesn't happen often … oh, wait, yes it does. All the bloody time, in case you missed the courses where they put you in a room with a teacher who looks like they haven't ever done the business they're telling you about. It happens all the bloody time."

"Oddly enough, I did miss those classes," I said, staring up at him from the bathroom floor.

"Well, that would explain how this might happen, then."

"What, you're going to sit here and berate a pregnant lady?" I asked, leaning my head against the wall.

"It's hardly a foregone conclusion," he said with a shrug. "Perhaps you're just acclimating after travel. Maybe you caught a bug on your flight. Or your body is reacting poorly to stress. Whatever the case, I wouldn't get all in an uproar about it quite yet." He smiled brightly. "You sure you don't want that tea? I'm having some."

"What is it with you Brits and your obsession with tea?" I asked, waving him off. "No thanks. And I never get sick. Never. Not since I manifested. Whatever this is, it's something else entirely."

"If you say so." He pushed off the wall and I could hear his footsteps heading out the bedroom door and into the small kitchen as I stared at the white porcelain of the bathtub's side. "I can recall being sicker than shite a few times since manifesting," his voice carried as I heard him clanging in the kitchen. "Of course, those might have more to do with the number of pints I had the night before than they did with any sort of sickness I might have picked up. Except this one time—"

There was a sudden bang and the sound of a door being kicked off its hinges in the main room. I sat bolt upright, almost hitting my head on the edge of the tub.

"What the—" I heard Breandan say, and then his words were cut off by the sound of suppressed gunfire. It doesn't sound like it does in the movies; it's still incredibly loud. Behind it I could hear thumping of bullets hitting wood, impacting on what I suspected were the cabinets in the kitchen.

I was moving on muscle memory alone, on my feet and out the door, my nausea put aside as easily as a thought. I could feel the adrenaline flowing, any memory of what I'd been talking about with Breandan only a moment earlier completely thrust out of my mind. As I cleared the door to the bathroom I saw a man in full tactical gear—vest, hood, all black—linger with his back to the door of the bedroom. He gave me such a choice view of his back, I couldn't help but abuse it.

I hit him in the kidney with a hard punch and he screamed. I hung my left arm around his neck and dragged him behind the doorframe for cover as bullets hissed past me. On television, suppressed gunfire sounds whisper quiet. It's not. The sound of the bullets whipping out of the barrel and shattering the thin walls was still quieter than the bark of the shots ringing out, but they were only quieted a bit, not silent.

The man I had in my grasp decided to fight, and with more of his comrades in the next room, I had no time to deal with the possibility he could rise up and catch me from behind while I went to stop his friends. I broke his neck cleanly the way Glen Parks had taught me to, killing my second human being in less than twenty-four hours. I felt the rough assurance from inside that I was doing the right thing, the smart thing, but a small voice within cried at the thought that I was even in this position.

I pulled his submachine gun off the strap, gripping it in my hands as the first of his fellows burst through the bedroom door. I was ready and ripped off a clean three-shot burst that caught him in the chest. It staggered him and I followed it with another that caught him in the black-hooded face, splattering the wall with blood and grey matter. He slumped and fell as another submachine gun peeked around the doorframe and fired blind above me, showering me with plaster dust where I was hiding, covered over by the body of the man whose neck I had broken. I tried to keep my eyes open, the gun trained on the door's aperture, waiting for the next one to appear.

He did, barely showing his head around the frame, and I peppered him with a three-shot burst that would have made Parks proud. It was flawless, impossible save for the fact that I was in close proximity and possessed of a steely calm brought about by hundreds of hours of training. A puffed cloud of red turned the air a subtly different color for a brief second before the body pitched forward. I would have let out a sigh but I had no idea how many more of them there would be.

I heard movement behind the doorframe and I saw a flash of black shadow against the bright of the kitchen lights. There was a burst of gunfire and I felt heavy impacts to the body that was lying atop me. Six bullets hit his tactical vest, thumping his corpse into me, hard, like miniature earthquakes jerking his body and bruising me with each hit. I lost my breath from the impacts, but I could tell from the force of them that none of them had penetrated through to me.

I flung the corpse toward the door, not really aiming so much as trying to buy a moment's time; if the shooter had any more uninterrupted seconds to take aim, he'd surely be able to hit me in the head, and I was beginning to think I might have more than just myself to be worrying about. The corpse flew forward, reminding me of a time when I'd done something similar to a table in my living room on the day I first left my house. I heard the wet smack of it hitting the doorframe and collapsing as I ripped off two quick three-shot bursts. I rocked my body sideways and rolled to a crouch, waiting just inside the door to see what came my way. I edged closer to the frame on the chance he'd reach a barrel inside. It would only take another moment and I'd be close enough to grab a gun if it came through the door.

Unfortunately, I was still a step away when it happened. I saw the barrel poke in, and I looked up it as it pointed down on a perfect arc toward my head. My meta-enhanced eyes allowed me to see the subtle rifling at the closest end of the barrel, and even though I jerked my weapon up, I knew I wouldn't make it before a burst of gunfire put my lights out for good. The smell of blood, of bile, of my own recently re-experienced vomit hung in my nose along with the heavy odor of the gunpowder discharge. That sharp, familiar aroma of a hundred days on the range was unmistakable, and more pungent than my recent digestive explosions. I looked down the dark barrel and waited for the flash that would end it, everything—and I felt a moment's pity for the fact that I had left so damned much undone.

There was a sound of a soft click, then another, as the hand that held the gun pulled the trigger again and again to no effect.

"Well, now," came an Irish voice from outside the door, "looks like you're having a spot of bad luck." The sound of something hard hitting flesh, and then a body hitting the wall was followed by the submachine gun that had been pointed at my face falling to the ground in front of me with a clatter. "You in there?" Breandan's voice came around the corner.

"Yeah," I said, my every muscle tense as I leaned against the wall, still clutching the gun to my chest, the stock hard against my shoulder. "You all right?"

"Me?" Breandan's voice came back. "I'm quite fine. Made it to the floor before they destroyed my kitchen with a flurry of bullets. I'm not really sure I need that tea anymore, though, as I'm now quite awake." He peeked his head through the door and looked at me. "You know, if you hadn't distracted them and started tearing them up one by one, I'm quite sure they were planning to murder me."

I sighed, ragged breaths coming more quickly than I would have liked. "Same here. That last one, the weapon jamming—"

"Bad luck," Breandan said with a smile. "Doubt I could have pulled that off with all of them, but when it was down to one, it seemed easy enough to change his odds." He extended a hand toward me. "Do you think there are more outside?"

I looked at the bloody mess on the floor of his bedroom, extending out into the main room as I took his hand and let him help me up. I tore it away from him after a moment and saw the surprised look in his eyes. "Sorry," I said, "bad touch, remember?" I looked at the bodies piled around me. "You think these are Omega thugs?"

He looked them over. "Omega? Maybe. I've heard they have something called 'sweep teams' for their dirty work. Why?" He eyed me. "You piss 'em off?"

"Yeah, I took the mickey out of them," I said, leaning over the nearest dead body, one of the ones who had caught a few bullets to the head. I pulled the mask off of him and looked into a destroyed face. "I ran into an Omega sweep team once; they had tattoos on their chests."

He shrugged as he nudged at the open collar of one of the bodies. "Don't see an obvious one on this bloke. You could ask the last one who he's with." He pointed to the fellow whose gun had jammed on him when he tried to shoot me. I could see him, lying against the wall just outside the bedroom door, his black tactical gear a stark contrast against the dirty white walls of the flat. "I think I left him in a hurting way, but still lively."

I walked through the door into the main room to find the door to the outside hall broken open, hanging off the hinges. I glanced back at Breandan, who shrugged. "Common sight in this building, I'm afraid. Neighbors won't give it a second look."

I turned back to the man lying unmoving against the wall, his head slumped over. I pulled his mask off and found his eyes closed, face slack. He'd had a pistol on his belt, but I could see Breandan had removed it when he'd knocked the man unconscious, and I pulled the tactical vest from him and slipped it over my own chest. Couldn't be too careful when people were shooting at you, after all. I slapped him lightly in the face (lightly for me—it still rocked his head back) and his eyes flew open with a shock. "Hi," I said in a sweet voice tempered by irritation. I was still holding the submachine gun that I'd pulled from the first man I'd killed, and with the tactical vest I'd taken from this one I had several fresh magazines. I kept the weapon handy, unafraid that he'd be able to wrest it away from me before I pulled the trigger on him. "Who are you with?"

His hair was dark and his face was pale, with a set of scars that looked as though someone had taken shards of glass and mashed them into his forehead above his right eye. "Who are you?" he asked me, staring back, awfully unconcerned for a man with a gun in his face.

I smiled and used the barrel of the gun to whip him hard in the scars. I broke the skin and a thin trickle of red made its way down his face as he looked back at me more in anger than shock or fear. "Let's try this again," I said calmly. "I ask the questions, you answer the questions. Very simple ground rules for our time together, and if you follow them, I won't shoot you in the leg and then play around by sticking my finger in the bullet hole."

There was a subtle hint of fear at that across those inscrutable features. "I can see you've been shot before," I said. "Hurts, doesn't it? Try to imagine me twisting your nerves, ripping at your wound, causing you so much pain ..." I let my voice drip with sincerity. "Now ... are you ready to talk?"

He sneered at me, chin jutting defiantly out, face like flint. "I'm not saying a word."

I looked back to Breandan, who shrugged as though indifferent, and then I sighed. "Okay." I tossed my gun backward at Breandan, who caught it, then I thrust my palms flat against the man's cheeks. "Hold still. I wouldn't want to have to hurt you as I'm ripping the memories out of your head."

His eyes went wide and he started to struggle, but I ended that with a solid punch to the nose that broke it. He tried to slap at me with a hand, but I broke that too, at the wrist, and he cried out, but I ignored him. There was a building sense of pressure in my body as he began to jerk in my grasp. There was a sweet burning feeling at the tips of my fingers, like I'd stuck them in something that was making them tingle in all the right ways. I felt the man try to stand, but I leaned in and put my weight on him, straddling him, to keep him down. He screamed and I hammered him with an elbow to the midsection that knocked the wind out of him and left him gasping for air. All the while I kept my fingers on his face, locked on, my short nails digging into his skin as he tried to get a ragged breath in.

I could see the flash of memories, of things coming from his mind, facts and thoughts. I knew his name was Roger McClaren, that he was an American, a mercenary, hired by a group who he didn't even know. I saw him in a room with the others that had come. There was a man giving him orders, a man who seemed vaguely familiar to me even though I couldn't place him. He was tall, with a mop of hair that was out of control, and he stood before the mercenaries.

"He's an Irishman," the man told the mercs in a flat accent, his head distorting in the memory as I watched it. "Name is Breandan Duffy. Should be a soft target. Sweep him up and we'll have another for you to hit by the time you get back. I want London ops wrapped up by this time tomorrow so we can start heading north to deal with a few strays before we clean out that cloister in Scotland." His eyes flashed. "There's work to do between now and then, so get done with this one quick."

"Question, sir," came the voice of one of the men outside McClaren's field of vision. "What type is this one? Should we expect much resistance?"

"Our telepath says he's a luck-changer," the man at the front of the room said, his dark eyes never moving off the man he was speaking to. "That jibes with the intel we got on him from an interrogation. Swarm him, hit him fast, you'll not have any problems. He's unpredictable in his habits, though, as he's some sort of petty thief, so waiting for him to come out of his flat at a certain time is out. His offensive capabilities are minimal, and the telepath puts his disposition as more of a risk of flight than fight. He's on the seventeenth floor so you should have him trapped." He shook his head, his dark hair flopping about his face. "Minimal resistance risk. Take him down, report back. We'll have three more down by sunset and the day after tomorrow we can get up to York."

Another question came from behind McClaren. "This can't be all of their kind in London. I thought there were more of them."

The man at the front of the room smiled. "There are. And we'll be back, with some help. We've got some resources in country that have already wiped out one cloister. They're on their way to do the job to a couple in Ireland before they meet us back here after we finish in Scotland. We've got a lot of work yet in London, but we'll need more than just guns to do it."

I sensed the mood shift in the room, as though someone else was about to ask a question, but McClaren stood up and sketched out a rough salute to the man in the front of the room. So McClaren was the squad leader. "Yes sir, Mr. Weissman. We'll get this Duffy stitched up and be back in a couple hours."

Weissman smiled coldly, his thin face not capable of much warmth or sincerity. "I have no doubt."

The world faded around me and I came back to a screaming in my head, a searing at my fingertips, and I pulled them off McClaren's face with great reluctance as he slumped to the ground, unconscious. I looked down at him and shook my head. "Quit whining. Any other succubus on the planet would have eaten your soul just now just for the cheap thrills, and frankly, knowing them, that would have been worse for you than you can imagine." I turned to look back at Breandan, and I realized that I'd only been in the memory for a second or two, even though it had shown me minutes worth of time in Mr. McClaren's life. "They were here for you."

"Well, yeah," Duffy said, unsurprised. "They did break down

the door to my flat, after all." He frowned. "Wait, did you think they were here for you?"

I watched him, in near disbelief. "There are people after you, trying to kill you?"

His face etched surprise. "There are people trying to kill you, too?"

I gave him a look of pure annoyance. "You could have mentioned that people were trying to kill you before you let me sleep in your apartment!"

He gave me a wide, unexpressive shrug. "And when were you planning to mention that someone was gunning for you?"

I scowled. "After I slept."

"Look," Duffy said with a slight grin, "clearly, we're both in some sort of peril here. It could have been either one of us that caused this spot of bother to descend on my flat—"

"No," I said, looking back down at the unconscious McClaren, "they didn't know I'd be here."

"Yet I'm quite thankful that you were," Duffy said, "as if you hadn't been, I'd be dead." He seemed to think about it for a moment before his face turned serious. "I guess having you catch me pickpocket you was a lucky thing for me after all?"

I stared back at him and pursed my lips. "Don't get all sappy on me now. I get the sense that this sweep team is only one piece of what this organization has available in the U.K." I reached down and ripped McClaren's belt off, then stepped back into the bedroom to start gathering magazines from the other fallen mercenaries.

"You 'get the feeling'?" Duffy looked back at me with alarm. "I'm not too up on what succubuses are capable of—"

"It's succubi. If a bunch of us got on London double deckers, that'd be succubuses."

"Ah ha ha!" He laughed weakly and sounded fake. "The point is, did you just rip the soul out of the man?"

"No," I said as I stooped to pick up three narrow magazines and a pistol, which I tucked into my belt. "I pulled his memory from the briefing he got before he came here."

"And saw what?" Breandan asked, watching me wide-eyed.

I stopped and stared back at him before I answered. "A guy at the front of the room giving the order to kill you. His name's Weissman. I think he's a meta and almost certainly a member of Century."

"Sorry, who?" Duffy gave me the look of a man who'd missed a step. "What's Century?"

I tried to find a way to say it that didn't sound absurd. "They're a group of metas that are planning to kill every other meta on the planet … except for them." Nope, that wasn't it.

Breandan's face got comically screwed up again. "Right. And this Weissman, he's the James Bond villain sitting atop their little organization? Stroking a fluffy white cat as well, I trust?"

"Didn't see a cat," I replied and pulled three more magazines out of the belt of a dead commando, "just him, by himself, right now, in a warehouse not terribly far from here."

"And you are picking up all these bullets because …?" he waited expectantly, though I could tell from the tone he knew what was coming.

"I'm going to go have a chat with this Weissman," I said, taking a deep breath in through my nose as I stood to look at Breandan. "You see, he and his little henchman's club, they killed someone a while back that I cared about, and I haven't been able to properly repay them for it."

Breandan looked down on me with his superior height, but I could see the skepticism in his face. "Oh, yeah? Who was that? Your mother?"

"Oh, God no," I said, almost laughing. "I said someone I cared about." I looked around soberly, trying to decide if I'd pulled everything of value from the bodies on the floor. "No. Her name was Andromeda."

"Andromeda?" he asked, and I could hear the little noise from him that told me he was beginning to wonder not *if* I was crazy, but just how crazy I was. "That was her given name?"

"Hell if I know," I said. "I only knew her for a few hours." I watched his expression change, and I knew that telling the truth wasn't doing my cause any favors in his eyes. "Listen ..." I said softly, "maybe you should stay behind. What's going to happen with this Weissman could get messy."

"Oh, messy?" Breandan gave a wave to indicate all the dead bodies around him on the floor. "Well, all right then, I should definitely keep clear of it if it's going to get messy. Because it certainly isn't at all messy here, no, bodies on my floor is a perfectly normal effing day!" His eyes got wilder, and I saw a tick in the light crows feet around his eyes as he waved a hand around. "Are you serious? There are dead people on the floor of my flat, ones who came here to kill me!"

"Yeah," I said with a little cringe, "see, this is why you should stay behind. I don't know if you can handle what could happen with Weissman—"

Breandan extended the pistol in his hand to aim at McClaren's head and fired it once, then jumped like he'd been the one shot. "Jesus!" It sounded like he said "Jay-sus!" Blood had splattered on the wall, and McClaren's corpse was now lifeless on the floor, dropped by the momentum of the shot.

"What the hell did you do that for?" I asked, looking from the body to him in quick order.

"Well, I didn't mean to!" he said, looking from McClaren's corpse to me with panic in his eyes. "I was going to point it at him to show you how serious I was," he waved the pistol toward me and I slapped a hand on his, twisting the gun out of his grip while keeping the barrel pointed away from me. "And it just went off!"

I stared at the pistol in my hand as I took a step back from him. "They do not just … go off. You have to pull the trigger for them to go off."

He waved at it, clearly agitated. "Well, it … don't they have a safety or something to keep that from happening?"

I held up the weapon. "It's a Glock 17. No, it does not have a traditional safety. First rule of guns—do not point one at anything you do not want dead."

Breandan looked back to McClaren's corpse. "And is he … is he …?" He kept trying to form the question, but it was clear his emotions were getting in the way.

"Dead?" I finished for him. "His brains are all over the wall and floor, so yes, I think we can safely say he's dead." It occurred to me I'd seen entirely too much of that recently, as though somehow in the moment I killed Glen Parks I'd opened a floodgate on an orgy of violence that had come dropping into my life.

"Dear God," Breandan breathed. "I didn't mean to." He looked tense enough to crush an apple between his buttcheeks. "You're awfully calm about this!"

"I didn't kill him."

"Yeah, but you killed these lot!" He waved his hands at the other bodies. "How can you be so damned still about it!"

I shrugged. "They were trying to kill us. I find it hard to dredge up much moral outrage about them being the ones who died instead of us." For some reason, I didn't mention that it hadn't been long ago that I had felt as he had. I looked over the scene of the chaos again. "Even with the suppressors, those gunshots were loud." I eyed him in mild accusation. "Especially that last one. We should probably get out of here before the police come."

"They won't be coming for quite some time, if at all," Breandan said quietly, too stunned to pull his eyes off the carnage around us. "Sadly, this is not the first time I've heard what sounds like gunfire in this building."

"Marvelous," I said. "Well, I'm going to go pay a visit to this Weissman and see what I can find out from him."

"And the fact that he sent a heavily armed group of men to kill us doesn't concern you at all?" Breandan looked me over. "Your first instinct is to go charging after him now you've learned who he is?"

I nodded slowly. "It's the first time I've ever had a straight line into this organization. The first time I've ever seen anything of them but men in black carrying guns, other than a telepath who kept pretty quiet about who he'd dealt with. These people are the bogeyman of the meta world, and they're scaring the hell out of everyone around them. I want to turn that around for a bit."

"You're ballsy," Breandan pronounced.

I looked down at my figure with a frown, as though I had to check. "Quite the opposite, actually."

With one last forlorn look around his flat, he said, "I don't suppose it's going to do me much good to stay here. Sooner or later the police are going to show up and it'd be best if I weren't here for it."

I frowned. "This was all self-defense. It'd be hard to explain to the police but not impossible."

"Then why aren't you staying?"

I thought about it for a beat. "I've got things to do and explaining myself to the cops isn't one of them." I reached down and pulled the wallet out of the back pocket of one of the men, trying to decide if I wanted to risk using one of his credit cards to get a room. Probably not until I took out this Weissman, one way or another.

"Let's just say my explanations to the police might fall on deaf ears, given my previous history with them," Breandan said with a grin as he opened the sliding door to his closet, now stained red from the fight, and pulled out a small canvas bag. "Just give me a few minutes to pack and we can take off."

"You understand what's going to happen here, right?" I asked, dead serious. "I'm going to drive to the address I have for this Weissman, and I'm going to brace him hard, like I just did to McClaren. I've had a lot of questions dangled in front of me about this organization, Century, and it's time I got some answers. When I say it could get messy, I mean it, because I'm going to walk in there prepared to bleed Weissman until he starts answering or until he forces me to milk his brain dry. Do you understand?" The quiet, hushed tones of my voice had drained all the color from Breandan's face, and he gave me a short, sharp nod of acquiescence. "Good," I said, and felt the wave of nausea crash over me again, both from what had happened five minutes earlier when I woke up coupled with the realization of what I'd done and who I'd killed in the intervening time. "Then if you'll excuse me, I'll be needing to vomit again—and after that, we'll go find this Weissman, and kick down his door."

Chapter 21

We took the assault team's van. Breandan drove and I rode in the passenger side, head over a garbage can I'd taken with us from his bathroom. I sat over it in misery, the sick feeling I had in my stomach still mysterious in origin. I honestly didn't know how much of it was from the clangor of voices that was occasionally rising in my head, the possibility I was pregnant, or if it was just stress and nerves from killing so many people in the last twenty-four hours.

Or it could have been Zollers. Maybe he had planted these Adelaide memories in my head. As fun as it was to glimpse into the past, I could do without the severe nausea.

I hoped that it was more the latter. Part of me worried it was the possibility of pregnancy, which would be … well, I didn't know quite what it would be. I hesitated to say disastrous, but on a gut level, that's how it felt.

You don't want to be a mother? Zack's voice asked me.

I looked at Breandan out of the corner of my eyes as he drove down the road I'd pointed him toward. I had sifted directions out of McClaren's memory and was letting him know every few minutes when he'd have to make a turn. "Not sure I'm ready," I said quietly, without opening my mouth, and hoped Breandan couldn't hear it. "Not in the world we're living in now, with my kind being hunted to extinction."

I could hear the sadness in Zack's reply. *It'd be the only thing left of me in the world. The only sign that I was ever in the world, that baby. If there is a baby.*

"Try to imagine me explaining to him or her how their father is still watching them," I said, looking at Breandan for any sign that he was hearing me. He appeared edgy, nervous, naturally, but he kept his eyes on the road. "This is not the preferred method for raising a child."

But we could—

"Let's talk about it later," I said, and threw up again into the depths of the pail. "Take a left turn up ahead," I said as I came up again and pointed at the approaching cross street.

Breandan glanced sideways at me. "Finished talking to yourself?"

I glared at him. "I wasn't talking to myself. I was talking to …" I let my voice trail off.

"You hear voices?" Breandan said as he guided the van into a turn. It was a bleary day, and the dark sky above us looked ready to rain down at any moment. "Normally I'd say that's a sign of being crazy."

I kept my calm as I favored him with a bleak smile. "But in my case, it's not?"

"There are plenty of other signs that you're crazy," he said, shaking his head as he straightened out the wheel. "Besides, I think the voices in your head are actually real."

"They are." I used a hand to smooth out the shirt I wore under my tactical vest. It was the same one I'd been wearing for over a day, without bothering to change. I glanced into the back of the van, where my bag waited, along with the MP5 submachine guns I'd taken from the hit squad. "I know the rest of the story sounds crazy. But in the last six months, almost a third of our kind has been wiped out globally."

He looked at me seriously and gave me a brief nod. "I believe you. Even if we left aside the fact that in the last sixty minutes, almost all of me was wiped out," he said with a calm he couldn't have produced only twenty minutes ago, "I get the feeling you're in the middle of some things I would have preferred to remain out of if I'd had my druthers. Unfortunately," he said ruefully, "it would appear that my druthers are well nigh irrelevant since you're the only reason I'm presently alive."

"You didn't have to come with me," I said. "This is going to be dangerous. Could be deadly. I have no idea what kind of powers this Weissman has at his disposal. You could have run, gone to ground. They might not have found you."

"They shouldn't have been able to find me this time," he said, keeping his eyes on the road. "But since they already want me dead anyway and have shown an apparent talent for making it happen, absent your help, I don't think me sticking about and trying to hide is going to do me much good." He shook his head. "No, I think my best bet is to cling to someone who actually knows how to fight these bastards off." He looked over at me with a grim smile. "That means I'm going to be stuck with you for quite some time yet, methinks."

"Oh, yay."

"You could act a little happier. I did give you a place to stay in your hour of need, after all."

"Sorry," I said. "I don't do well in groups." Because I was already a group, all by my lonesome, just me and the ghosts of the people I'd killed.

The van bumped along as we went, the smell of gun oil strong in the air as we slid through the streets of South London. I considered briefly the idea that Breandan could be right, that I could be a mother. It wasn't a fun thought. I had a house, true, but it wasn't much of a home. After all, there was still very obvious proof in the basement of how my mother had raised me there, a steel box designed to keep me confined. The world around us was going to hell, and if I went back to live in Minneapolis to raise a child, would I be very smart if I didn't try to keep us on a low profile the way my mother had? After all, someone was trying very hard to wipe out every last member of our species at the moment and they were making a damned good show of it. If I didn't want to be another body on the floor of a church basement somewhere, I'd need to keep out of their sight. Or at least out of the range of the telepaths they were apparently using to track us.

"Telepaths," I breathed, and I heard a chorus of agreement within.

"What?" Breandan said.

"In the memory I took, Weissman said they were using telepaths to identify metas," I said, drumming my fingers along the plastic-leather coating of the van's interior. "If we could find those telepaths, take them out of the game—"

"You mean kill them, don't you?" Breandan asked.

"Then Century's scheme comes crashing down, doesn't it?" I wasn't asking Breandan. By this point I was staring out the front window, trying to figure it out. Was Weissman a telepath? How many did they have? I narrowed my eyes. My real question, which I wasn't sure I wanted to admit, was how many would I have to kill to succeed at waylaying their plans? "Without trackers, it's going to be damned hard to find their targets."

"Uh, if you say so," Breandan said, nudging me back to reality.

"Turn here, then left again," I said, pointing at a warehouse ahead. "It's there." I looked at the visor above his head and hit a button that caused a heavy metal garage door to open. Darkness shrouded the interior and I reached back to grab one of the guns and checked to make sure a round was chambered. "I think you might want to wait here."

"I don't know that that's so wise," Breandan said. "How about I follow two paces behind you?"

"Not such a grand idea," I said, scooping up the second submachine gun we'd brought and strapping it around my chest. "I've seen you use a gun, and I don't want you to handle another until you've had some basic lessons in safety drilled into your head." I gave him a sympathetic look. "Sorry. But you're more dangerous to me with a gun than you are to them."

"Oh, I see how it is," he said with a look of hurt. "You shoot one bloke in the head by accident and it's all over, then."

"Yes," I said, opening the door, "that's how it is. Because I'm attached to my head, and I don't need any more holes in it."

"Bloody violent Americans."

"Says the man who just blew some poor, unarmed bastard's brains out."

Before he could respond I hit the ground in the warehouse moving like Parks had taught me, sweeping the corners for hostiles. If this Weissman was a telepath, there was no way I was going to sneak up on him. If he had surveillance cameras of any sort, I similarly had little chance to catch him by surprise. If he didn't, then theoretically he should be expecting his own men and would be surprised by a girl with a submachine gun creeping into his lair. Theoretically. This was the problem with theory; it wasn't proven. A thousand things could go wrong that I could think of and countless more that I couldn't. What if the team was supposed to call him on the way back to check in?

"Maybe this wasn't such a great plan," I whispered.

I wasn't going to say it, Bastian said, *but I'm glad you realize it now.*

If you see this Weissman with a gun, Eve said, *try to jump out in front of it, will you? Catch the bullet in your teeth. You can do it. I believe in you.*

"I get the feeling that Eve's decided not to be a team player," I whispered. "Somebody do something about that, please?"

There was the sudden sense of motion in my mind and it was as though I could see Eve being attacked, thrown to the back of my mind by shadows, tossed into the nether regions while screaming in protest. It was almost as though there was a clang, a damnably familiar sound for some reason, and her presence was gone. I shrugged. "Thanks."

I was in an open bay, spread wide along the largest part of the warehouse building. I dived through McClaren's memory in a flash, and saw that there were offices to my left. The whole room was shrouded in shadows, like ink had dripped down and covered the walls outside of the places where lamps broke the dark. I could see the outline of the door that led to the offices, still shut. I knew from McClaren's memory it was to keep out the chill that was ever present here in the bay.

"Where are we going?" Breandan said from behind me. I didn't bother to turn back, just made a slow motion with my offhand (the one that wasn't on the grip of my weapon) that showed him we were moving forward. "Oh, okay."

I fired him a sizzling look, then whispered low. "We don't know if Weissman's a meta. If he is, he may hear us. Go silent."

Breandan nodded once then continued to crouch like an idiot, as though he could somehow hide by bending his large frame forward to sneak. I wanted to tell him he looked like a moron, but he was the only backup I had, so I chose silence as a form of tact. There was a faint sound of water dripping in the corner, and the smell of oils were thick here, along with something else, like this place had been around a while and hadn't ever been exposed to the elements much. My feet made low, quiet noises with each step I took toward the door, and I wondered what I'd find waiting beyond.

McClaren's memories told me that Weissman was most likely in his office, which was at the end of the hall behind the door. I crept toward it, even steps, covering ground quickly and quietly. Breandan, for his part, did much the same, only marginally noisier than I was. When I opened the door, I tried to assume a normal tread. I was only going to get one shot at this, and if Weissman was out of position, I'd be ready, but if he wasn't, just walking in pretending to be his returning raiding party would probably allow me to catch him by surprise. Probably. Well, hopefully.

The hallway was a hundred feet long, and the walls were a dim brick, like the rest of the building. The lighting wasn't any better here than it had been out in the bay, and I started to wonder why the place was so dark. I pondered and realized that it wouldn't surprise me if Century had vampires working for them. They were sensitive to light and excellent trackers, which would be just the thing for the outfit that was looking to find and eliminate all the meta-humans on the planet.

I crept down the hall, trying to walk normally, not muffle my steps, and I saw Breandan looking at me wide-eyed. I waved him forward and walked at a casual stride but kept my gun up as I came down the corridor, ready to wheel at the slightest notice of any danger. McClaren's memory told me the place was clear, but his information was only as good as his most recent visit, which had been a couple hours ago. Just because he thought there was no one else coming didn't mean he was right, after all.

I reached the last door and searched through McClaren's thoughts again. A simple knock would suffice; that measure of courtesy was perfectly normal for how he'd treat Weissman. I gave one sharp thunk on the wood, and heard a voice from inside. "Come in." It was high, and a little nasally. It was exactly as I'd heard it in McClaren's mind.

I turned the knob and flung the door open, bursting in with my gun up and the barrel aimed straight at Weissman. He was exactly as I recalled—thin, a mop of dark hair up top. His age was tough to gauge, but he looked around forty, without any sign of grey hair. Wrinkles were also strangely absent, and he covered his shock reasonably well as he stared down the barrel of my gun.

"Sienna Nealon," he said with a careful swallow as he leaned back in his chair, his hands raised where I could see them. He seemed deeply unconcerned.

"You know me," I said. I wasn't asking. "Should I be afraid?"

He chuckled. "You're the one holding the gun, not me."

"Now, now," I said. "Perhaps I should have asked, 'How do you know me?'"

He gave a slight nod, all calm assurance. "That is a better question. The answer is … because you're the only meta-human in the entire world that I'm not allowed to kill."

Chapter 22

I looked over the man across the desk, his slicked-back hair and oily demeanor reminding me of every joke I'd ever heard about greasy salesmen. He smiled, and I suddenly wondered exactly why he was so damned happy to be looking down the barrel of a gun. "Well, now, isn't that a change from just a few months ago when your people tried to put me in the ground right after Andromeda?" I asked, getting the sense that I should pull the trigger and save myself whatever trouble he was cooking up.

He grimaced slightly. "Things change." His face took a moment to readjust back to a smile. "It's such a pleasure to finally be able to formally meet you."

"The feeling is not mutual," I said. "McClaren wasn't impressed with you as a boss." I lied. I hadn't drained enough of McClaren to get that impression, and what I'd gotten from him at the meeting this morning had been fairly limited, mostly focused on the assignment.

"So you killed him?" Weissman nodded subtly. "Good for you. I'd heard you were on the killing floor now, off the bench, as it were." He smiled again. "Zollers thought you'd never come around to it. I told him he was wrong, that everyone can be a killer if they're pushed hard enough, but I think, really, he was just afraid to give you that push."

"Maybe he was afraid of what would happen to whoever did the pushing," I said, but I didn't smile.

"Oooooh," Weissman said, gleefully, almost ominously. "I like the sound of that." The relish was evident in his voice. "I heard you did in all of M-Squad. One by one, brutal when necessary, clever by turn, and even improvised a couple times when you were backed into a corner." He leered at me, and something about him reminded me of Rick. "Shame about Old Man Winter, though. Were you surprised when he ran from you? The big bad? The Old Man, running from the little girl?"

"Not really," I said. "If the choice was run or die, wouldn't you try and get away?"

"Oh, come on," Weissman said with a chuckle, "you don't have to lie to me. He broke your hand off and threw you from a plane. You were no threat to him at the end. Maybe at the beginning, if you'd taken that shot at the plane window, but once he'd disarmed you?" He laughed again, presumably at the pun. "Nah. I wouldn't want to be him the next time you cross paths, but he beat you. Fair and square. The game was over, and you lost." He cocked his head and pretended to be concerned. "How'd that feel?"

I glared down at him. "Would you like to find out?"

"You don't need to threaten me," he said coolly, without an ounce of concern.

"Why?" I asked. "Because you'll do what I say and answer whatever I ask?"

"Hell, no," he said with a deeper laugh, one far more sincere than the last. "Because you couldn't intimidate me into talking if you emptied every bullet you had into the most painful nerve endings on my body. Because you could beat me to within an inch of my life and it'd still be amateur work compared to what I've seen before." He shrugged and laughed lightly. "Because even if you had any power over me—which, hey, smart girl—you don't," his voice went cold as he said it, "you couldn't intimidate me because I've been intimidated by the most frightening men who have ever walked the earth." He folded his fingers across one another, steepling them. "But you can give it a try, if you want. Ask your questions. I'll answer some of them." He pulled one of his fingers out of the steepling. "But if you get uppity with me? You'll find out why I'm the one holding the power in this room. And you do not want me ... as your enemy."

"I kinda think you already are," I said, with only a brief glance back to Breandan to find him white-faced, staring blankly at Weissman. "So ... Sovereign."

"So ... what?" Weissman fired back. "Is there a question in there somewhere?"

"Why does Sovereign want all the metas in the world dead?" I asked, looking down the sights at Weissman.

Weissman laughed, loudly and tonelessly. "Sovereign could not care any less about killing all the metas of the world." He leaned forward, putting his elbows on the desk, and I caught a glimpse of some meanness in him, buried deep, a dark sliver of something terrible. "That's my program, not his."

I blinked, trying to reconcile what I knew of Century to what Weissman had told me. "Isn't Sovereign your leader?"

Weissman smiled a nasty grin. "Sure. But he doesn't call all the shots."

I chewed that one over for a minute. "If Sovereign doesn't care if the metas of the world are killed ... why do you?"

Weissman seemed to sink back in his chair at that, like he could draw back into the shadows against the wall behind his desk. "Because they're a threat, obviously."

"Oh, well, obviously," I said in total sarcasm. "Except your leader doesn't seem to think so." I considered that for a moment and felt a tingle that came with realization. "He doesn't think they're a threat to him. But they're a threat to you?"

Weissman smiled, this time less nastily, but only a little less. "I'd heard you were smart. Not bad. Yeah, they're a threat to me. Minor at best, but still. Sovereign ... as you call him ... he's not what you'd consider a real 'hands-on' leader. Day to day, I'm in charge. And my job is a lot harder with three thousand metas walking the earth, interfering in my plans."

I blinked at him, trying to process that information. "You think that in a world without metas, you can conquer humanity?"

He laughed, and leaned forward with a conspiratorial grin. "Sweetheart, I know it for a fact."

Kill him.

I pulled the trigger instinctively without thinking about it at the first words from Wolfe, and only after the shot rang out did I reconsider. It didn't matter, because the moment the muzzle flared, Weissman was gone. The shot hit the empty chair and padded stuffing flew out of the back, creating a little cloud of rubberized foam that settled quickly.

"Uhm …" Breandan's voice echoed in the small office, "where is he?"

I heard the thump of something being hit and spun to find Breandan, wide-eyed and flung toward me. I didn't have time to react before he caught me in the side and the two of us went crashing into the desk. I felt a rib crack and I cringed as I went down. I suppressed the temptation to scream in pain.

"The real question," Weissman's calm, assured voice came from where Breandan had been standing only a moment earlier, "is *when* is he?" He looked down at us, running his tongue around in his mouth as he leered down at us, totally unworried.

Breandan groaned in pain as he sat up, and I followed after he lifted his weight off me. "Is this a riddle of some sort?"

"If so, I expect you'd fail, Irish," Weissman said, examining his fingernails as if there was something trifling beneath them. "I warned you I was the one holding the power in the room."

"And here I was trying to figure out why you were so damned arrogant." I propped myself up and didn't bother pointing the gun at him. "You can control the flow of time."

Weissman smiled. "You really are a clever one. Most people don't get that until it's far too late." His smile grew into a grin.

"Of course, if it weren't for the special instructions I have regarding you, it'd be too late for you by now. As it is, I'm afraid I'm going to have to kill your friend now—"

"Wait," I said, and Weissman cocked his head at me in curiosity. "If you have control of the flow of time—and I presume you can, what? Speed it up?" He nodded. "Slow it down?" He nodded again. "Make it stop?"

He smiled. "If necessary."

"Then why the need for all these gun thugs?" I asked, slowly getting back to my feet. "Why the kill teams, why send the metas up to Ireland to wipe out those cloisters?" I watched his reaction for this, but he didn't bat an eye, didn't reveal a thing. "You could do it yourself, every bit of it."

He gave me a grudging nod. "I could, technically."

"You could, but …?" I waited a moment. "But it bores you? It's beneath you?"

He laughed. "Probably. But no. You're fishing. All right, fine. Here's a nugget that won't get you anywhere." His eyes turned serious, but the laugh lines remained at his eyes even as a little worry crept in at the corners. "Because there's another meta out there with this power, this ability I have. If I stop time, it stops for both of us. Same if he were to do it. Now, he doesn't—or does it exceedingly rarely, anyway. Call it a gentleman's agreement between the last two of us left—we don't inflict this slow-stop stuff on each other."

I thought about that one for a beat. "Aren't you about to wipe out every meta on the planet?"

"Close," Weissman said, this time with less smile, less assurance. "But not all."

"So your friend with the same power as yours," I said lightly, "he doesn't take kindly to you messing with his world?"

Weissman's irritation flared. "That's not what I said."

"But it's what you meant." I gave him an infuriating smile.

"That was the subtext, outside of your puffery, that this other guy, with your power, he scares the shit out of you. Enough that you won't push the boundaries because you're afraid of him."

Weissman gave me a humorless smile, started to say something harsh but waited until he'd calmed for a second. "Like I said, you're smart."

"And you're scared." I licked my lips. "How do you think this friend of yours will take it when you end up wiping out most of the metas on the planet?"

"Oh, he doesn't care about that," Weissman said, and the genuine, mean and nasty smile returned. "He's far too preoccupied with his own navel gazing."

I smiled back, and this time I saw a flash of annoyance from him. "So this guy ... you're scared of him? And he's not Sovereign?"

Weissman rolled his eyes. "You're a little too clever for you own good."

I wondered how fast he could move; if he could stop time in a blink. "Why, thank you, Mr. Weissman. I don't suppose you'd kindly tell me where this meta is? This one you fear, this one that you're not going to mess with, even as you exterminate every other on the planet?"

Weissman laughed. "I wouldn't worry about him. If the day comes that he works his way toward being a threat, Sovereign will take care of him. No, I'd be worrying about your little friend here." Weissman gestured toward Breandan, who stood with his back to me, eyes on Weissman.

"Why would I worry about him?" I asked. "You already said you're going to kill him. I can't hit you, I can't hurt you. Ergo, he's screwed." I shrugged at Breandan, who looked back at me with a sort of muted horror. "Sorry. I can't stop time, or slow him down, and he basically has the ability to teleport anywhere in the room, or show up behind us, or just leave until we're gone. He could sit here and watch us until we've left, then follow us back to where we're staying and kill us there." I looked at Weissman. "Except you can't. Because if you stall time for too long, he'll get pissed at you, whoever *he* is." I smiled. "So ... how long can you stop time before he gets mad? Or does it have a cumulatively annoying effect?"

Weissman sighed. "Long enough to kill him and then leave town, which, if you really took McClaren's soul, you'd know I was planning to do anyway."

"After you kill another few metas, as I recall," I said. "Your business in London is hardly concluded."

"So you want to be a pain in my ass, huh?" Weissman said coldly. "Keep in mind that while I can't kill you, my orders say nothing about beating you into unconsciousness and chaining you to a radiator for the next forty-eight hours."

"You know what, Dr. Time?" I grinned at him. "You're welcome to try. You'll probably even succeed, being the amazing badass you clearly are with your abilities. But I wonder if you can—"

"Just stop right there," Weissman said. "If you're waiting on some mythical meta I told you about to come save your ass from me, don't. I assure you, I can pulp you and your pal with the greatest of ease and leave the area without raising his eyebrow."

"Now we're learning," I said. "Let me ask you something about your power—"

"Enough fishing," he snapped. "We're done with the conversational portion of this meeting."

"So that just leaves the fighting, then?" I quipped.

"I know you meant that to be funny," Weissman said, almost with an air of pity, "but it's not going to be quite so hilarious when you're stepping in a pool of your friend's blood.

"Well, go on then," I said, waving him toward Breandan, who turned back and gave me a *how could you?* look. "I can't stop you, he can't stop you." I locked eyes with Breandan. "Looks like my luck's run out." His widened, and then he gave a subtle motion of the hand toward me.

"I think you mean his," Weissman said with a leer.

"Sure," I said and snapped off a shot from the hip at him.

True to form, Weissman disappeared before the bullet struck. I spun and fired from the hip at the empty space in front of Breandan, who didn't even have time to react before the bullets were on their way, whizzing in front of his face. There was a scream of pain and suddenly a figure was lying prostrate on the floor in front of Breandan, clutching his shoulder. I was on him a second later, my hand around his neck, my fingers wrapped around the soft flesh, choking him and willing my powers to work faster.

"Now, Mr. Weissman," I said with a smile as I knelt astride him. He grunted in pain as he held his wounded shoulder, "Let's see what you know."

"Lucky shot," Weissman hissed through gritted teeth as I gripped his throat tighter and felt the first stirrings of my power at work on him.

I shot a glance at Breandan, who looked to be trying to catch his breath. "The very definition of one."

"You think you win on a lucky shot?" Weissman said, the pain entering his voice. "Let me tell you something about me, about Century. It's gonna take a hell of a lot more lucky shots to take us down than you've got in you." He gave me a burning glare of defiance and then was gone, disappeared from my grip as I fell to the ground from where I had been kneeling atop him.

"Oh, shite," Breandan said in alarm from above me. I looked up at him and swallowed heavily, waiting for the blow to fall. The air was still and quiet in the office, and as I started to stand something slammed into my back so hard I was driven to my knees. A moment later I saw Breandan fall, flipping behind the desk after a blow to the face.

"Did you think you could beat me?" came Weissman's voice from above me. "Did you really think you could conquer someone who has mastery over time?" Fingers grabbed me around the back of the neck and drove me into the floor, hard. The concrete rushed up to meet me and I felt something break, a stabbing pain above my eye telling me that things were most certainly not all right at the moment, at least not in the realm of my face. "You are such an arrogant little twat. If I didn't *have* to spare you," he spun me around and held me by the front of my shirt, "you'd already be dead." He clubbed me across the face with brutal speed, and my head snapped back, dazing me further. "So you get to live. But," he said with a smile, "I'm gonna leave you in so much pain that you'll wish for the next twenty-four hours that I'd killed you." He hit me again, and I heard cracking in the back of my neck from the force of the blow. I tried to lift a hand to grab his, but there was no feeling in my fingers, or my feet, or anywhere else in my body.

Weissman stood. "And I'm gonna start by slaughtering your little friend while you watch." He straightened the cuffs of his suit coat. "By the time I'm done, I'm gonna have to keep you from drowning in his blood." He pointed a thin finger at my face. "Remember—it could have been easy. Now it's gonna be long, drawn out and torturous. And it's all your fault. Watch and learn, little girl—"

There was a stir in the air, and it took on a savage ferocity, like a storm blasting through. Something whipped through the air and caught Weissman, flinging him. Whether he couldn't use his power or something was stopping him, I didn't know, but he hit the back wall of the office and came to a landing behind the desk. He sprung to his feet a moment later, holding his still-bleeding shoulder and staring at the office door. I wanted to turn to see what he was looking at, but I couldn't move my neck.

"Well, well, well," Weissman said, almost snarling, "I didn't expect to see you here."

"No?" came a familiar voice from the door. It was youthful, vibrant, something so reassuring about it. "I'm guessing you didn't expect to see anyone here. But the problem with you Century guys is that the longer you're running this little extinction operation, the more time you give us to hunt your asses down."

"Congratulations," Weissman gave a faux clap of his hands, like a little round of applause that was limited by the awkward way he had to hold the shoulder I'd shot. "You're way behind, but hey, you finally found our London base. Now ... do you honestly believe that you can stop me before I leave?"

"No," came the voice in reply. "But there are six of us and one of you. I may not be able to stop you right off, but I bet I can keep you tied up until your friend across the world gets pissed off and decides to intervene." There was a pause and I saw Weissman's face fall. "Yeah, I know about him. So ... you wanna rumble? Because I just tossed your ass once, and I'm thinking I can probably do it again if necessary."

"Lucky shot," Weissman said.

"I've got more where that came from."

Weissman clicked his tongue. "You played this all wrong. You could have come at me, put up a hard press. You might even have gotten me, if you'd just given up the girl." He smiled, and it was cold, brutal, mean—everything I'd come to expect from Weissman after just one encounter. "But hey ... fair enough. You win. I'll walk away for now." He gave the figure in the doorway a near-salute. "See you real soon." He cast his gaze to me. "Don't think this settles anything. You can't protect her. Not from me if I came for her, and damned sure not from *him*."

"*He* better not come anywhere near her," came the reply, along with a slow, even, near grinding of teeth along with the words.

"You think you can stop Sovereign?" Weissman said with

that same smile. "Oh, that's a laugh. You are so out of your depth. Good luck. I believe I'd give it up if I were you. He did kill your father, after all; I doubt he'd have much more trouble with you."

"Don't bet on it."

Weissman rolled his eyes. "What is it with you kids these days? Fine. Die, then. You're destined for it anyway. Just don't be surprised when it's ugly and painful and bloody and everything you've ever feared." His eyes locked onto the figure at the door and stared him down. "The worst part will be that in your dying moments, you'll have to live with the knowledge of what he might do to her after you're dead." Weissman's nasty smile came back full force. "Hell of a thing to die thinking about, wouldn't you say? I hope she's worth it."

"She's worth it."

Weissman shrugged. "If you say so." With a blink of my eye, he was gone, but I heard the last thing he said before he disappeared and I fell unconscious. My eyes closed slowly, and things around me faded to black as the last words echoed in my head.

"I damned sure wouldn't die like that for my sister."

Chapter 23

"Do you want to die here tonight?"

There was a subtle quiet on the London street, a pale twilight that hung in the air as the sun fell behind the buildings. The words echoed across the apartment blocks, and I knew it was South London, that it was the eighties again, and I could see that Adelaide had changed since last I'd seen her. The mohawk was gone, replaced by neck-length hair. Her jeans weren't ripped and torn anymore; she was in a skirt now, something so out of character for her I wondered if she felt the same about it as I did. She wore black leggings and knee high black boots and stood at the mouth of an alley while someone stared back at her from the opposite end. "I don't want to die here tonight, no," she replied to the man at the other end, "but I don't think there's a great danger of that at present."

"Oh, no?" came the voice from across the way. "I don't fancy your odds, luv."

"I don't mean to insult you," she said, her boots clicking as she came down the alley, shedding the tweed jacket she wore over a white blouse, "but I don't think you know a bloody thing about me."

"I know you're an Omega assassin," the man replied, holding his ground, "and that's about all I need, really. Come at me, and you'll die. That's all you need."

"I don't know about that," Adelaide replied, continuing her slow stroll toward him. I wondered how she could walk in those heels, much less fight in them, but I suspected based on what I'd seen of her so far that I'd be finding out shortly. "In fact, I think it's going to go quite the opposite way."

"Told you to kill me, didn't they?" The man asked. "They would. I know things," he said, his flabby paunch hanging over a truly sloppy pair of trousers. "Things they don't want getting out. Things about their golden boy, Wolfe." The man wore a self-satisfied expression that was hiding something else entirely. "He's a murderer, you know. Kills anything he wants to. Men, women, children. The Primus and the ministers just look the other way. He's a stone killer, has been for thousands of years."

"I've heard rumors about that," Adelaide said with a glacial reserve. "Don't expect it matters much to anyone in Omega."

"So you're another that doesn't care what Omega does so long as you get your piece of the action, is that it?" The man waited, his hair long around the sides of his face. "It doesn't bother you that people who used to be gods have sunk to petty criminality to finance their lifestyles?"

"I wouldn't be very good at my job if I let moral concerns get in the way of my work," Adelaide said. I couldn't see even a glimmer of emotion from her.

"They tell you to even try bringing me back alive?" The man asked.

"They weren't specific, this time," Adelaide replied. "If you gave yourself up, I could be persuaded to bring you back—"

"Don't wanna go back," the man said, and I saw some age on him at that moment. "I'd rather kill you than go back."

"All right, then," Adelaide said tightly. "Give it a go, then."

The man wore a look of almost-remorse. "You'll be sorry you asked for this, luv."

"I don't think I will," Adelaide replied.

The man leapt at her across the last ten feet, and he soared through the air with all the strength I'd come to expect from a meta. As he did so, his chest bulged under his ill-fitting clothes, turning him from a paunchy sort to a wide-bodied beast. His face filled out on the jump, his neck widening and pushing his collar open to reveal raw muscle that hadn't been there a moment before. He landed and Adelaide dodged backward, just missing a heinous punch from him that would have smashed a tree in two.

"Ever fought a Hercules before?" the man asked with a confident grin. "All I've got is the strength to beat you to death twenty times over. You run, I catch you. You fight, I beat you. You try and hit me, I break you to pieces."

"Well," Adelaide said in a defensive posture, standing back from him a few paces, "you've certainly got me there. Whatever will I do?"

"I told you—die," he said. "You could have run away before, but now I can't let you tell them where I am."

"If that's the way you feel about it," Adelaide said, "maybe we can come to an understanding." She eased a step closer to him, watching his hands.

"Oh?" the man asked. "Now you see what I've got, you think it's time to deal?"

"Not really," Adelaide said, her accent clipping, her tone ambiguous. "I just wanted a moment to get closer to you." She threw herself at him and he swung at her. She ducked his blow and came up with one of her own, an open-handed slap to his face that lingered there, giving me pause.

He laughed at her and caught her hand. "A slap? Really? I would think you could do better than that."

"Quite right," Adelaide said, and brought her other hand around in a slap that didn't so much as sting but stayed attached to his face, held on by her grip.

He laughed out loud. "This is supposed to hurt me, luv? Why don't you try about three feet lower?" He wagged his pelvis at her.

She smiled. "You want me to?"

He laughed again, bubbling with mirth as she held on to his face. "If you're offering …"

She hung on to him just another moment before I saw the first flinch from him at the pain. "Wait a minute," he said, his voice a low grunt.

"Sure thing," she breathed, holding on tight, "I'll wait."

"No!" He swatted at her and she took the hit, not letting go of his face. Her head came back up, nose bloodied, and she pushed tighter to his skin as he hit her again, this time rocking her head back. She jammed her thumbs into his eye sockets, wrenching a scream from him that tore through the alley like the howl of a beast echoing through a canyon. "Let me … effing … go … !"

"'Fraid I can't do that," she said, lowering him gently to the ground as his strength gave out, his body shrinking, returning to its normal chubby proportions. "You know by now," she said to the blinded, swollen man that she held gripped by the head like a volleyball, "Omega doesn't let go until we're through with you."

"P-please!" he said, begging. "I have a wife and daughters! They're … they're like you!"

"Like me?" she asked, and I could feel the amusement flee as she tried to ignore the truth of what he was telling her and focus on the words purely on the surface level. "Funny? Strong?" She hesitated, and I heard the death rattle leave him as she let go of the body, and he crumpled to the dirty floor of the alley. Adelaide let out a little breath. "Succubi, eh? Maybe we're all related somewhere back up the line."

She took a couple steps back from him and leaned against the wall, the spotted, aged bricks standing out against her pale skin in the dark. "Sorry it came to this, but here we are. Now Omega's done with you … Mr. Nealon."

Chapter 24

I woke in the dark, gasping for air again, my head spinning with what I'd just seen, with everything that had happened of late, and that damned nausea back again. There was a smell in the air, something sweet, like honeysuckle, and it soothed my nose a little. My breathing was ragged, and I could feel cool sheets underneath me, my mouth dry with thirst. I smacked my lips together until I heard a click, and a light came on to my left.

I turned to find a table lamp on a nightstand. Next to it was a ragged old cloth-covered chair upholstered in some terrible shade of orange that surely hadn't been in vogue since the 1970s. Sitting in it was a very familiar face, one that brought tears to my eyes and a lump to my throat.

"Reed," I said with a light gasp.

His dark hair was pulled back in a ponytail. His tanned skin was almost orange by the glow of the lamp, and his eyes were flinty; I couldn't see any happiness in them; it was as though he were looking at a stranger and not me. "Sienna," he said with reserve.

"What are you doing here, Reed?" I looked around the shadowed room. It was wood-paneled in an old style that reminded me a little of my mother's room in our house. "I should probably ask where we are, too."

"Still London," he said coolly and leaned back in his chair. He wore a simple leather coat, his constant companion, and a pair of jeans that allowed the black cowboy boots he wore to hang out of the bottoms without interference. "You've been out for a little under a day. We brought you back to our safehouse here after your tango with Weissman."

"Weissman," I said, sitting up and feeling an ache run down my back. "He was Century's advance man in London. He was conducting the extermination here."

"Extermination, huh?" Reed asked with bitter amusement. "That's a good way to describe it."

I felt my joy at seeing him deteriorate. "What's happened?"

He shrugged lightly. "Their 'extermination,' as you so eloquently put it, is proceeding pretty quickly, much faster than we knew when last I saw you. They're just about done in Africa. Asia is pretty well knit up. They hit Australia months ago; we didn't even really notice. They've done some island hopping in the Pacific to clean things up there, and now all their attention is focused on closing out Europe before they move to the Americas." He smiled ruefully. "I heard it's started in South America. A favela in Rio de Janeiro got burned completely out last week, left nothing but a mountain of scorched corpses." His fingers tapped out a rhythm on his leg. "Dead bodies everywhere, all over the world."

I let myself fall back onto the bed. "Damn."

"'Damn'?" Reed looked back at me and I tilted my head so I could see the accusation in his eyes. "That's all you have to say?"

"What else would you like me to say?" I put a little heat on my question. As if there was anything I could do about all this?

"How about an explanation?" Reed said, firing back with a little heat of his own. "You disappeared off the face of the earth! I left for Rome for a few days and when I get off the plane, they show me satellite imagery that the Directorate is in rubble." He thumped his chest with an open palm. "I thought you were dead!"

I stared back at him, stunned. "You don't know, do you?"

"Know what?" Reed asked, leaning forward. "I don't know anything! I left to get help, and when they told me the Directorate was destroyed, I assumed you'd call me." He lowered his voice.

"When I didn't hear from you, I figured you were dead." The last word came out as a hushed whisper.

"I'm not dead," I said numbly. "Almost no one died in the attack on the Directorate. Sessions, Perugini, I think. Scott was already gone; he took off after Kat couldn't remember him. Kat," I said, almost rambling as the emotions of that night came back full force, "she betrayed us to Omega. Resumed her ... earlier personality." I watched Reed's jaw drop slightly in shock. "But Omega held back. Janus didn't aim to kill anyone, the ones that died did so by accident. He was just there to knock us over. It was ..." I swallowed heavily. "After they were done, Winter ..." I felt a twitch in my eye, even after the week or more that had passed since it happened. "It doesn't matter. Zack's dead," I said numbly. "So's M-Squad."

"What?" Reed's head shook as he blinked away surprise. "I thought you said almost no one died in the attack." He paused, and got quiet, and I felt his hand brush against mine in a reassuring stroke. "I'm sorry about Zack. How did it ... how did he ...?"

I thought about lying. Part of me wanted to. "Winter," I said, and Reed's neck bent to the side as he cocked his head at me, brow furrowed with concern. "Winter killed him. With M-Squad's help."

"Holy shit," Reed breathed. "And they—"

"Like I said," I cut him off, "they're dead."

Slow understanding dawned on him and his head slowly dipped back as he leaned against the back of his chair. "Did *you* ...?"

I couldn't meet his gaze. "I did it, yeah."

"God, Sienna ..."

I let a silence hang between us like a curtain. "I almost got Winter, too," I said, "but he got away." I looked up at him. "I'm sorry I didn't call. I'm sorry I didn't ... dreamwalk to you or something."

"Why didn't you?" he asked, leaning forward again, his hand resting on the sleeve of my clothing. "Why didn't you tell me?"

I bit my bottom lip to keep it from quivering and waited to steady myself before I spoke. "I didn't want ... to admit what they did. And after I did what I did ... I didn't want to admit that to anyone, either." I looked at him and felt my eyes water. "I've killed people, Reed. A lot of them, lately. Not all of them deserved it." I felt my arm shake under his grasp. "It's like I can't stop, like I can't control myself. I don't know if it's me, or Wolfe—I don't even know if there's a line between us anymore!" I heard a quaver in my voice. "When he says to kill someone, it's like I just start moving without thinking." I brought my other hand up to my face to cover it, as though I could hide from him. "I ... killed the Primus of Omega."

There was a shocked silence. "You ... did what?"

I pulled my hand away and looked at him. "I killed the Primus of Omega. I beat him to death in his own office."

He frowned. "Is that why they appointed the new one? Rick?"

I shook my head. "No. That's the one I killed."

Reed took a sharp breath. "Oh, wow. We didn't even know that he was dead."

"It just happened yesterday." I brushed some of the dampness from my cheek with my sleeve. "He was trying to intimidate me by talking about how powerful he was, how insignificant I was, and I just snapped and ... beat him to death."

There was a quiet for a moment after that, and when I looked at Reed's face, I could see he was trying to come up with something reassuring to say. "You know, Omega's not exactly an organization built on sweetness and light. If this Rick was running the show, he was not a good guy. I wouldn't lose a lot of sleep over it if I were you."

I bumped my head against the headboard of the bed. "I don't seem to be losing sleep over much of anything lately." I blinked and looked sideways at him. "What do you know about my family?"

He looked stupefied. "Uh … you mean, other than that I'm your brother?"

I sighed. "The Nealon side."

He shrugged. "Nothing, really. Why?"

"Because," I said, trying to put together the pieces of what I'd seen in my dream, "I'm pretty sure I just saw an Omega operative kill my grandfather."

Reed looked left then right, as though surveying the room for something he'd missed. "Um … maybe we should get you off that pain medication."

I studied my arms for an IV. There wasn't one. "I don't think I'm on any pain medication."

"Then we should probably get you some."

"I'm not delusional," I said, annoyed. "I saw it in a dream. Like a flashback. I think it came from Zollers, like he put it in my head so I could see it. I keep seeing this Omega operative named Adelaide, doing work for them here in London back in the 1980s." I felt a stir inside at that, and I knew who it was that was taking an interest. "She was a succubus, and she was trained by Wolfe."

Reed sat up, his eyes focusing on me in rapt attention. "Why do you think she killed your grandfather?"

"I'm not a hundred percent on it," I said, "but she called him Mr. Nealon, and he was a meta who said his wife and daughters were succubi." I shrugged. "Just a hunch. Maybe we're unrelated. Just seemed like an odd thing for me to witness if it's pure coincidence."

"Coincidence in this instance does seem a bit farfetched." Reed shook his head and squeezed my forearm again through the cotton sleeve of my shirt. "I really am glad to see you. When I thought you were dead, I …" He swallowed heavily. "You're the only family I have left, you know."

"Same goes, bro," I said with a weak smile. "I'm sorry I didn't call or … anything. I just … I'm sorry. I couldn't handle it at first. I just retreated from the world. Afterward …" I let my voice trail off, and when I spoke again it was quiet. "I think I was probably too ashamed of what I was going to do … and since then what I've done. I just didn't want to drag you into that."

Reed rubbed his eyes. "I would have been there for you, you know that, right?"

"In a heartbeat," I said with a weak smile. "But you shouldn't have had to be there. Not for that." My smile disappeared. "Not for what I did."

I could see the unease as he nodded. "I have to go … talk to my boss. Fill her in on what happened to Rick. This is important. I have a feeling she'll want to talk to you herself."

"Wait," I asked. "What happened to the guy I was with?"

"Breandan Duffy?" Reed asked with a smile. "He's fine. Playing cards with some of our hired hands here. He's under our protection now. We're trying to get as many metas as we can under our roof here in London so we can all band together."

"How's that going?" I asked, hopeful to hear something good in return.

"Bad," Reed replied with none of the optimism I'd hoped for. "We've only been here for a couple days, though." He hesitated. "We had to get out of Rome pretty quickly."

I didn't frown, exactly, but that didn't sound like good news. I put it aside, though, remembering something more urgent. "Weissman was sending someone up to Ireland to wipe out a couple cloisters up there," I said. "He was planning to hit one up in Scotland himself, with his team of mercs. Since Breandan and I killed them, I don't know what he's going to do now, but someone should warn them—all of them—what's coming." I felt a tremor inside, a fear for those people I didn't even know. "I saw the handiwork of whatever he sent to Ireland. There were bodies …

everywhere." I let the last bit out as a whisper, and in my mind I saw them again. In a flash, it reminded me of all the corpses I'd left on the ground lately.

"We've got someone on their way up there right now," Reed said. "We're hurrying. It could be tight. Century's in full motion now, scrambling to get everyone they can on the playing field to kill every meta possible and we're thin on resources." He ran a hand through the hair on top of his head. "As much as I hate Omega, they're nothing compared to this threat. At least with them, these metas stand a chance of survival."

"And what about with you?" I asked quietly.

He smiled, faintly. "We're not played out yet." He gave me a last squeeze of reassurance and headed back through the door.

After he shut it, I waited in the quiet and pondered Reed's words. He could try and reassure me all he wanted, play the big brother card with all its authority, but it didn't matter. I'd seen what Century had done to a room full of metas already, wiping them out without a fight, without hope, without remorse—and I wondered if they'd be able to do just the same to all of us who remained.

Chapter 25

I stood up a few minutes later, testing my strength. The faint smell of Reed lingered in the room, and I cracked my neck to see if it was all better. It was. I couldn't remember if I'd had a broken neck before, but it wouldn't have surprised me. The benefit to healing quickly and being in as many fights as I'd been in was that it was incredibly hard to remember all the injuries I'd accumulated in my year of battle. And it had been only a year, unbelievably.

I was still wearing the same clothes I'd had on when I confronted Weissman, minus my purloined tactical vest. I didn't see any dressers or any sign that there was any other clothing available for me to change into, which wouldn't have been so bad if not for the fact that I was feeling grimy. I wondered if anyone had bothered to collect my travel bag from the van in Century's warehouse, and I ultimately decided I'd just retrieve it myself later, if necessary. I had reached the point in my life where I needed to decisively handle things myself. I'd relied on my mother for all the years I'd lived at home, then on the Directorate when I was in their employ. I didn't want to rely on anyone like that ever again. It made me feel too weak and vulnerable when they decided to pull up stakes and leave me on my own.

I was doing a full, slow stretch and cracking my back into place when the door opened softly. I turned to see Breandan walk in, a smile on his face. "Good to see you," he said, closing the door softly behind him. "At least it's good to see you up and about. I think you've been unconscious more since I've met you than you've been awake, actually."

"That seems to be a fairly common state of affairs nowadays,"

I said, rising off the bed to greet him. "How are the cards treating you?"

He grinned. "These Alpha fellows seem to think it's my lucky day."

"I can't imagine why."

He shrugged lightly. "Who am I to disabuse them of the notion that their fortunes are merely off for the time I'm at the table? It'll probably be another game or twelve before they tumble to the notion that I might be cheating. At that point, they'll ask me what my power is. Probably better if I quit while I'm ahead, eh?"

"For some reason, I thought you didn't like to gamble," I said.

"Oh, I like gambling," he said amiably, "I just don't think it's good for me. But that's something else entirely." He looked me over. "You look well. Especially considering how unwell you looked when we carried you out of that office where Weissman beat the holy hell out of us."

"I heal fast," I said, running a hand over my dirty blouse. It wasn't exactly top quality to begin with, just a little above casual, but it was what I had.

"You're not even joking," Breandan said. "It was well over a day before I could safely take the cotton out of my nose after our scrape on the tube. But you—you're a right mess less than a day ago and now you're fit as a fiddle."

"I'm a powerful meta," I said absently.

"What's that have to do with it?" he asked, wrinkling his nose.

"Something about the power scale," I said with a shrug. "Some meta types are more powerful than others, and with that comes faster healing, more strength, dexterity, all that. It rises correspondingly."

"Very fancy," he said with a smirk. "Those of us with only the ability to idly fiddle with luck, I suppose we're on the low end of your power scale?"

"I don't know. I've never really seen a chart comparing and detailing the different types, to be honest."

The door opened again and I leveled a semi-serious glare at it as Reed entered. "No one around here seems to understand the polite art of knocking, apparently."

"Sorry," Reed said, "I've got someone I'd like you to meet."

"Oh, good," I said, looking down at my ragged clothing, "I'm well dressed to meet your boss right now."

He smiled faintly. "I maybe should have been more clear about this. When I said 'My boss,' I didn't just mean my immediate supervisor."

"Geez," I said with a certain feeling of dread discomfort. "You're introducing me to someone way up the chain, aren't you?"

"Right at the top, I'd estimate," Breandan said softly.

"Yeah," Reed said, looking sidelong at the Irishman. "The founder of Alpha."

"By all means," I said with a feeling of surrender. "Bring him in."

Reed scrunched his face up at me then slapped the door once as though to signal someone outside. "She."

"Fine," I said. "Bring she in." I smirked. "Or did you mean 'her'?"

"He meant her," came the voice as she opened the door. She was fairly tall as women go and ridiculously elegant, even clad as she was in a pantsuit. "I am definitely a her." She surveyed me with cool eyes, grey as a stormy sky, her hair a faded platinum that she clearly wasn't bothering to conceal. Age looked good on her, better than on most women, but it was still obvious in the lines that had crept in on her face. As a young woman, she would have been considered stately, but probably not beautiful. As an older one, she looked commanding, severe, and not like someone whom my first instinct would be to cross. "It's quite an event to meet you after all this time," she said in a dry tone, sharp and crisp. "I must admit with everyone in the meta world scrambling to get hold of you over these last few months, I rather expected you'd be taller." She let a smile show the irony, and it took me only a moment to realize she was joking.

"Thanks," I said, not quite sure how to take that. "I tend to find that my stature makes people underestimate me."

"No doubt," she said. "But, before we begin," she turned to Reed, "perhaps you'd like to make a more formal introduction."

Reed gave a subtle nod, and I saw his Adam's apple bob as he swallowed almost comically. "This is my sister, Sienna Nealon," he said to the woman, giving me a cool look as he did so. "Sienna, this is my boss—the head of Alpha." She turned to face me as he spoke, keeping her arms folded across her chest, her suit not even creasing as she did so, maintaining the elegant lines. "You've probably heard of her before.

"Her name is Hera."

Chapter 26

"I'm standing in the presence of a famous one," I said dryly as I cast a look sideways at Breandan, who smiled weakly back. "Hard not to have heard of the wife of Zeus."

She didn't flinch, but I saw a flicker of amusement, tempered by annoyance. "Yes, I get that all the time," she said, with an air of exaggerated patience. "Some of our mistakes are forgotten as quickly as they're made. Unfortunately, that one appears set to haunt me until the end of the world."

Breandan looked at her with his eyebrows raised about halfway up his forehead. "Sorry. Marrying Zeus was a mistake? Is that what you're suggesting?"

"Did I suggest that?" she asked wryly. "Let me make it more clear—it was a disastrous mistake, and one I wish I could take back a thousandfold. Not only was it ridiculously short-lived by the standards of our race, but every myth surrounding it at this point makes me seem like quite the shrew." She rolled her eyes. "Now I'm the mythical equivalent of Kim Kardashian."

I held my tongue, tempted though I was to make some witticism about myth being rooted in fact. I assumed I had matured in the last year because there was a time when I'd never have been able to keep from saying something as juicy as that. I knew there was still an insufferable smile perched on my lips, though, and Hera noticed it too. "I wouldn't worry about it; you're nowhere near as well known as Kim Kardashian, at least not to the current generation." Well, it wasn't as bad as what I could have said. I gave it a five on the harshness scale. If we were grading on a curve. "Bad reputations notwithstanding," I said, changing the subject, "perhaps we oughta get to business."

"Sure," Hera said with a subtle nod. "Have a seat." With a wave, she indicated my bed, which was the only thing other than the chair beside it that could be sat on in the room.

"No, thanks. I'd really rather stand after the last day or so's action." I didn't intend to patronize her, but I'm sure it came off like that. I really just didn't want to sit. Or feel like I was in her charge at all.

"Right." I noticed she remained standing, too. "So, you know what's going on out there."

"I've heard," I said. "I told Reed what I know about Century's plans. Any chance you're going to be able to save those people in Ireland and Scotland?"

"We'll try," she said, her face grey with what looked like the weight of that thought. "It's a pretty big burden to carry. I don't know if Reed's told you much about us, but we're hardly as well funded or connected as Omega. We're stretching the limits of our resources at this point." She lowered her head slightly. "At the rate metas are being killed, though, it's not looking too pretty for us as a race."

"Do you know what's carrying out the killings?" I asked and caught a trace of curiosity from her. "I was at a village, a site of one of the massacres a few days ago, and it was like nothing I've ever seen before." I paused. "And I've seen Wolfe at work, so it's not like I've never witnessed a massacre."

"True enough," she said. "We're not exactly sure. As you probably know, Century has a hundred members. A very tight-knit cabal, and those members were chosen very carefully for their skills and abilities. They're powerful. They don't have any weak links." She edged a glance toward Breandan, who flushed under her gaze. "Anyone you run into from Century is either a mercenary or a member of their inner council. They've certainly not been hesitant to use bloodthirsty men with guns, but most of the damage is being done by metas."

"What types do they have at their disposal?" I asked, curious. "And how did they recruit them?"

She gave a light smile, and it was like a beacon in the dark of her wearied expression. "Near as we can tell, they were approached one by one over the last few years, chosen by Weissman and Sovereign. If someone decided they didn't like the sound of it, decided they didn't want to come along for the ride … well, let's just say they weren't seen again." Her smile faded. "Now that's speculation, since no one's told us about any such meeting. But some very high-profile metas have disappeared in the last few years, unexpected and unexplained. For those types, that's just not usual. Some of them were very well known within the community—people like …" she hesitated, "Persephone, for instance. Loki. Set." She shrugged. "Quite a few others. All gone, all disappeared. I'd have to guess most are dead."

I narrowed my eyes as I thought about it. "So if they were recruited they wouldn't have resumed their place in meta society? You assume none of them said yes and … I dunno, went back to Century's secret undersea volcanic lair?"

She smiled again, this time carefully. "There might be some lingering out there, but I would think that the temptation would be to have them exert their influence in the name of the conspiracy that they were now part of. After all, if some of their members are highly placed in the meta community, they could use that influence to press for calm while this storm started blowing their way. And they might have done just that. It's not like we didn't see signs of this years ago. We just didn't know what we were looking at. The puzzle was missing almost all its pieces. Now that more of them are on the table, the picture is starting to appear, and I don't care for the shape of it at all. We're down by two-thirds of the meta population already." She said this with a little bit of a drawl, and I realized that she really didn't have much of an accent.

"I suspect they mean to finish the task at hand in the next few months, and then … whatever their plans are for humanity, it'll be showtime."

I thought about what she'd said, and something didn't add up. "I knew someone who worked for them, a meta."

"Oh?" She eyed me. "You're talking about that doctor that worked at the Directorate?"

"Zollers," I said. "I don't think he was part of the inner council, not by the way he talked about it. I mean, maybe he was, but he was supposedly going to have to go on the run from them."

"Sounds like he'd be a veritable wealth of information about them if we could get our hands on him," she said. "I doubt he's within easy reach, though."

I frowned. "Maybe not." I looked around the room for a moment as I pondered whether I should mention that I thought he was out there, trying to influence me in some way. I decided to pass on it for now. "You know, Omega's trying to do something similar to what you're doing. Trying to limit the damage. Help metas." I shrugged. "Or so they say."

Hera pursed her lips, deepening the already-present wrinkle lines around her mouth. "And they probably are, too. I despise most of those bastards with every damned fiber of my being, but this is the sort of crisis that puts even us on something approaching the same side.. These aren't the times when we're making a mad dash to grab metas up to solidify our own power, or to draw our own lines, increase our little fiefdoms. It's all or nothing days now, life or death. Tends to put things in perspective."

I smiled. "If that's the case, why don't you put aside your petty differences and work with Omega on this?"

She gave me a smile right back, but it was thin and patronizing. "I don't know. Why don't you do the same with Erich Winter?" She gave it a second to sink in and stayed cool. "Because of bad blood. After enough of it passes between you, it becomes a river you have a hard time crossing. I don't want to go back to them, hat in hand, and I doubt they much want to face up to me. So for the next little while, we'll each just ignore the other and keep scrambling to do everything we can to keep Century from destroying our world."

I sniffed, trying to ignore the faint smell of her perfume. It was fit for an old lady and not much else. "Have it your way, I suppose."

"Besides," she went on as if I hadn't spoken at all, "I still haven't forgiven those bastards for some of the things they did in the olden days. I bet they could say much the same about me."

"When you say the olden days," Breandan interjected, "do you mean like … um …"

"Xerxes's invasion of Greece," Hera said, almost indifferently. "That one caused some major ripples in the hierarchy at the time. A lot of us were in different countries around the world, only getting together for special occasions and content to rule our own little lands, managing the humans from a distance, exercising our power judiciously. Everybody did their own thing. We were fragmented in our own states, but it was working."

Her expression hardened. "Then some meta-jackass named Xerxes gets his loincloth in a twist and decides to declare himself a living god and starts invading the lands of others. He was hardly the first to try it, but … you know what an Athena-type is?" She looked rather pointedly at me.

"Sure," I said. "I met one just the other day."

"That boy could rile an army," she said with a smile. "I never did get the whole story, but I suspect one of his parents was an Ares. It wouldn't have been so bad if he hadn't taught them how to fight us. Made a mess out of our defense at Thermopylae." She let her smile fade. "That was the beginning of the end for us, and a great many of us weren't happy about it. Omega, though, they took it the worst. The Primus at the time was—well, guess."

"Your hubby," I said, and she let her amusement show.

"We were about done by then, but yes," she said. "The power of the gods, our ability to control man by annunciation and revelation, was fading. I said we should step into the shadows. We, who lived longer than most, who knew human whim and desire better than the shorter-lived humans did themselves, we could exert control without being blatantly obvious about it." She smiled again. "Leave it to a man to think that he needs to use a hammer when the touch of a hand will do. He never did quite get that lesson. Fortunately, when his brother took over after Zeus's death, he understood it."

I raised an eyebrow at her. "Poseidon?"

"Hell, yes," Hera said. "You didn't think I meant Hades, did you? No offense, but he would have made a worse Primus than Zeus, bastard that he was. Besides, he was dead by then, thank the stars."

There were a few parts of what she said that flagged my attention, and I started to ask some questions, but she went on and I found myself listening along.

"Poseidon took over Omega, backed by the four ministers," she said, "and he, with considerably less ego than his brother, recognized that there were other ways to rule the world. So he took us into the shadows, behind the scenes, made us legends and whispers. It took a while to make the transition, but he made money the tool by which we got what we wanted from mankind, and it worked pretty well for a couple thousand years, if I may say."

"Why did you break off from them?" I asked, the less pressing questions fading to the back of my mind for later.

"Because Poseidon died," she said. "And because the man who replaced him had not near the integrity of Poseidon, and took Omega in directions I didn't think it should go."

I raised an eyebrow at her. "I'm sorry, what? What directions did they go?"

She shrugged. "I think there's plenty of money to be made by legitimately supplying humans with what they want and need. Owning corporations, merchants, employing people was a way that we made gold hand over fist for millennia. The replacement Primus, the one who ran Omega until his son Rick took over a few days ago, was a servant of my late husband. His right hand man, if you will. He considered organized crime to be the last frontier for increasing the margins and the control Omega exercised over people, and so he took them into a very different place." She leaned toward me. "Now understand, we were gods. Our hands were not clean, by any means. We killed people, sure. I tried not to, but it happened from time to time, usually while I was avenging some wrong done to one of my followers. It's not as though they had a very good criminal justice system back then, and crimes on women tended to go unpunished.

"But I tried to steer us hard away from the course of being bloodthirsty killers," she said with narrowed eyes. "That was what Hades was. What his little triad did, those Cerberus boys. They were the scum of our kind, and most of us didn't want to sink to their lows, didn't want to be compared to them. Hell, some of us had even died trying to bring his ass down. But that was all lost on Rick's father."

"Who was he?" I asked, interrupting her. "The Primus? Who was he in the old myths?"

She shrugged again. "His name was Gerasimos, but the only way you would have heard him mentioned in myth was as Alastor, which was a nickname way back, a sort of curse that mortals wished on each other to signify what he had done, which was carry forth vengeance for Zeus, to strike down those who offended him for whatever reason." She rolled her eyes. "Often nonsensical and fueled by alcohol. Anyhow, he took over after Poseidon's death, and we had a bit of a clash, he and I. He earned that name by killing people. I didn't approve, but it didn't matter so long as Zeus was in charge. Which is another reason I hate that man to this day. Poseidon had reason, less ego, would at least hear you out." There was something behind her eyes that was akin to longing. "He shouldn't have died. He was the one who united the old-world gods, brought us together, expanded influence from Europe to Asia, even made inroads to South America." She shook her head again. "I don't suppose this all matters, but you know why I'm telling you all this, don't you?"

It was my turn to shrug. "Because I asked?"

"That's close enough to true," she said with a smile. "I've heard that Erich Winter tended to feed you a little at a time and keep the rest to himself, doling it out whenever he felt like it. I expect after what happened, it might have made you a little suspicious."

"So you want me to trust you?" I asked and sent a canny look toward Reed, whose face was neutral. After that, I looked to Breandan, who wore a poker face of his own. "You're drowning me in exposition so I won't think you're keeping things from me?"

She wore a maddening fragment of a smile, and I watched her tap her fingers on the side of her legs while she seemed to contemplate something. "Is it working?"

I thought about it for a second before answering. "It's not hurting your cause. What do you want me to do?"

"I don't suppose you've heard the tales?" she asked, watching me for a reaction. "I call them tales, but they're more like rumors, straight from the fields of west Asia and the eastern Mediterranean, from people who have seen things like you found in that church basement."

"You mean about how death is coming for them?" I asked, drawing a nod from her. "About how death is reaching out his hand for the metas, again? Just like what happened before." Her expression was carefully guarded, but her lips were upturned just the slightest in the corners. "They talked about it like it was Hades, right? Like it was him all along, back again?"

She finally broke into a smile. "So you have heard."

"Janus said he's dead," I replied. "So did you, just a few minutes ago."

"And so he is," she said and glanced at Reed. "Get the car ready, will you?"

He nodded and brushed his way out of the room, his ponytail swinging behind him. He didn't even protest or ask her why, just did it. I wondered at that but only for a moment before Hera got my attention again.

"I'm having him get the car because I think it's time you learned what use I would have for you," she said, almost quietly. She gave a nod to Breandan. "You can bring your friend with you if you'd like, but the next lesson I've got for you is going to require a little trip back in time, and I can't do that here. I need a little help."

"Back in time?" I asked. "Like … really back in time, turning back the clock?"

She laughed lightly. "Figuratively. I want to show you something, something that will help to explain things better than I could without the visual aid. Will you come with me?"

I hesitated. It's not like I wasn't squarely in the middle of her safehouse right now. It wasn't as though she didn't already have the ability to persuade me, to push me along. Still, she could have tried to force the issue but she was going for the delicate approach. It was the opposite of manipulation and yet carried the fingerprints of it still. "Sure," I said, overcoming that hesitancy. "Where are we going?"

"To show you where you came from," she said, stepping over to the door that Reed had just gone through a moment before, "to show you where your family originated." She smiled. "And to hopefully answer for you, finally, just one of the reasons you're so damned important to everybody on the planet."

Chapter 27

The luxury sedan cruised the rain-slicked streets of London. The weather had turned in the last day while I was unconscious, and the chill had been palpable as we had gotten in the car. Hera sat in the back with me, her platinum hair short-cropped around the top of her head as she leaned it back against the leather seat rest. Breandan was quietly nervous up front, and part of me thought about asking him why he was here with me. I didn't bother, though, because a second after I thought of the question, the answer came to me—he was still worried some Century sweep team was going to jump out of the shadows and kill him the moment he wasn't around me. Somehow, I'd become a good luck charm to a man who could control luck. Go figure.

Reed was up front with him, driving, and we rode along in silence until we crossed Tower Bridge heading north. I saw the Tower of London across the water. I had meant to check it out but that obviously hadn't panned out. As my eyes followed it while we passed, they came back to Reed in surprise. "Hey, aren't you used to driving on the other side of the road?"

"Yeah," he replied. "So?"

"So," I said, "isn't it kind of confusing, trying to remember you're not going the right way? I mean, I've only been in the passenger seat so far for a couple of drives and it messed with my head."

He shrugged. "It's no big deal. Just takes some thought."

I raised an eyebrow at him and thought about giving him a glare as he stared back at me in the rearview mirror. "What are you trying to say?"

He stared back while we sat at the traffic light, waiting for it to go green. "That it takes some thought." I saw his grin flash in the mirror. "Don't go looking for an insult where there isn't one."

"Oh, okay," I said. "You're just saying that so I won't be expecting one later and—BAM!"

He looked back to the road. "You know me too well."

"Oh, yes," Hera said, her eyes closed and her head back. "I haven't seen a brother and sister this sweet on each other since Artemis and Apollo."

I frowned. "Janus's parents? Wait, are you saying they were like … Cersei and Jaime Lannister? Cuz, if so … eww."

She raised a drooped eyelid enough to stare back at me with a commanding green eye. "That's exactly what I was saying. It sounds more incestuous than it was in most cases, though, because you have to keep in mind that myth isn't fact. What looks like family was more like an organization. What appeared like a father figure was more like a … Director, I suppose." She gave me an elusive smile. "His children were actually his lieutenants. Brothers—well, Hades and Poseidon actually were his brothers. But none of the kids were related."

That shut us up for a while. An uncomfortable silence persisted even as we slid through the downtown area, the tall buildings towering above us as I stared out the window and tried to crane my neck to look straight up. The rain dotted the glass like little diamonds, refracting as the sunlight peered out from behind a cloud and hit them. Prisms of rainbow light were as small as little beads within the drops, and I watched them refract as we drove on.

It took us what felt like an hour to arrive at our destination. My internal map was totally screwed up, and we passed a hundred parks along the way. It seemed like every few blocks there was a square that was empty save for greenery, with a fence wrapped around it so it could be closed at night, I presumed. "Looks like Russell Square," I murmured as we passed another. I wasn't really thinking about it as I spoke; all these squares looked alike to me, surrounded as they were by fairly similar buildings to my untrained (and uninterested) eye.

"It is Russell Square," Hera said quietly, causing me to sit up in surprise. "We're almost to our destination."

We parked a few minutes later and walked under cloudy skies down a street toward a building hidden partially behind a wall. Grey, weathered columns marked a massive facade, and as we climbed the stairs I turned to Breandan and whispered, "Where are we?"

He shrugged, a look of complete obliviousness plastered to his face. "Never been here before myself. I wouldn't know."

"It's the British Museum," Hera said, not able to disguise her irritation. "Don't you live here?" she asked Breandan pointedly.

"I've only been here for a few years," Breandan replied. "It's not like I'm some tourist who has all day to sit around scratching myself while pondering the great sculptors of ancient Carpathia." He thumped his chest. "I work for a living!"

I shot a look at him sideways. "You pick pockets on the tube a couple hours a day."

He gave me a look of great personal affront as we climbed the steps to the entrance. "Also downtown, sometimes." His pale cheeks flushed slightly crimson. "You know, just … to be clear for the record."

There were only minor crowds as we entered the building. It was a little darker. Not dim, but the light was plainly reduced. The smell of the place was clean and reminded me of shopping malls but with a hint of age to the whole thing, as though this was a place that had been around longer and carried great importance. "This way," Hera said, leading us forward into a well lit room beyond the entry.

As we walked through the doors into an open courtyard, my eyes widened. Above us was a dome that covered a massive room.

Had it been outside, it would have easily been large enough to be a stadium. In the middle rested a circular structure all on its own, with a spiral staircase wrapped around it on either side. Small restaurants and shops were scattered around the courtyard, and I felt a craving for a strong cup of coffee. I walked on, though, following Hera's lead, and marveling at the impressive white space of the courtyard around me. It was surprisingly brightly lit, especially for such a cloudy day.

Hera took us to the left, and I caught a glimpse of Reed at the rear of our procession, his eyes darting around, looking for any threats. Part of me wondered who would even be able to find us here, but after only a moment's thought, I remembered I had been found by enemies in odder moments and with less reason to believe they'd be looking for me.

We passed fine stone carvings and art from ancient Egypt, and my head swiveled as I walked by a display. I halted to read it—a sculpture of Bastet excavated from Bubastis. I rejoined the procession as Breandan gave me a look that indicated he was wondering what I was thinking. "Nothing," I replied to his nonverbal question.

I had seen a memory from Zack that detailed the moments before Omega destroyed the Directorate headquarters. Bastet had been there, and she and Winter had plainly been familiar with each other. When he had greeted her, he had mentioned that it had been "a long time since Bubastis." I had wondered about it at the time but had been more focused on other things that happened in the course of the memory. It was a skill I had, bouncing around from detail to detail without getting mired in anything but what I needed to focus on now. In some ways it was helpful. In other ways it wasn't. At the moment it was helping me distract myself from the possibility that I was pregnant with the child of my dead lover.

We made our way through a corridor filled on both sides with Persian carvings that were brilliantly done. I didn't have much experience with sculpture, but it looked like the work of years to create something so detailed. I caught Hera looking as well, and she flashed a reserved smile when she realized I had seen her. "These artisans did impressive things. Now you could craft something smoother and more perfect in sand in a matter of hours."

"You're talking about sandcastle sculptures?" I asked, my eyes tracing over the lines of the work as we continued to walk.

"Yes. It still impresses me what they can accomplish," she said.

"But those don't stand the test of time," I said. "I doubt any of them will be in a museum in a few thousand years."

"That's not the point," Hera said. "The point is that with technology and knowledge, man has advanced to a level where it's not only possible to surpass many of the things the gods used to do, but it's trivialized much of the making of art. Rather than a chisel and a piece of marble, a power tool can make a sculpture like these," she indicated with a wave of her hand to encompass the Greek gallery we were entering as she said it, "in hours or days. It used to take considerably longer." She smiled ruefully. "Just like killing men, really. It used to take battles or pillages to kill thousands or tens of thousands." She snapped her fingers. "Now you can do it in an instant." Her smiled faded. "It used to take a Hades or an Ares to do such a thing."

I glanced at her sidelong as we passed a gorgeous sculpture of one of the goddesses of ancient Greece crouched. It seemed well preserved, the white marble still looking clean and bright after what had to have been thousands of years of existence. "To do what? To fight a battle to kill tens of thousands?"

"No," she said, and stopped in the middle of the gallery. There were only sporadic groups around now, the museum drawing close to closing time. "Well, yes, in Ares's case. But Hades," she said with a shake of her head, "he was something else entirely."

"You keep mentioning him," I said. "And others, that Athena I met—she came from a cloister in Greece—she said that the old metas, the ones that had lived as long as you," I caught the twitch of her eye at my mention of her age, but she said nothing, "thought it was like Death had returned. Death with a capital D."

Hera seemed to consider this for a moment. "Death with a capital D. That's as good a way to describe him as any."

I thought of the village that had been destroyed, the bodies all piled in the church basement, and I stared down Hera, who was now pensive. "What was Hades's power?"

She blinked, not really in surprise, but looked at me almost as though she were amazed I was asking the question. "He could rip the souls from mortals to imprison them within himself."

I felt myself flush with heat, as though it was an embarrassment that he was like me. "He was an incubus."

She shook her head, dismissing that idea. "No. Your kind has to touch to drain a soul. By necessity, even if we threw you naked into a pit of other naked bodies—which has been done, rather cruelly, I might add," she said, "you could only drain a few at a time. Hades could rip the life out of every person standing within a hundred meters of him." She seemed to grimace. "If he focused hard enough on someone miles away, thought really hard about him, he could rip the soul right out of them at that distance. Touch had nothing to do with it. You could touch the man all day—not that I did, other than once—and nothing would happen." She shook her head again. "No, he wasn't an incubus. Close, though."

Very close, Wolfe whispered.

I kept my gaze on Hera. "There's more, isn't there? Something you're not telling me?"

She smiled slyly. "Something I'm not telling you *yet*. Give me just a minute." She turned and we began to walk again, this time toward a far wall. Two sculptures sat posed next to each other in thrones, the marble weathered with time and age, pieces flecked off it from ill care. The man's face was utterly missing, but his muscled body was still present, one hand gripping the arm of his squared throne, the other broken off at the wrist. It was sculpted in such a way that it could have been holding a staff, or a piece of fruit—anything, really.

To his left was his queen in a smaller chair. Her face, too, was missing, but her body was more complete. Her robes were flowing, but the curves were exquisite, and one breast was displayed. Her feet were lost in the furls of her dress, but there was a simplicity and elegance to her that caught my notice.

"A fine piece of art, here," Breandan said casually as we ambled up to it. "I wonder how much that would fetch on the open market?"

"I think you mean the black market," Reed said, "since you'd have to steal it in order to sell it, and I doubt that Ebay would be very excited to have you place it with them."

I looked at the inscription on the placard in front of them. It read, *Hades and Persephone*.

"The King and Queen of the Underworld," Hera said dryly. "I felt bad for her, you know. Demeter didn't deserve to lose her daughter because Hades was a depraved maniac who was utterly insatiable and unwanted by any reasonable woman." Her eyes narrowed as she regarded the sculpture. "Still and all, Persephone was quite a shrewd lady. Rather than be dominated by that beast of a man, she managed to wring some concessions out of him, got him to curb his bloodthirsty ways—at least for a time. And when the moment came that she realized what he meant to do, she killed him herself." Hera's smile went broader, and I could see the measured respect in it. "I would have done the same." Her face darkened for a moment. "Hell, many's the time I wish I had. Then again, Zeus was a bastard and a murderer but nothing on the scale of Hades."

"What did he do?" I asked quietly, taking in the lines of the sculptures, the king and queen sitting in their places and looking down on me. The statues were taller than I was, even without the plinth they rested on. Where I stood, I could almost imagine being in some shadowy cave, in the darkness, being stared down at by the two of them. Now faceless. I wondered if the sculptor had been in their presence when he had made the statue, or if it had been simply inspired by them.

"Hades?" Hera asked. "He got it in his mind that humanity was unworthy of continued life. So he went from town to town, drawing out the souls of everyone he met. He was on a mission to walk the earth until he had killed every-damned-body on it."

I took a step closer to the statues. I wanted to reach out, to run my hand over the smooth marble of the surface, but the signs made it obvious that I shouldn't. I could almost taste my desire to connect with these figures from the past, but for what reason I didn't even know. "Why?"

"Because a mob killed his eldest granddaughter in Troy," Hera replied. "What was her name?" She paused, her fingers on her chin. "Hell if I can even remember; it was so long ago. Anyway, the girl stole something while she was out of her mother and father's sight. Harmless enough, right? She was twelve or so, took some trinket not thinking anyone would notice. But she got caught, and the stallkeeper grabbed her, and he and another man held onto her until they died." Hera watched me carefully, waiting for my reaction.

A tingle ran over my scalp with the slow understanding. "Persephone was a Persephone-type."

Hera smiled. "Indeed."

"And Hades could steal souls," I said, almost whispering. I looked back to the statues, and this time my hand did reach out and touch the base of his leg, felt the smooth marble beneath my fingertips.

"Some of their children came out as Persephones," Hera said. "I didn't think any of them came out like Hades. Most of them came out different, hybridized, as it were, with his power, but restrained and mixed with the limitations of hers. You had to be able to touch directly to the flesh to be able to use it, rather than work at it from a distance, as he could. They had quite a few children, you know, over the next thousand or so years." She smiled lightly. "They weren't very welcome among our kind. Shunned, really, by all but a few. Some had children with humans, some bred within their own ranks. Not many of our kind were as brave as Janus, marrying one. Some got killed by mobs like the one that killed his little girl. Some were wiped out by Zeus after Hades died," Hera said darkly. "A large majority of them, actually. Now there are only three succubi left that we know of, and only two confirmed incubi."

"You said you didn't think anyone came out like Hades." I looked up at the statue of my forebear.

"I didn't think they did," she replied. "Apparently I was wrong. We all were. Because it's beginning to look a hell of a lot like there's a Hades-type out there working for Century." She glanced up at the statue. "And if that's the case, let me tell you something—there's only one type of meta that is immune to that power and therefore only one that can kill him." She smiled at me again, but this time it was grim, and there was no joy in it. "Would you care to guess what type that is?"

Chapter 28

"So you need me to stop a Hades," I whispered. Then, louder, "Why not just use James Fries?"

"What?" Hera asked, puzzled.

"If Omega needed me to stop a Hades," I said, "why not just use Fries? He's already on their payroll."

"Because stopping this Hades is not what we were after you for," came a voice from behind me. I spun to find Reed and Breandan already turned, facing the source of the voice, hands raised and ready to throw bad luck and wind at him.

Janus stood behind me, Eleanor, Kat and Karthik with him, arrayed in a rough pentagon with Janus at the head, his arms folded in front of him, crumpling the neat lines of his suit. "I am not looking for a fight," he said, offering open hands in our direction.

"You may get one anyway," Reed said, his face twisted in anger.

"Reed," Kat said, soothing, drawing his attention. Her hair was curled in a way she'd never done it while she was at the Directorate, and she wore a suit with a skirt. She looked older, more professional, and for the first time she seemed like a century-old presence and not a kid playing teenage games. "There's no need. We're not here to hurt you or anyone. We just want to talk to Sienna—and you."

"I'm listening," Hera said, interjecting herself into the mix. She gently brushed past me, her hand resting on my arm for a moment longer than necessary as she passed, in a reassuring way. She placed a hand on Reed's shoulder, and I saw him lower his a second later. "What do you have to say, Janus? Care to pick up my story of Hades where I left off and fill in the details of your personal experiences with the matter?"

I saw a flash of anger buried deeply in Janus, but when he spoke, it was about something else. "The cloister outside Cork, Ireland, has been wiped out." Janus's face was worn, tired. He looked like he hadn't slept in a week. "Our people are moving quickly toward the one outside Connaught, but based on what they found outside Cork, it will likely be too late."

"Assuming they could even stop a Hades," Hera said.

"It's Connacht," Breandan tossed in. When everyone turned to look at him, he blushed. "Well, get it right, you bloody English."

"They cannot stop a Hades," Janus agreed, turning his attention back to Hera. "I have sent for James Fries to hurry to London, but unfortunately he is somewhat … unresponsive to my messages." He sent me a look—not accusing, but pointed. "I can only imagine it has something to do with the fact that I ordered him to remain in a position where he once more got himself shot."

"He earned that all by himself," I said.

"Perhaps he did," Janus agreed.

Reed turned to me. "You shot Fries?"

"Only a couple times," I said. After a moment's thought, I added, "Maybe three." A pause. "On a couple different occasions."

His expression turned grudgingly respectful. "I guess you have changed."

"Yeah," Kat agreed, "you're really becoming your mother's daughter." Her words were acid, and I wished I had a gun to shoot her with right then. I sent her a nasty look instead.

"There are people in danger," Janus said calmly. "People are going to die." He was watching me, those eyes like ice. No, not ice. I could see some melt in them, other emotions. Fear.

"You're afraid," I said, watching him.

He didn't even blink. "Only a fool wouldn't be, at a moment such as this. They are hunting every one of our kind to the end of our lives. A type of meta we didn't even know still existed has re-emerged, and it is the worst kind of news for us. They will destroy every last one of us."

"But this still doesn't explain their intentions for humanity," I said. "After they've killed all the metas, how are they going to exercise that newfound dominance without every government in the world bombing them into atomized dust? This whole play makes no sense. Fine, stage one is wipe out the competition so you've got the monopoly on meta-human powers. But I've yet to hear what stage two is."

"As much fun as it might be to speculate about this stage two, to sit around and spitball, I think you call it—about what comes next, it is ultimately irrelevant." The frustration bled through in Janus's voice. "We need to stop the first stage, or else the cultural legacy of all meta-kind comes to an end." He paused, and looked slightly chagrined. "I don't think meta-kind is a word, but you get the point, yes?"

Hera was the first to speak. "I understand your gist. First things come first."

"Yes," Janus said. "Thank you. We must halt this genocide. I am all in favor of helping to keep the humans safe from Century's predations, but the only method we have of determining their next phase at present is either base speculation or waiting to see what they come up with after finishing their task of wiping us all out. And as effective as the latter would be, I submit that none of us would be here to see it." He clenched a fist and hit it lightly against his other palm. "We need to act now, to save as many of our people as possible."

I swallowed deeply. "I'll go to Ireland."

Janus shook his head. "I think it is too late for that. You will need to go to Scotland, immediately, or risk the loss of that cloister while trying to play catch up near …" his voice trailed off for a moment, " … Connacht." He nearly mangled the word in his accent.

"Oh, yeah, that's right, throw the Irish to the wolves," Breandan said mildly. "You may not be an Englishman, but damned if you haven't got the same attitude." He watched us all for a beat. "Kidding! Only kidding. It's what needs to be done, I get it." He turned to me. "I'll go with you."

I frowned at him. "You'll be safer here. I'm going to go face-to-face with a man who throws death like you toss luck."

"Well, then you could use a little luck on your side now, couldn't you?" Breandan gave me a grin, his mustached face born down by a little weight that was peeking out from behind the facade.

"I'm going too," Reed said, tossing a look at Hera, who raised an eyebrow at him.

"Might as well make a foursome," Hera said, looking dryly at Janus. "If you don't mind having me around."

Janus smiled then dropped his eyes slightly. "It has been quite some time since we have been on the 'same side.' I don't mind at all."

"Good," Hera said, and I caught the hint of something much deeper going unexpressed between the two of them. I could feel Wolfe's grin inside me, but he said nothing.

"We have a helicopter waiting," Janus said, gesturing back toward the door through which we had come. "If you'll come with me?"

"You parked a helicopter on a London street?" I asked, leading the way. He touched me lightly on the back for just a second as I passed.

"No," he said with amusement as he fell into step beside me. "We have it back at headquarters. It is fueled and ready to make the trip to Scotland."

I took a few steps before I spoke, the footsteps of our party echoing through the quiet gallery. "So … who's the Primus now?"

There was a subtle change in Janus's face, a hint of discomfort. "I don't know. The Ministers have yet to make a decision. The entire organization is in utter chaos. I have had to take the initiative to get this mission off the ground while they … debate."

I looked at him as we walked. "How did you find us?"

It was Eleanor Madigan who answered. "We have a facial recognition software program that scans the results from the surveillance cameras around London. It caught you getting out of your car outside the museum."

"I'm suddenly very thankful I haven't posed for many pictures," Hera said from just behind Janus. "I'd hate to think you were watching my every move."

"We actually were," he replied, "up until this crisis. Now, we're understandably short of manpower for such a task."

"And here I thought Alpha was Omega's number one enemy," Hera said as we crossed into the Egyptian exhibit. I could see the white courtyard ahead of us, with the massive tower in the middle of it. "I suppose this is a time of shifting priorities, a time when maybe we can finally let some old feuds die out."

As we entered the courtyard, the light flooded down from above, the smooth lines of the dome leaving faint shadows on the floor where the beams crossed. It was starting to darken outside as the day reached its close, but the clouds had dissipated and left a clear sky above. The crowds had almost disappeared as well, as the last few museum patrons were beginning to file out. One of the nearby coffee kiosks was giving off the most wonderful smell, making me want a cup for myself. I halted as Janus did the same, stopped by someone standing in front of him.

"Or not," Janus said simply.

They were arrayed around us in a semi-circle—eight people, with Bastet near the fore. The three of them closest to her wore dark suits, dressed interchangeably the way agents had been clad in the Directorate. But the other four …

The other four were impeccably dressed, two women and two men. Not young like the "agents" who flanked them but older, more august. One was a woman of stunning beauty, who in spite of looking like she was forty was a knockout. She could have modeled on any catwalk in the world and probably outshone competitors twenty years younger than she was. Another woman looked a little haggard, her hair a mess with streaks of purple highlights, and she fiddled with a smartphone while watching us with one eye.

One of the men was horribly disfigured, his face bearing a sort of general scarring that looked as though his skin had been scraped off and healed. One of his eyes was white and sightless, the other brown and fixed on me.

The last man was dressed well but pale, terribly pale, making me look like a well-tanned sun baby by comparison. He almost faded into the walls but he was muscular to the point of ridiculousness.

Janus turned to me, almost ruefully, and hesitated for a moment before he spoke. "I am sorry. I didn't know they would be coming."

I looked at the group arrayed against us and ignored Bastet's grin. "Oh, wow, a B-52's cover band," I cracked. After a pause in which there was no laughter, I asked, "Who are they?"

Janus gave a nod to the woman who I had thought of as a model. "Aphrodite." Then the one with a smartphone. "Eris." He turned to indicate the scarred man. "Hephaestus." Finally he came to the pale man. "Heimdall." He let himself deflate, visibly, and I felt the first hint of worry.

"Nice to meet you all," I said, with utter reserve. "I suppose it's not every day you meet some of the old gods."

"Not just old gods," Hera said, and every word she uttered was tense beyond anything I'd heard from her thus far. "Not even just THE old gods." She hunkered down slightly, into a stance I could only think of as defensive. "What you're looking at here is nothing less than the ministers of Omega. The powers behind the throne."

"Well, they certainly do look like the suction behind the toilet." Still, no one laughed. I looked at them with new eyes, understanding now the nervous fear that crackled from Bjorn and even Gavrikov, the sort of tense discomfort that came from knowing that I was horribly overmatched, that they had ill intent for me and I didn't know what it was.

"She's coming with us," Hephaestus said in a low, gravelly voice, his scarred face surveying us. "Move aside, Hera, and we can make this quick."

Hera gave me a look that was indecipherable, inscrutable, and I realized she was weighing things in her mind. Why would a woman who had lived for thousands of years throw her life away, outnumbered three to one in a meta battle with old gods? She was frozen, and her look ticked from each of the Ministers, one by one.

"You're coming with us anyway," Hephaestus said to me, and his lips stayed even. I would have expected a smile, but maybe his face was too scarred to allow for it. "There's no need for any of you to die in the course of this." He gave me a solid look, that white, sightless eye almost glowing as he looked at me. "We will kill them if you make us—Hera, your brother, even that Irishman. Right here, while you watch." The corner of his mouth twitched. "And not give it any more thought than you'd put aside for snuffing out Erich Winter. Come with us, and we'll spare them all."

I should have felt angry, furious, but there was nothing within, just a gaping void. This wasn't the first time I'd had others used as hostages against me. Zack was empty of suggestion, as was Bastian. *Whatever,* Kappler said. Gavrikov and Bjorn were quaking in their metaphorical boots.

Go with them, Gavrikov said.

You do not want to cross them, Bjorn said. *They are not to be trifled with.*

"You're afraid," I said out loud, loud enough that everyone could hear me.

"Damned right I am," Breandan answered into the shocked silence. "There's like … twelve of them! And I'm not that much of a fighter."

"Were you talking to me?" Hephaestus said. That blind eye kept on me, staring.

"No," I said. "Mind your own damned business. I'm trying to have a conversation here."

You should be afraid, Bjorn said. *They can destroy you, right here. Right now.*

"You know, it's funny," I said and no one spoke. "I *should* be afraid, staring all of you down." I looked from Aphrodite, smiling a benevolent smile like a pageant queen, to Eris, who had yet to look up from her phone, over to Heimdall, who almost faded into the white background, then back to Hephaestus, his marred flesh like a beacon turning my gaze back to him. "But I'm not."

I wasn't lying to them. For some reason I couldn't define, I was steely calm.

And then it got defined for me. Real fast.

Kill them, Wolfe said. *Kill them all.*

Chapter 29

I ran at Hephaestus without thought, came at him low, at high speed, before any of them had a chance to react to my suicidal maneuver. I suspected he was fast; he was one of the old gods, after all. Old being the operative word.

Me, I was young.

I streaked in under his guard, kicked his legs out from under him in a slide, kneed him in the guts and was atop him before he had a chance to do anything but throw up his arms ineffectually. I straightened my index finger and drove it hard into his remaining eye, spearing him right in the pupil. He let out a scream and I kicked him hard in the groin before rolling off of him in the direction of one of his suited flunkies.

I grabbed the man by the lapels and yanked him hard toward me. His arms pinwheeled as he fought to recover his balance. I flung him on, speeding him up as he passed and sending him like a projectile into two of his fellow men in black. They wouldn't stay down for long, but I didn't need forever.

I moved with fluid grace, a thousand hours of practice in a basement, in a training room, in the field, all coming together with the thousands of years of experience of a heinous beast who lived in my head and had nothing but a thirst for blood. I feinted my way toward Aphrodite, who looked at me wide-eyed, as though the thought of an actual fight had never occurred to her. The way she made a defensive move told me otherwise, but I didn't care. She was a princess, living a life of a woman of privilege, treated like a queen and pandered to for thousands of years.

I'd been locked in a house my whole life, and when I was

really bad, in a steel box that I'd beaten my way out of with my bare hands. Her jaw broke under the strongest punch I could throw, and while she was busy crying about that, I hit her again and shattered the bone above her eye. Then I tossed her into Bastet, sending both of them into a gift shop display that caused stuffed animals to go flying everywhere.

You can either be a princess or a badass, not both. It takes way too much time and effort to fit in either one of those boxes, and the choice of which my time would be spent on was made for me, long ago. I had no regrets about it, either, given the many kinds of hell that had been unleashed upon me since the day I broke out of the box. It hadn't even been a year.

I came at Eris as she fumbled to put away her smartphone, as though saving it was worth the beating she was about to take. I knew that by now some of the flunkies I'd attacked would have to be coming back to themselves. Also, if Janus and his crew were going to come at me, I'd be dealing with them shortly. I'd gone left, wiping out their flank, and I'd still have to come back to the center and the right, deal with Heimdall and whatever else was left. For now, I listened, and heard only scuffling in the distance, nothing directly behind me, so I kept going for Eris. She was the last of them I'd have to deal with in this direction. If I was very fortunate, Janus would just stay out of it.

I heard lightning crackle behind me, and I knew that was a foolish notion. Part of me wanted to look back and see who he'd thrown in with, but it wasn't going to do me a bit of good until I'd taken out Eris. Then I could make my way back through them without fear of getting attacked from behind.

"So, you're Eris, huh?" I said as I kicked her in the knee. She was moving far too slow, a thousand years of being indulged having taken its toll on her too, I supposed. "You're the Goddess of Chaos, aren't you?" I punched her in the face and followed it with a knee to the guts that doubled her over. "You should appreciate this, then." I spun her around and clasped my fingers to her throat, allowing me to choke her out and get a view of the battle that had been unfolding behind me. I didn't really have the luxury of time to suffocate her or let my powers drain her dry, though, so I just squeezed her with all the strength in my fingers and crushed her larynx. "I do know how to create a bit of chaos, after all."

And I had. Bast was in a fight with Reed, and I saw her pitched through the air and against the center tower. She managed to turn about and catch herself on the side of it with her feet then bounced nimbly down to land on the stairs. She sprang back into the fray at Reed and he blasted her with another gust.

Breandan was in a knock-down, drag-out fistfight with one of the suited thugs. He was bleeding from a cut beneath his eye, and he hammered the man with a blow to the midsection and caught a hard hit to the side of the head in return. Hera and Madigan had Heimdall double-teamed, but it looked to be going poorly for them, as he was moving faster than either and showed none of the hesitation that the other ministers had made obvious to me. He was a fighter and clearly in practice. Madigan's lightning couldn't even catch him, his reflexes good enough that he was dodging every strike she made at him.

Janus and Kat each had a black suit of their own occupied, going fist to fist with them. It appeared they were holding their own, but Karthik was dominating the last one, had him clearly on the ropes.

I let Eris slip out of my grasp to fall limply to the floor, and I knew where I was needed most by the whisper in my mind and my own tactical experience. I hit the black suit who was fighting with Breandan with a running clothesline to the back of the head as I passed and felt his neck break from the force of the blow. It hurt me. It hurt him a hell of a lot more.

"Thanks!" Breandan called out as I kept on, jumping into the air as I made for the fight between Madigan and Hera on one side and Heimdall on the other. He was taking them both at once, a flurry of fists being exchanged, up close and personal—and he was beating them both. Madigan looked like she'd been in a fight or two, but Hera was absolutely out of practice. Her punches were slow, and she was dodging at a vastly underwhelming pace. I watched her take a hit to the belly and then the jaw that sent her to her knees as Heimdall turned all his attention to Madigan. She lasted another five seconds and I saw her get staggered. She started to go to her knees when Heimdall blasted her with a kick that sent her body cracking and rolling twenty feet across the floor, limp. I didn't know if she was dead or alive, but I suspected the former much more than the latter.

"And now a real challenge arrives," Heimdall said quietly. The frenzy of his motions only a moment earlier had subsided. He was peaceful, calm now, an island of tranquility in the midst of chaos. "You are a warrior."

"You too," I said. "Your friends? Not so much. I guess a couple thousand years of being the kings and queens of the world made them soft." I looked him up and down; he rippled with muscle, and not in the normal way a meta did, just by sheer genetics. He was toned in a way few were. He worked on it. His reactions showed he'd never lost his edge. This was a man that time hadn't made soft and flabby. He was a sharpened blade, just looking for a place to strike. "They don't know how much work goes into being ready to fight," I said, and he nodded subtly. "But you and I do."

"In my time," Heimdall said, and his voice was deep, resonant, "I have been beaten only twice."

"Really?" I tried to keep the surprise out of my voice. "I've been beaten a lot. So I guess if we're going by fighting records, you've got the advantage."

He smiled. "I always do."

I smiled back. "Of course you do." I paused. "How do I beat this man to death?"

Heimdall's smile faded. "What?"

Touch him every chance you get, brief little touches, only a second each time, Wolfe said. *He'll hit you but try and dodge it. If you can't, take the hit and trade contact time for it. Keep him busy until your power finally starts to drain him. Then eat him up like—*

"That'll do," I said and extended a hand to Heimdall. "Well? You ready to see who's better?"

He never lost his calm. "There is no doubt in my mind."

"Awww," I said, feigning embarrassment, "it's so sweet that you know I'm going to beat your ass. But you're willing to fight anyway! That's courage." I gave him an exaggerated thumbs-up. "You are a special star!"

His nostrils flared. "I have been the strongest warrior on earth for thousands of years."

"Really?" I gave him a pitying look. "Then why haven't you gone looking for a fight with Sovereign?"

His eyes widened and he was moving without warning, coming at me in a bare-fisted attack. I turned aside his first blow, slapping his wrist to the left. When his next one came, I grabbed it, pulling him forward and using his momentum against him. He snapped it away before I got a chance to hit him, but neither did he manage to counterstrike, so I considered it a fair trade.

One …

He came at me again, follow up punches turned aside, and I clasped his arm this time and pulled him into a punch of my own. I didn't hold back; it was a strong hit, and it stunned him enough that I got another in before he slipped my grasp and hit me with a backhand that caused my head to rattle a little.

Two, three, four …

I kicked him in the leg. I had been aiming for the chest but had to adjust due to the speed at which he came at me. It hobbled him and he stumbled. I pressed the attack by punching him in the head again then the gut. I grabbed his wrist and tried to spin him around in a pirouette like a dancer. It was a clumsy move on my part, but it brought me unfettered access to the side of his head and I pounded him in the skull three times before he landed a hard elbow to my stomach that made me take a few steps back.

Five …

We circled each other warily, his head bleeding from minor cuts where I'd struck him. I felt a pain in my belly from the last hit, and one of my cheeks stung. So far I was winning, but I knew that the moment I underestimated him or tried too hard to press my touch, it'd turn. He was a canny bastard, that much was obvious, and if I didn't play it cool, he was going to realize what I was up to sooner rather than later.

I came at him again with full fury, blocking one of his punches in a way that hurt both of us, probably equally. Neither of us let it show, though, and we traded a punch each. Mine hit him in the gut, his hit me in the side of the head, a glancing blow that still caused a brief flash in my vision. His stomach was like iron, and while we were tangled up close, he tried to grab me. I let him, and he pulled me closer for a headbutt, which I allowed. I angled my head in such a way that it landed skull to skull. You don't run into too many people that know how to really execute a headbutt, or how much it effing hurts when you do it wrong. I knew, and I knew it was going to cost me some serious pain, but I tangled my hand up with him and waited for the hit, knowing that if I could hold onto him after the impact it would easily buy me ten seconds—and probably reveal my plan.

Our foreheads met, bone on bone, and the pain was so bad I thought my life flashed before my eyes. It was like the end of the world had come, like the universe had sent the big bang out at us for another round. The only thing I focused on other than the exquisite, screaming, shearing anguish in my forehead was the sensation of my fingers, still locked around his wrist. I felt him staggering but held on, even as I hit my knees. A meta-strength headbutt was the sort of thing that would turn a normal human's skull into pulped mush. I suspected I'd lost enough brain cells in this attempt that permanent impairment might follow, but I'd have to survive the impending cerebral hemorrhage first. It felt like someone had taken a sledgehammer and turned it loose on the top of my head, then poured lighter fluid over the remains of my skull and had Gavrikov blow up behind my eyes. The only saving grace was that I could feel my fingers tingling as my power started to work. Or else the paralysis from brain injury was setting in. Either or.

"You …" I heard Heimdall whisper in fury.

"Yes, me." I blinked and threw out my other hand blindly in a snapped punch that caught him in the jaw. "You were expecting Bugs Bunny?"

His eyes were slitted, watching me, and I knew this because I'd only just gotten my own back open. The world was still spinning around me, and I realized it was a wonder the two of us hadn't fallen over. My balance was shit, and plainly so was his. He was woozy, I could tell, and I was just starting to feel better.

"You … cannot …" he said, grunting, staggering unbalanced on his feet. He looked even paler than he had when we'd begun, which took doing.

"Can." I hit him in the throat with my free hand and he expelled all his remaining air and looked at me with a shocked expression. "Will." I hit him in the face with a hard cross and he fell to his knees, his eyes blinking, stars filling them. I felt the thrum and pull of my powers ripping at his soul, clawing it out of his body. I didn't want it, but my body did. "Have." I kicked him like I'd seen him lay into Eleanor Madigan and he flipped backward, end over end like a combination between a bowling ball and a ragdoll until he hit the wall of the white tower and lay there, unconscious. "Did." I wiped blood off my forehead from the headbutt that had ended the world. "I guess that makes me number three, huh?"

"Holy shite," came Breandan's voice from behind me, and I turned, giving the museum battlefield a look of cold fury that I had lately reserved for Kat. He was ragged but still standing next to Kat and Janus, who were attending to the fallen Madigan. Reed was glaring at Bast, who was glaring right back, trapped between him and Karthik. The suits were all down, as were the four ministers of Omega and Hera. "I appear to have lucked out in my choice of guardian angels," he breathed then flipped his hand toward Bast, who was sitting very, very still, as though trying to decide whether or not to pounce. "Give it a go, if you want. See if your luck holds out."

Janus looked up at me from where he sat next to Kat and Madigan, his face drawn but serious. "You have become something very different than the girl I met in the basement of the Directorate."

I felt a wash of emotion through me and pushed it aside. "Is that good or bad?"

Something tugged at the corner of his mouth as he forced a weary smile. "For the rest of the world, I think it is a good thing." The smile evaporated as suddenly as it had appeared. "For your own sake, I think the opposite."

I looked over the carnage and my eyes came to rest on Bast, who watched me through narrowed, predatory eyes. "I need answers," I said to Janus. "I need to know why Century wants me alive. I need to know why you've been after me this entire time." I cut my gaze over to him. "I need the truth."

Janus gave me a slow nod then looked to Hera, who lay on the ground, dazed and bleeding, and she nodded. "You deserve the truth," he said softly, and turned back to look me in the eyes. "If ever there was someone who deserved to know why everyone has been vying for your attention since day one, it is you." His gaze softened. "I am sorry for not telling you earlier, but the truth of your situation is possibly the most closely guarded secret in the entire old world of meta civilization, and one that threatens to destroy us even now. No one knows this but the oldest of our kind, and it is information sealed away by a pact so ancient that most of us were little older than you when we made it."

He reached out to me and placed a hand on my shoulder. "The truth is this: you have the power to save the entire world, or destroy it. And it is not something that should be used lightly, as—"

His eyes froze in place then bulged, and his jaw fell in shock. His mouth moved open and closed several times, and I saw him gasp for air. A slow drip of something red fell on his shoulders, and it took me a moment to realize that it was blood. It flowed freely, turning into a drift that ran down his suit on either breast, dripping from the back of his head where something had appeared behind him, hazy, and only for a moment before it was gone again.

"NO!" Kat screamed and lunged at him from behind. She caught him in her arms as he folded at the knees and dropped. There was a gaping wound in the back of his skull, I saw, as he fell forward and I caught him. I took care not to touch his skin as he lay, supported by Kat and I, his face slack.

"You killed Eris," came a voice from my left and I turned, in shock, to see Weissman sitting there with a knife in his hand the size of my forearm. He shrugged lightly. "Saved me some time." I tore my gaze off of him to look to Aphrodite. Her throat was slit, her eyes glassy and lifeless. Hephaestus was dead too, similarly cut, his head nearly off from the savagery of the attack. I tossed a look back to Bastet, but she, too, was lying in a pool of her own blood, dead, as was Heimdall where I had left him in a broken heap. I looked to Hera for any guidance, but she, too, was finished, the last of her kind. Her empty eyes rested on me, her blood ran red across the tile floor, and I could see by the angle of her neck that there was no hope for her, either.

"I heard Heimdall say that he'd only been beaten by two people in his whole life," Weissman said, looking down at the edge of his knife. "You were number three, huh?" He smiled, and looked at me over the edge of the blade, which dripped dark red on the white tile. "I guess this made me number four."

Chapter 30

I made a move toward him and he pointed the knife at me. "Ah, ah, ah," he said as he wagged the blade. "I'm running short on time, but don't think I won't gut you and leave you in a pile to heal while I kill every last one of your friends." His eyes flashed, and I could see he wasn't lying. "Don't test me right now, because if I have to push the bounds and use my powers more, I will make you—and them—suffer." He waved the blade over the gory mess that was the courtyard floor, the marble floors slick with blood. "My part here is done, as far as I'm concerned. I spoiled your sweet revelation scene," he waved the blade toward the body of Janus, "killed anyone else who might tell you the truth—" He grinned. "It's a shame. If they'd just been honest with you earlier, you know? We'd all be screwed. Trust the powerful to protect that power at all costs, even if it means their own lives." His smile was so heartfelt I could tell he was enjoying the hell out of himself. "Good thing I was here to stop them from screwing everything up."

"How did you get here just in time?" Breandan asked the question that was on my mind.

"It's easy when you've got a spy reporting everything back to you," Weissman said with a casual shrug, as though it were no big thing. "Isn't that right, Eleanor?"

I turned my head to see Madigan pulling herself up from the ground. Reed's eyes met mine. He was a little bloody, but otherwise all right, standing not far from Eleanor, where he'd been standing off with Bast. I saw a hint of frustration from him, and I shook my head subtly. Not yet.

"So," Weissman said, looking around at the carnage before us, "it looks like this is it for now." He gave me a salute with his knife blade. "Don't try and follow us," he said with a voice of amused warning. "Because … blah blah blah, gutting, pain, intestines used as party streamers." He waved the blade at us. "You know. Just don't. I'll get creative in ways to make you suffer but not die." He shrugged. "Til we meet again, Miss Nealon. You keep running, though. You're like a little hamster on a wheel, trying to stop us. It's kind of fun to watch—til it gets boring." He grinned. "Good thing I'm not in charge of deciding your fate, because I think you know what would happen when you got boring." He turned, and Eleanor followed him, casting nervous looks behind her on their way out, watching to see if any of us followed.

She needn't have worried.

"Dammit," Reed said as he sagged to the ground, resting on his haunches. He lay back, and I watched him close his eyes as he stared up at the dome above us, the wire-frame ceiling that was holding back the sky from falling on us.

There was only a moment of silence before Breandan spoke. "I don't mean to be the downer—not that we need any more of those—but we need to be getting out of here, and fast." He waved a hand about. There were a few humans left cowering behind displays. I saw one girl quaking as she watched us from behind an overturned table. "I don't fancy explaining to Scotland Yard how I came to be acquainted and associated with all these bloody corpses."

"Who gives a damn?" Reed asked, still tilted toward the ceiling. "We're done, now."

"It's not over yet," I said, sounding stronger than I felt. I made my way to my brother's side, and he sat up to look at me. His eyes were nearly squinted shut. "It's not over. Call your headquarters, get them to send some more help." I looked to Kat, then Karthik. "We can rally with Omega, what's left of it—"

"Don't you get it, Sienna?" Reed said, and he let out a hysterical laugh. He bit his lip and sniffed, and I got the feeling he was only centimeters from losing it. "This *was* Omega." He waved to indicate the bodies on the floor, and it came to rest with his finger pointing at Hera's corpse. "And she *was* Alpha." He looked ghostly, pained. "Our headquarters in Rome was destroyed by Century three days ago. She was the last of the surviving leaders of Alpha. I'm all that's left, except for the mercs at our safehouse. Not one of them is a meta." He rested his hands on his knees, and sat with them in front of him, like I used to sit in the box. I thought maybe he'd rest his head on his legs, but he didn't. "It's over. Everyone who had any chance of organizing metakind to fight Century just died in this room."

Chapter 31

"Not quite," Kat said, her voice soft. She lifted Janus up in her arms. "Close, but he's not dead yet."

"He got stabbed in the back of the head," Reed said from his sitting position. "You can't tell me he's going to be of use to anyone." His words were bitter, rueful.

"Maybe," Kat said, and I caught her hesitancy. She licked her lips as she cradled him. "But I won't know until we give it some time." She nodded toward Breandan with her head. "Your criminal friend is right—"

"Oh, well, thanks for putting it that way," Breandan said.

"We need to get out of here," Kat said. "I suggest we go back to Omega headquarters, since it's the most well-equipped location to serve as a base of operations."

"I really want to go strolling into the heart of enemy territory," Reed said. "It's high on my list of priorities, getting murdered."

"Reed," I said gently and then yanked him to his feet, letting the gentleness go. "Get your ass moving."

He blinked at me in surprise. "Okay," he said, and I could hear the chagrin in his tone. "Okay, then."

I looked around again, quickly, taking stock of what we had left. "Karthik?" I asked, and the young man seemed to come out of a stupor. "You with us?"

"Sorry, yes," Karthik said, nodding. "I am. Let's regroup."

"Maybe you should let Breandan drive," I said to Reed.

"We have a van," Karthik suggested. "Parked in the rear of the building. May I suggest we use that exit? More cover for us, perhaps less likelihood of running into the police on their way in here."

"Fine," I said, and Karthik took the lead, Breandan a few steps behind him. They headed to our left, following the courtyard and the curve of the white tower until it opened into a new section of the museum. We tromped through empty halls, Kat carrying Janus in her arms like a baby, and made our way down stairs and through hallways until we reached the back exit. The smell of the place was heavy, almost musty, though I couldn't shake the sense that there was blood coming with us, blood on everything, filling my nose and mouth like I could taste it.

Tastes good, Wolfe said.

"Shut up," I whispered.

"What?" Karthik asked, turning back to look at me.

"Sorry," I muttered. "Talking to myself."

As we burst out the back doors we found a police car waiting. The sirens were flashing in the dimming light of the day, and two police officers were waiting in carefully crouched positions.

"Look out!" Karthik called, "there are men with guns behind us!"

I paused for only a second before I realized he was lying. For a moment I actually thought he was telling the truth, enough to get me to look back through the brass doors to see that there were, in fact, men with guns inside, standing just in front of the glass.

"RUN!" I shouted as I dodged to the right and out of the line of fire. I saw the cops dive behind their car as Reed turned to see what I saw.

"Keep going!" Karthik shouted, and I felt him come up behind me. He grabbed my collar and pulled me back to a run then did the same to Reed. "Trust me!" he shouted, and took off with us. "They're just illusions that I created with my power to distract the police while we escape." This he said at a whisper, low enough the police wouldn't hear him.

We cleared the back courtyard and found Kat already opening the doors to a navy blue panel van. She was gingerly sliding Janus into the back with Breandan's help. As soon as he was in, Breandan jumped into the passenger seat as Karthik slid into the driver's side. Reed leapt into the back, neatly avoiding landing on Janus, and I followed, managing the same feat. I also managed not to crack Kat in the back of the head with my elbow, but it was a near thing on that one.

The van's engine roared to life as the sound of sirens filled the air around us. "We might need to take a detour or two," Karthik said as he slammed the vehicle into gear and started it forward. "You know, to avoid the police."

"They're gonna have us on surveillance cameras," Breandan said nervously. "Our pictures will be everywhere, won't they?"

"With Omega's connections, I think we can minimize the fallout," Karthik said. "At least for now. Possibly not much longer, though, not with the ministers dead." He ran a hand over his forehead and then through his dark hair before bringing it back to the steering wheel. "They were the power behind Omega. Without them, we're going to be out in the cold with the government soon. They've always managed to keep a lid on these type of incidents before."

"Looks like the whole nasty cake is about to collapse on itself," Reed said with a sneer that vanished quickly. "If this was any other time, I'd be positively ecstatic about it."

"Like to glory in the fall of your enemies?" Karthik said from the front seat as he weaved the van through traffic, shaking those of us in the back from side to side. I braced against the wheel well as Karthik eased us into a turn.

"Omega is a criminal cartel," Reed said with a laugh. "You people own half the organized crime in Europe, using your metas as muscle to keep the rackets in line. Yeah, forgive me if I don't weep on a normal day if you guys get kicked over." His amused smile came to an end. "The fact that we've come to this, to the point when your organization is basically all that's left in Europe between us and the end of our species …" He let his voice trail off, but everything he'd said up to that point had been laced with contempt.

A silence settled over us as we weaved through London's rush hour. It wasn't desperately packed; it kept a good flow, save for the few times I heard ambulances go rushing by. I felt the change as we headed down a slope and realized we were entering Omega's underground garage.

We pulled to a stop a minute later and I cast Reed a look. "Are you gonna be okay with this?"

He gave me an inscrutable one in return. "Allying with Omega? No." He paused and looked over at Kat, who was still ministering to Janus, keeping her hands clear of him. "But I'll keep my objections to myself, since all I've got left at the safehouse are hired guns who will probably be in the wind the moment they find out Hera's dead and thus their paychecks are at an end."

I nodded at him then turned to find Kat staring at me wide-eyed. "What?" I asked her pointedly.

She shook her head, as though she wished I hadn't caught her looking. After a moment or so of thought, she spoke. "I just … was amazed to hear you ask him if he was going to be okay with this since, like … two days ago you killed our leader and crashed through a window to get away from us."

I glared at her. "Don't forget that I broke your nose. Twice."

She flinched. "Restraint?"

"You've just about seen the last of it," I said. "Don't push me."

The van door slid open and Karthik waited outside. Breandan joined him a moment later, studying the parking structure with all the skepticism of a man walking into a jail cell. Kat carried Janus in her arms without help as we passed the glass box where the security guard had been reading the paper only yesterday and got in the elevator. She stopped at the floor below the main level, carrying Janus to their medical facility. I thought about going with them but decided it was pointless.

When the elevator dinged and opened on the top floor, I walked out onto a quiet cubicle farm. Only a dozen or so people were still here, and when I flashed a questioning look at Karthik, he shrugged. "We furloughed all the non-essential personnel yesterday on Janus's order. Non-critical operations have been suspended."

I led the way past Janus's office without thinking about it, and burst through the doors of Rick's old office without stopping. Breandan and Reed followed me, while Karthik peeled off and headed toward the other side of the floor. "Be with you in a moment," he said, and I trusted he would. I walked through into the space that Rick had begun to convert into modernity, the last vestiges of the old world charm still there in the form of paneled wood and that robust cigar smell that lingered even now.

"So this is the seat of Omega," Reed said, taking in the whole room with a sweep of his eyes. "It's kind of how I always imagined it."

"Actually, that was the seat of Omega's power," I said, pointing to the wreckage of the chair that still rested behind the desk. I looked over the edge to see smears of blood still there, and I hesitated before I stepped around to look closer. The smell of it was heavy, and I could almost taste it because of how much of it was dried on the floor. "Janitorial must have been furloughed, too," I muttered to myself.

"What?" Reed asked.

"Nothing," I said, not taking my eyes off the space where I'd last seen Rick, a bloodied mess of flesh and bone splattered all over the floor. I looked back to Reed. "So …"

He looked back at me then to Breandan, who watched us both uneasily. "So … what?"

"Well," I said, "Janus wanted us to go to the cloister in Scotland, try and save them from this Hades-type."

He stared at me with a blank look. "Sorry … is that a thought, a suggestion, an order?"

I frowned at him. "I'm not your boss, Reed. I can't give you orders. I'm not in charge."

Breandan looked from Reed to me. "Really? Then … who is, might I ask?" He looked down at the space behind the desk. "And is that blood?"

"Yeah," I said. "Their last leader met a somewhat grisly end."

"Ouch," Breandan said. "Looks messy. When did that happen?"

"Oh, I don't know. An hour before I ran into you in King's Cross Station?"

He looked at me for a moment before it registered. "Oh! You! You killed him. I get it now." He let his thumb and forefinger rest on his face. "You really are racking up quite the prodigious body count, aren't you?"

I put my fingers over my eyes and rubbed my face, as though I could scrub away all signs of my identity, be someone else for a while. "It's been a confusing few weeks."

"This isn't like you, Sienna," Reed said quietly.

I looked at him through weary eyes. "I'm pretty sure it's not all me."

His eyes widened in slight alarm. "You mean …"

"Wolfe," I said calmly. "He used to be able to take control of my body. Now it's more subtle. He says, 'Kill them!' and I'm moving before he's even done speaking." I leaned to rest my backside on the desk. "The sad part is, I don't even disagree with what I've done in some of these cases." I turned my head to look at the bloodstains behind the desk. "Some of them seem to strain the moral compass, though."

"Dear God," Reed whispered. "You say it like it's nothing. Like you just cracked an egg. 'Oops, killed a whole bunch of people. Better luck next time.'"

"Honestly," I said, and felt a tired that had seeped into my very bones, like the London rains, "given what's going on right now, is anyone even going to notice the drop of blood I've put into the bucket?"

"Well," Breandan said with excessive cheer, "it's nice to know that my guardian angel is actually an avenging angel, ready to kill over the slightest offense." He stiffened and held out his hands peacefully. "Which I am not trying to give. Please don't be offended, oh murderous angel."

I sighed. "It's not like that." I looked out the window. "At least I hope it's not."

Reed came to sit beside me. "What happened to the girl who struggled with the fact that she'd killed Wolfe and Gavrikov?"

I didn't blink as I looked at the skyscrapers on the horizon, lit in anticipation of the coming night. "I think I left her in the box."

"Bad news," Karthik said, breaking the silence as he re-entered the room, shutting the old wood door behind him with a gentle click.

"Is there any other kind lately?" Reed asked.

"There's the *Daily News*," Breandan said. "No, wait, that's bad too."

"We have confirmation from our agents that the cloister in Connacht was wiped out," Karthik said, reading from a piece of paper in his hand.

"But finally an Englishman who can pronounce it," Breandan muttered.

"In point of fact, I'm from Mumbai originally," Karthik gently corrected him.

"I was trying to be culturally sensitive. Inclusive and all that, you know."

"Ah," Karthik said. "So now the last bastion of metakind in the English isles is to be found in Scotland." He read a thin readout. "Population is only thirty or so." He pulled a piece of paper from underneath that one. "It looks as though the job is just about done over here." His dark eyes were tinged with sorrow, and his voice was weighed down with it. "This is the last cloister in Europe. North and South America are all that remain after this. That and whatever stragglers aren't cloistered that haven't been swept up yet."

"Dear God," Reed said, letting his hands cover his eyes. "Scotland it is."

"The helicopter will be ready in fifteen minutes," Karthik said. "There is one thing we need to discuss first, though."

"What?" I asked. "I mean, we know what we're dealing with—a Hades-type. We know I'm the only one who stands a chance against it. And we know that—"

"We have no one to lead us," Karthik said. "With the ministers and Bastet dead and Janus out of action, Omega's line of command is officially finished."

"What?" I looked at him in utter disbelief. "Your organization landed something like fifty metas on U.S. shores not two weeks ago when you went to destroy the Directorate. You can't tell me that there aren't any field commanders for those metas—"

"Most of them are dead," Karthik said quietly. "The toll of Century's efforts on our continental operations has been quite steep the last two weeks. When the crisis began, we had something on the order of a hundred metas on payroll. We did send fifty to deal with your Directorate, and with the exception of our American operatives, they all returned within a couple days. However, we've had major setbacks as our operations were destroyed in every European capital in the last two weeks. It was a blitzkrieg, nothing less. Every single field agent on the continent is now out of contact. The last—an office of five metas in Paris—went quiet this morning. Their last report indicated that the final major cloister in southern France had been destroyed in a blaze of fire."

"So …" I said, "for next moves, I guess we can assume that Weissman's intended return to London is going to include a visit to this location."

Karthik gave me a slight nod. "That seems likely. We have about twenty-five metas here, not counting yourselves. Most are young, like Athena, the girl you brought in the other morning. Only a few of us have any offensive power or combat training."

I rubbed my forehead. "Dammit," I said. "Dammit."

"What?" Reed asked, growing alarmed.

"When she gets worried, I prepare to panic, personally," Breandan said.

"We can't go to Scotland," I said. "We have no idea what method of transport that Hades-type is using. He could be there already, in which case we'll miss him and he'll be back here before we can return." I thumped my hand against the desk. "The only thing I know for sure at this point is that this is his last stop. He'll kill everyone in this office before he can declare the job done and move on."

"So you're suggesting we write off that cloister in Scotland?" Reed asked, looking at me, dazed. "You're suggesting we let those people die?"

"I'm not suggesting it, Reed." I looked back at him tenderly. "I'm saying it flat out. They're dead already. As much as I wish we could save them, even if we reach them in time, there's no guarantee he's going to be on his way there. He could be heading here right now." I looked at the stripped-down office. "He's coming here, guaranteed. He may hit Scotland now, he may hit it later, but he's coming here, for sure, and nothing is going to stop him unless I'm here to do it." I thumped my hand against the desk again, harder this time. "I can't gamble with the lives of the people here on the chance of being able to save those folks in Scotland."

"How thoroughly practical of you," Reed said coldly. "Looks like Old Man Winter has taught you well."

"What did you say?" I let the chill creep into my voice.

"You heard me," Reed said. "You just let the emotion bleed right out. 'There's no guarantee …' As if there's a guarantee of success if you stay here?" He jabbed a finger at me. "You realize Weissman and Madigan are out there still? Madigan knows her way around Omega HQ, she can show them how to get in without any difficulty. You're writing off those people in Scotland—very coldly, I might add—calculating that the odds are better that you'll be able to save the people here. I'm telling you that you might not be able to. It's not just a Hades that's going to be coming. Weissman has out-thought us at every juncture, and he's gotta know he just put all his remaining enemies in one camp. That means he's not worried about us. He's not worried about you," Reed amended. "He's gonna finish Europe by rolling over us here and then we're done. Say goodbye to the whole eastern hemisphere, because Century will own it when it comes to the meta world."

"What do you want me to do?" I yelled at him. "I mean, seriously? I'm one person. I'm eighteen years old, Reed! Until two weeks ago, I was just a follower, riding along on the coattails of other people who were smarter and more organized than I was, okay? I have one thing in me, and that's that I know how to fight. That's all I have to bring to the table. So when I tell you that making our stand here is the smartest move because otherwise we're going to lose the cloister in Scotland as well as get everyone in this place killed, you can take that as the word of an eighteen-year-old girl who's both scared and more than a little pissed that she's having to play janitor and protector to the remains of a group of people who have hounded her since day effing one, okay? This is a mess, all right, and it's not mine, but somehow I seem to be the one that gets to mop it up. And I get to do it all less than two weeks after my first love was killed and while I'm trying to figure out if I'm pregnant with his baby!"

Reed staggered back like he'd been slapped. "You're …" His face narrowed in horror and his voice went to a hushed whisper. "You're pregnant? HOW?"

"The whole family needs remedial education in that, I suppose," Breandan said to no one in particular.

"Dr. Sessions made a … suit …" I said. "For Zack. Before he …" I shut up, watching both Karthik and Breandan find immense interest in their shoelaces and the London skyline, respectively. "Anyway … I don't want to be in charge of saving the world of metas, because we're probably gonna fail." I rubbed my hand over my face. "So, seriously. Who wants to be in charge? I'd vote for any of you."

"Yeah, no," Breandan said, "my vote's for you." He looked around sheepishly. "You know, if I get a vote. Not really sure what the Parliamentary procedures are here, being someone who rather drifted in and all."

I brushed aside my hand and focused on Karthik. "This is your party, Karthik. Your house, your rules."

Karthik shook his head. "I'm afraid that while I am a fairly good tactical leader of a squad, I lack the long-range vision and experience to run even the fragments that remain of Omega. I defer to your experience."

"My experience?" I asked with amusement. "My experience is running a baby squad of metas for three months after I finished training."

"You're the most powerful of us," Reed said in a strangled voice. I looked at him, and he looked back, giving me a shrug. "Probably the most experienced team leader, too, given that Karthik just deferred to you."

"You were just bashing the hell out of my decision to make this our defense point a minute ago," I said, trying to see if there was something behind his eyes that he was hiding, some sarcasm I wasn't detecting.

"I was bashing the lack of emotion behind it," he said calmly. "I didn't question the logic of it, I just hate that you've had to come to a point where you see it as a game of probabilities instead of a battle for the lives of people."

I felt my mouth dry out. "There are numbers behind the people." I lowered my voice. "Two hundred and fifty-four."

Breandan cocked his head. "Sorry, what?"

"It's the number of people who died when Sienna first faced off against Wolfe," Reed said, never taking his eyes off me. "I honestly kinda figured you'd forgotten."

I shook my head slowly. "Never."

Reed gave me a slow nod of understanding. "All right, then. What's the play?"

"Umm …" I thought for a second. "We need everything we can get. Can you bluff those mercs at your safehouse into coming over here to help us establish a perimeter?"

"If you're okay with throwing away their lives," Reed said.

I sighed. "Is there anything … anything at all that you've got at your safehouse that could help us here?"

"Some guns," he said with a shrug. "Half of them were the ones you had with you when we rescued you."

"We could certainly use those," Karthik said. "We've had to ship out quite a few these last months, trying to arm human agents to shore up weaknesses in our roster."

Reed gave him a nod. "I'll get them over here and take inventory over what we've got, see if there's anything else that would help. I doubt I can get the mercs over here—I don't even feel good about trying, going into this fight—but I'll ask. See what I can do."

"All right, you do that," I said. "Karthik, I need a full assessment of what Omega has at our disposal. Every meta better be ready to fight if it comes down to that. This may be a game of seconds, if Weissman comes into play, and we'll need to stop him for as many of them as we can. Get me a list." I paused. "And something else—I need Omega's files relating to a succubus named Adelaide as well as whatever you have on me and my family, including my grandfather."

Karthik nodded seriously. "Do you have a name for him?"

I shook my head. "She called him Mr. Nealon when she killed him, and I never heard my mother mention his name, or that of his wife. Janus said they debriefed my grandmother later in life, though."

Karthik gave me a look that was filled with tempered optimism. "We have two analysts remaining, both metas who are staying here for protection. They know their way around Omega's systems. I'll see what I can get them to do. It'll be a good distraction." He gave the office a look. "We also need to decide where we're going to set up. Defending the whole building will be … problematic, especially from Eleanor. She's worked here for years, after all. She has more clearance in this building than I do."

"We make our stand on this floor," I said. "The open air layout is ideal for a fight if we can get rid of those damned cubicles."

He smiled. "I can pretty well guarantee that we have the muscle on hand to get those out of the way quickly enough. Anything else?"

"That should do it for now," I said and looked to Breandan. "I need you to get me a pregnancy test."

Breandan looked at me, slack-jawed. "Why does this particular chore fall upon me?"

I didn't glare at him, exactly. "Is there anything else you could be doing right now to help us prepare for the battle?"

He gave a slow, resigned nod. "Right you are, then. Old-fashioned or digital?"

I gave him a cocked eyebrow. "Picked out a few of them in your time?"

He shrugged. "For those who can make contact with the opposite sex, we do tend to enjoy the sort of activities that might lead to the tensest three days of one's life." He didn't smile. "Speaking hypothetically, of course."

I rolled my eyes. "Of course."

He tossed a look at Karthik. "Got a corner store nearby?"

"Sure," Karthik said. "I'll have one of our floaters show you the way."

"Thank you," I said, looking from the two of them to Reed. "Thank you all."

"You're the one in charge now," Reed said with a faded smile, "I think we should technically be thanking you."

"Don't thank me yet," I said. "Save it until it's all over."

"That's a good idea," Breandan agreed. "Wouldn't want to go thanking you before we survived, after all. What if we went and gave you all this gratitude, and then we ended up dying in this little last stand? Truly a waste, it'd be." He slapped Karthik on the back, dragging him toward the door.

Reed lingered as Karthik shut the door behind them. "What is it?"

"I don't know," I said. "I just keep waiting for the other shoe to drop. I keep waiting for the next betrayal, for Breandan to turn around to me and be like, 'I've been working for Century all this time!' before he stabs me in the back."

Reed squinted at me in deep thought. "From what you just described, it sounds like he'd be looking you in the face. Hard to stab you in the back from the front. Unless he was a contortionist." He pondered that for a moment, dark face turning into a deep frown. "Are there contortionist metas?"

I let out a little noise of impatience. "You know what I mean. Kat betrayed us before the Directorate went down. My mom left me just before things went all to hell. The people I placed my trust in turned out to be liars and murderers." I felt my face drop into my palms. "I just wish … I knew what to do. You're all looking at me like I'm a leader, and I'm gonna do everything I can, but I'm sitting here terrified, wondering who's going to turn on me next. I feel like I don't even know who my enemies are anymore." I laughed mirthlessly. "I'm running Omega, Reed. Take a moment to marvel at the irony of that."

He put a hand awkwardly on my shoulder. "Life's not clear like that, Sienna. It's not a collection of straight-line paths to your objectives. People don't yell out, 'Ha ha! I am betraying you!' just before they break your heart. In spite of how you're feeling, not everyone's a bad guy." His look turned sour. "Hard for me to admit, as we're currently not just in bed with Omega, my worst enemy, but fully … uh …" He peered at me and his olive skin grew flushed. "Never mind. Bad analogy, given … uh … What I mean is, when it comes to trusting people, you've had a damned unlucky run. But I think … even the Irishman seems to be genuinely afraid. And we're all looking to you because you're a fighter." He made a mirthless chuckle. "We're all looking to you because maybe it's obvious that you're the one of us that's most prepared for this … *because* you've been through all those things."

"I'd rather have been through none of it and be able to sit at the back of the room with Zack, unnoticed," I said. "I don't want to be the kind of person that it's going to take to win this fight." I felt a lump in my throat. "I don't want to be the kind of person who kills so casually and never feels anything bad about it … a monster. I never wanted to be a murderer, Reed, never wanted to be some thoughtless killer who could do what Charlie did and just drain a man, or be like Fries and casually kill because I wanted to, because it sated some thirst in me." I wiped my eyes. "I thought I was different. I thought I could just be me."

"That was never gonna be part of the deal," Reed said, leaning some pressure onto the hand on my shoulder. "You've always been destined for this. Your powers decided it, your mother prepared you for it, and every step you've taken has made you harder, made you the kind of person that everyone looks at and says, 'I think she's tougher than me. I'm following her.' He wrapped his arms around me, and I felt the warmth of an embrace, something I couldn't recall feeling since the day Zack had died. "I think by the time this is all over, you might be the only person who's still sorry that you did go through the fire you have. Because the rest of us ... as unfair as it is ... are counting on this new girl to save us from the hell that's coming to kill us all."

Chapter 32

Reed left shortly thereafter, and I lay down on the couch while waiting for Breandan to return. Thoughts were blurring through my head, a thousand of them, a million of them. For the first few minutes I could hear the sound of cubicles being moved outside the doors of the office. After a few minutes I tuned them out, though, focusing instead on my own thoughts, on the smell of the smoke from the previous occupant of this office, the lingering sweet aroma of it. It settled in the back of my nose with the acid that my stomach was churning, begging me to eat something. I thought about opening the door, saying something to Karthik or someone else, but I couldn't get up. I didn't want to look them in the face. I wondered if any of the others, the ones Karthik was speaking for, thought I was a bad choice. I laughed at that out loud in the quiet dark of the office as the day drew to an end outside. If anyone wanted to stage a coup, they were welcome to the responsibility that I'd picked up purely by accident. I didn't want it.

My mind turned over the other responsibility I'd been considering, too. The idea that I could end up being a mother was downright bone chilling. I was eighteen, technically I was unemployed (doing volunteer work, I supposed), a single mother (unless you counted the voice in my head as the father, which sadly, for sharing responsibility, I really didn't—sorry, Zack). I knew nothing about kids, having never been around them. I tried to remember my own childhood, but everything I could see of it was all after we'd shut ourselves in the house, after mom had basically rolled up the carpet and closed up shop, locking me away from the world.

And if I failed to stop Century, it bothered me to admit, I'd just about have to do the same.

I ran a hand over my belly. It felt just as flat as it had a week earlier, two weeks earlier, a month earlier. There was no sign of anything amiss. If I was pregnant, it was soon into the goings, maybe a couple weeks along. That was still a big 'if.' The idea of what I'd have to do to protect a child made me nauseous. In a world run by Century, where a telepath could be hanging around a city at any time, waiting to find a meta to sic a team on, isolating yourself and hiding was just about the only recourse, unless you wanted to take on a hundred metas all by yourself.

That line of thought alarmed me. Just by contemplating these things, these fears, considering how I'd handle things, didn't that make me as bad as my mother? If my back was against the wall, would I do the same things she did under the pretense of keeping my daughter or son 'safe'?

Would I lock my child away to protect her from certain death if we were found? I swallowed heavily and wondered if that was what Mother had been thinking when she did all the things to me that she did. Once upon a time, only a couple weeks earlier, I had believed that I was the sort of person who wouldn't cross lines, who believed that there were certain things that were just wrong, that I wouldn't do in the name of winning, of beating my enemies. There was a time when I couldn't even bring myself to kill.

Now I wondered if there was anything I wouldn't do to stop Century from killing every meta on the face of the planet.

Sometime after I had that thought, I drifted off into sleep, and the world changed around me. I was with Adelaide again, and time had shifted. I watched as the darkness took form, becoming the office around me, the same one I had been lying in when I had fallen asleep.

"He'll be along shortly," Janus said, shifting back and forth on his feet. Janus wasn't a man predisposed to show his nerves, at least not in my short experience with him. His discomfort was tangible, and he stood there with a file folder, shuffling it back and forth between each hand.

"Why am I here?" Adelaide asked, and I could see her nerves showing as well. She stood next to one of the bookcases, eyeing the titles on the shelf. She looked up. "Is this about my next assignment?"

"I am not sure," Janus said, taking a look toward the couch, the one I had been sleeping on. It was empty, unoccupied, the yellow upholstery looking to be in slightly better repair than what I was lying on some twenty-odd years later. "Would you care to have a seat?"

"No, thanks," Adelaide said. "I should … probably just keep myself out of trouble." She pulled her hand away from the bookshelf, as though she were afraid of damaging the dusty, leather-bound volumes.

"You are no trouble," Janus said with quiet calm. "You are … one of our best, if I am being honest."

Adelaide gave him a weak smile in return. "If you're being honest? Does that mean you're not honest that often?"

Janus chuckled. "It means I'm often not allowed to give a frank assessment. Unbridled truth often gets sacrificed on the altar of the greater good."

She watched him with eyes that showed a clever intelligence, and I wondered what she was thinking. "Does that mean you have to hold things back in order to be good at your job?"

Janus stared out the window, his reaction not immediate. "I suppose it does," he said after a moment. "If we are being honest," he flashed her a smile, "that galls me as well. Since the day I was old enough to associate myself with the world our kind created, I have been a servant to others who had more power than I. True, I was an influencer, an advisor, but a servant nonetheless. I have always tried to do the right thing in every circumstance." He cast his gaze down and pulled off his glasses. He tugged a handkerchief from his pocket and began to wipe the lenses. "At times, it has meant telling one person a particular kind of truth and telling another a completely different one."

There was a flash of amusement. "Doesn't that kind of make you two-faced?"

He finished wiping his glasses and put them back on the bridge of his nose, adjusting them to look down at Adelaide. "It would hardly be the first time I was accused of such things. The problem with being an empath who walks the corridors of power is that you always know what the person you are speaking to wants to hear. If you possess within you the desire to ultimately please people, it is very hard not to bend your words in the direction of what they want." His face sagged. "Bad news is never a welcome guest, but of late it seems particularly interested in overstepping its bounds."

Adelaide's interest was purely casual, at least on a surface level. She was pretending to pay attention to other things, but all the while I got the idea she was listening intently. "Oh?" she asked. "Lots of bad news lately?"

"Having you kill Mr. Nealon was unfortunate," Janus said, watching her carefully.

She froze. "You did want him dead, though, right?"

"Of course," Janus said. I saw the release of tension from Adelaide after the moment's silence. "And you did very well on that. But … we have a bit of a new problem."

"Oh?" She ran her finger over one of the bookshelves as she took slow steps, one at a time, her gaze falling over the shelves as she walked. "What is it?"

The door opened on the opposite end of the room, causing both of them to turn, and interrupting Janus's response. "I believe I will let him explain," Janus said.

The man who entered the room looked a little like Rick: dark hair that was beginning to show just the hints of grey, dark skin, confident. This one, however, looked ever so much older and wiser. His eyes were jaded, unworried, the kind of calm, cool darkness that I expected one might find in a man who'd done ugly things for any number of years. He smiled as he shut the door behind him, and I sensed an oiliness about him that caused Adelaide's skin to feel greasy.

"If it isn't our star succubus," he said as he strode across the room. His steps were slow, measured, and he seemed to take great pleasure in savoring his movement as he drew closer to her.

"Thank you," Adelaide said, blushing at the compliment. I was a little embarrassed for her at the reaction. "I appreciate the opportunity with Omega." She looked down, and I knew this wasn't feigned. "I know my kind doesn't tend to get many chances like this …"

"You are the exception," the Primus of Omega said with dark humor. "And you are turning out to be quite the worthy exception." He kept his distance even as he got closer, walking past where she stood on the wall of bookshelves to stand near a row of volumes that I'd noticed before. "We are always looking for exceptional talent at Omega. It makes our task easier. You have done fantastic work so far. Clearly a superior talent." The oiliness of his smile nearly made me gag. The flattery was so thick I was surprised Adelaide wasn't choking on it.

Janus didn't seem all that impressed. "Perhaps it would be a good time to talk about Adelaide's next assignment?"

"Indeed," the Primus said, a look of real or feigned concern written across his face. "I want to talk to you about a very real danger; possibly the most dangerous threat we face in the world we live in today."

There was a pause, and Adelaide waited along with Janus for the answer. She looked around, and after a moment passed, she offered, "The Reds?"

The Primus laughed. "The Reds have something they believe in, for the most part. They're certainly dangerous, let there be no doubt. They are, after all, men possessed of extraordinary power in the form of modern weapons. If backed into a corner, they do have the power to unleash untold horrors upon the world we have so carefully constructed to our advantage." He smiled. "So, they are certainly a danger, but one I think we have well in hand. Because they're men. Flawed, corruptible, desirous of women, power, and all the worldly goods they seemingly eschew. No, we have a good handle on the Reds. So long as a man wants things, you have power over him. Leverage."

The Primus looked out the window. "No, I'm talking about someone more dangerous than that. I'm talking about someone who claims he doesn't want anything. Nothing at all." He looked back, slyly, at Adelaide. "Now, I think that's a bit of a fib. After all, a man who wants nothing is either a man totally satiated, who's achieved his goals … or he's a man with no ambitions at all." The smile froze, and the Primus looked back out at the vastly changed landscape of London, so different from the one I looked out at. "This particular man … he's not lazy or shiftless. I think all his talk of wanting nothing is just a cover brought about by a desire to avoid any possible harm. Either way, a man who desires nothing is dangerous. He has no pressure points. If there's nothing he cares about, that means there's nothing you can take away from him when you need something to twist on." He smiled at Adelaide. "Do you know what I mean?"

Adelaide shot a look at Janus before returning to the Primus. "Haven't the foggiest, sorry," she said with an embarrassed little laugh. "I mean, I understand the gist of the philosophy you're speaking. I get that you're talking about a man who seems to have no vulnerabilities, but I suppose I'm still waiting for the dots to connect on why you're telling me this."

"That's a good question," the Primus said with a chuckle. "And the answer is, I'm not really explaining it to you. You're simply here because I need you to be."

Adelaide's expression grew blank. "I'm sorry?"

The Primus turned his eyes toward Janus. "You understand, don't you?"

"He is not a threat," Janus said, shrugging expansively. "He has yet to tamper with our operations, he remains at a distance from us and the balance of humanity ... I don't see why you consider him a concern. This man ..."

"You know his name," the Primus said, and any trace of amusement was gone.

"I knew his name when he had one," Janus agreed, "but that was a long time ago. He prefers to go by the name Sovereign now, as I understand it."

"A ridiculous appellation," the Primus said, glancing toward Adelaide for only a moment before turning his attention back to Janus. "A man unto himself, apart from the world?" The Primus snorted. "No man is an island."

Janus gave a sort of one-shouldered shrug, as though to express his bafflement. "Quotations from Donne aside, he wishes to be left alone. You have read my report. We should leave him be. He has yet to show any sign of interest in things that he doesn't wish to involve himself in. We currently fit that profile. Best we keep it that way."

"I don't like to have threats looming over my head unchecked," the Primus said darkly.

"It is an exception we make for the greatest of nuisances," Janus said, "to keep our affairs running smoothly. We have made this exception before, for Akiyama, and I suggest we extend such courtesy to this ..." Janus looked sidelong at Adelaide for only a beat before turning his gaze back to the Primus, "... Sovereign. As you say, he professes to have no weaknesses, no interests, as it were."

"Every man has weaknesses, has limits," the Primus said, raising a finger in front of his face and waving it casually. "This one is no exception." The Primus's close-lipped smile grew broad. "He just doesn't know them yet."

Janus stared at him somewhat warily. "And you mean to expose them … how?"

The Primus turned to look at Adelaide for just a moment before turning to the bookshelf. "Nealon."

"What about him?" Adelaide said quietly. "I killed him like I was ordered—"

The Primus eyed her as his hand fidgeted. "Let me show you something." He reached over onto the bookshelf and grasped at one of the volumes. "First edition of *Hard Times*, by Charles Dickens. Broke my heart to do this to it."

Adelaide leaned forward as the Primus pulled on the Dickens novel, and there was a click as something released, and the bookshelves slid loose, some small machinery pulling them back on a track, swiveling them open to reveal a secret room. Adelaide peered in, just around the corner into the darkness hidden behind them. It was inky, all-consuming, ominous shadows that the light of the office couldn't penetrate.

And something reached out, catching her around the neck.

She squirmed, but the grip was like a metal collar, a bare hand that held her tightly around the throat, pushing on her windpipe and lifting her into the air. It was Wolfe, in all his glory, the horror of his black eyes and feral teeth bared in fury, his hot breath on her neck as he pulled her tightly closer. She stared in shock into his eyes then kicked at him hopelessly, every hit that landed on the beast's chest as futile as a mosquito kamikaziing into a human being. Wolfe didn't even react, save for his muted expression, no joy on his face at the kill he was executing. There was a pop in Adelaide's head, and I knew he had crushed her larynx as his hands slipped free and he staggered, just a bit, while he let her slip from his grasp.

"What in the devil did you do that for?" Janus cried as he fell to his knees next to Adelaide.

"Wolfe does as he's ordered," Wolfe said gruffly, without a single ounce of the pleasure I would have expected from him.

"Because I told him to," the Primus said. Adelaide writhed on the ground, clutching her throat, but no air was getting through and I could see the light beginning to fade from her bulging eyes. She writhed in a panic, grasping at Janus.

"Why would you do such a thing?" Janus said, running a hand along Adelaide's cheek. He met her panicked eyes as they fell on his, and she began to grow still.

"Because," the Primus said, "of Sovereign."

"What in the blazes does he have to do with Adelaide?" Janus's eyes locked on the Primus. "This is ridiculous. He is no threat to us!" He waited a moment, watching the Primus carefully. "What? What do you know that you are not telling me?"

The Primus said nothing and looked one last time at Adelaide as she glanced up at him, struggling for one last breath.

Janus watched him quietly, mind calculating, and then he spoke into the quiet calm. "Nealon."

Adelaide didn't move, didn't blink, didn't breathe, lying there in the middle of the Primus's office.

Adelaide was dead.

Chapter 33

"Sorry."

I awoke with a start, feeling a presence just above me. I restrained my hands, kept them at my side, fighting them for control of a feral desire to tear the throat out of the person who was standing there. The voice had been quiet; city lights illuminated the office.

"Sorry for what?" I asked the silhouette standing over me. I slid to the edge of the couch and sat upright, leaning my booted feet down to rest on the ground as I ran my hands over my face.

"For not waking you when I got back," Breandan said. "Karthik suggested it might be best to let you sleep until Reed returned and we had a better idea of where we stood."

"Is he back?" I asked, gingerly pulling myself up, using Breandan's shoulder for leverage.

"He's five minutes away," Breandan said, holding carefully still so my hand didn't touch anything but the cloth of his shirt. "Says he's got some things that might help, guns and such. I got that, uh …" He blushed in the dark. I couldn't see it, but it was obvious by his posture. "I got the thing you asked for."

"The pregnancy test?" I needled him.

"Yeah, that." He slipped a cardboard box into my hand.

"I suppose I should go find out if I'm going to be a mother," I said, staring at the shadowy box in the dark.

"Karthik says there's a private bathroom in the corner of the office," he said, pointing to a door built into the wood paneling at the far end of the room, behind the desk and next to the window. It was almost unnoticeable, just beside what I now knew to be the old Primus's secret room.

"Thanks," I said. "I could use a little privacy right now."

"Sure thing," Breandan said with a nod. "I'll leave you be."

"Why are you still here?" I asked his retreating back.

He paused before turning to me. "I told you, I'm sticking by my guardian angel to the end of this thing."

"The end of this thing could likely mean your death," I said, looking into the dark lines around his face. The shadows in the office were concealing him well; I couldn't really see what he was thinking, his expression. "You can't tell me a lone wolf like you wants to go down swinging with the whole team."

"Ah, no," he agreed, "that's pretty low on my list of priorities, actually."

"So why not just … disappear?" I asked. "You seem like the kind of guy that'd be good at that."

He gave me a nod, like he'd expected this question. "You know, it's a funny thing. You ever have a best friend?"

"Sure," I said quietly.

"See, so did I. Great girl, she was a Siren-type, if you know what that is?" He waited for me to react, and when I didn't, he went on. "Sweetest talker you ever met. When she spoke to a man, she could wrap him around her finger as easy as you could beat the crap out of a person. That was her power. Could sing and lure a man to his destruction—or not," he said with an easy grin that was visible even in the dark. "We met when we were kids, at the cloister up in Connacht," he said, and there was a dripping of dread as he said it.

"Oh," I said. "Oh …"

"She wasn't there," Breandan said, shaking his head. "Everyone we knew, everyone we grew up with, they were there, but not her. She was here in London with me. But see, we were on a train together in the tube. I was doing my routine, and she was doing hers. She'd distract the men, and I'd rob 'em. It was a shuffle. Except something went wrong."

I could almost see the flickering lights of the train as he said it.

"We got separated," he went on. "Normal enough. The way we'd work, sometimes you had to duck onto a train at the last second, sometimes you'd have to duck off one to avoid suspicion. I got off the Central Line at Tottenham Court Road. Had to, I'd nicked a fat purse and I had a feeling my luck was about to run out because I was giving it everything I had just to get the doors to open a second early. I locked eyes with her as I got off the train. It happened sometimes, just a hazard of the business. We'd always meet up at the end of the day, back at the flat." His face went dull. "She never came back. Wholly unlike her. I knew something'd happened."

"When was this?" I asked, the quiet almost oppressive as it hung in the office's stale, musty air. My office, now.

"About a week before I met you," he said. "I'd been looking every day, see." He paused. "I knew … knew there was something wrong. Knew she was … gone … before you ever said anything about an extinction." He nodded in the dark, his head bobbing up and down slightly, as if he had no control over it. "When those blokes with the guns burst through the door of my flat, I just thought maybe my time had come up, too. Figured it wasn't coincidence, you know? When you put 'em all out, I knew it wasn't luck, either." He lifted his hand and squeezed a tight fist. "Not sure I'd much believe in luck if I couldn't toss it out as easily as I do."

I felt like an idiot, totally dumbstruck. "I'm sorry, Breandan."

"Not your fault," he said with a light shrug. "So, anyway, that's why I'm not running. She was bloody grand at escaping, a natural, could talk herself out of any trouble she ever got into. Got herself out of more tight squeezes than anyone I've known, myself included. If she couldn't outrun these bastards …" I couldn't see

his eyes burn in the dark, but I could just about imagine it, "…
then I don't think any running I could manage would get me clear
of them. Having met Weissman, I know they're the sort that are
bound to hunt you until they catch you. Until they kill you."

"Yeah," I whispered. "That's the sense I get from them, too.
Like Weissman will be working for years just to make sure he
doesn't miss a single one of us."

"I wish I could say I admire their thoroughness," Breandan
said, "but I really just hate them. I'm hoping that you'll find us a
way to stake that bastard Weissman through the face. It'd be richly
deserved, I think, and personally satisfying."

"Yeah," I said. "I'm hoping I can pull that off too." I paused.
"But I have my doubts," I conceded.

"Who wouldn't?" Breandan said. "Fella like that, able to stop
time itself, reposition himself mid-battle? Kind of hard to beat
someone who knows what you're going to do before you do it."

My eyes grew unfocused for just a moment as I thought about
that. "Yes. Yes it is, isn't it?"

He peered at me in the dark. "You've just thought of
something, haven't you?"

He broke me out of my reverie, and I looked back at him.
"Maybe. Give me a few minutes?" I waved the box at him. "Get
Reed and Karthik together, along with whoever else we need to
meet with. I'll be out in …" I looked at the box and then back at
him. "However long this takes, I guess."

"Three should do it," he said, turning to head back toward the
door. "But I'll tell them ten, just in case you decide to take a few
after." He gave me a light grin and opened the door, flooding the
room, and him, with light. I could see the redness in his eyes, the
places where they looked a little puffy, and I said nothing as he
closed the door and left me alone again in the dark.

Chapter 34

I held the little stick in my hand, the little white wand that would tell me the course of the next few months and years of my life. I stared at it, the simple, unassuming thing, as white as the tile that covered the entire bathroom. There was nothing to do now but wait.

I sat on the toilet, the seat down and putting pressure on the base of my thighs. I took a long breath, in and out, and watched the stick like it was going to sprout arms and slap me if I looked away for even a moment. I was having a hard time breathing. Each breath I took was coming in gasps.

Worried, Little Doll?

"Damned right I'm worried," I said, almost hyperventilating.

This is hardly the end of the world, Wolfe said with a Cheshire smile that I could see in my head. Ironic bastard.

It'll be okay, Zack whispered. *Whatever happens, I'm with you.*

"It's not you I'm worried about."

What is it? Zack asked.

This kid is being born into a tactically unsound situation, Bastian intoned.

"He's being born as a member of an endangered species," I spat.

Bjorn was oddly quiet as he spoke into my mind. *You are running Omega now. You sit in a seat once held by Zeus himself.*

I looked down at the porcelain seat I was resting on. "I'm on the toilet. I kind of doubt Zeus held this particular seat."

Fear is for lesser people, Bjorn went on.

"Easy enough to say when you're dead."

It's gonna be okay, Zack said again. *I'm with you. The others ... you've got a good team. If anyone can beat back Weissman and these Century clowns, it's you.*

"I couldn't even stop Winter, Zack," I said. "I couldn't fight him off, and these guys scare the shit out of him."

You didn't know Winter was your enemy, Zack said. *You know Century is. You know they're coming.*

"I don't even know why I'm fighting them," I said, waving the pregnancy test around like it could speed up the results.

Because they stand for everything you don't.

I felt my mouth go dry, and I looked down at the white testing strip again. As it began to take shape, there was a cacophony in my skull, everyone speaking at once.

—We can kill anyone, Wolfe said, *I can show you how—*

—the Primus of Omega must never be afraid, Bjorn said.

—all comes down to tactics and strategy, Bastian threw in. *Absolutely a winnable war—*

—Klementina—

I'm with you, Zack whispered.

—whatever. Kill some more people, see if I care, Eve Kappler said.

The pain in my head was overwhelming, surging so hard I almost passed out. I fell to my knees, and nausea ran through me. "EVERYBODY JUST SHUT UP!" I screamed, never wanting anything more in my life. I took control of my breathing the way Mother had taught me, slowly in through the nose, slowly out through the mouth, and the voices stopped. I eased a shaking hand up on the edge of the sink and pulled myself up, continuing my breathing exercise as the nausea began to fade. My other hand clung tightly to the pregnancy test, and I didn't look at it, afraid of what I'd find.

I looked in the mirror, my pale complexion even more washed

out than usual. I stared at myself on unsteady feet, my dark hair tangled in a ponytail that was hanging over my shoulder. I wore a tank top that was a little damp with sweat. Something Dr. Zollers had told me ages ago, back when I first met him, bubbled into my mind:

"... if you don't know who you are, it's kind of tough to know what you want ..."

I stared at the face in the mirror. I hadn't looked at myself in a long time, maybe weeks, other than just to give myself a once-over to make sure I was presentable before I walked out the door to go somewhere. The face I saw staring back at me looked older than the one I remembered, and there were lines under my eyes, dark circles. My freckled skin was still a little mottled around my right hand where I'd lost it only a few days ago in a fight with Old Man Winter.

I took another breath and let it hiss out, with less force this time. "I thought I wanted to kill Erich Winter."

The words echoed in the bathroom, and I saw a face over my shoulder in the reflection, a dark one with black eyes and a razor-toothed smile. *Little Doll does want to kill Winter.*

Another face appeared in the mirror behind me, this one handsome, his sandy blond hair as wavy as I recalled it. *No, you don't.*

"The angel and devil on my shoulders, is that it?" I looked at my face in the mirror, balanced between the other two.

Opening the ice man's veins could be so sweet, Little Doll.

Hunting him is a pointless game that wastes your time at a moment when people NEED your help.

The others started to chime in, too:

—*Klementina*—

—*tactical advantage*—

—*leader*—

—*whatever*—

"Enough," I said, calmly but with feeling, and the wave of nausea that had started to build at the cacophony of their voices subsided before it had even truly begun. "Silence." I said it as a command, and it was finally obeyed. I saw the faces in the mirror, mine, Wolfe's, Zack's, and all the others, quietly watching me. I surveyed them, saw the judgment, saw them watching with their own ideas about what I should do, how I should do it, where I should go, what should happen next—

I took a long breath, and I ignored all the rest of them, now nearly quiet compared to the deafening chorus they had been only moments earlier. They weren't silent, but I didn't hear them because there was something else pushing them to the back of my mind. A certainty that hadn't been there before.

"I know who I am." I held my fingers up to touch the mirror, right in the middle, to the reflection of the face in the center of them all. "I know who I am, and I know what I want."

With that, there was silence, and when I looked back at the others who had been standing behind me in the mirror only a moment earlier, they were all gone. I stared at the girl in the mirror, and I realized she didn't really seem all that familiar to me. Probably because she wasn't a girl anymore.

I clutched the pregnancy test tightly in my hand as I left.

Chapter 35

"I need a status report," I said as I closed the office doors behind me and stepped out into the main bullpen of Omega. The whole place smelled of dust, and I resisted the temptation to sneeze as I looked up to see little particles floating through the air that had been disturbed by the moving of cubicles. The floor that had once been filled with the cubes was now just dirty brown carpet with stains where the cubes had rested. I could almost taste the dust, the air was so thick with it. My eyes locked on Reed and I gestured to the air as I coughed. "And … can you …?"

"Sure." He raised a hand and I felt a subtle gust blow through, opening the door of one of the offices off the main room. A wall of solid dust followed it, along with a few unsecured papers, before the door slammed shut behind it, leaving us with clear air.

"You're a handy one to have when there's a high pollen count, I'd wager," Breandan said, his arms folded, leaning against the wall.

"He's also useful when you're lying on a beach in the hottest part of summer and the wind has died down," I said absently. "Where are we with everything?" I looked from Reed to Breandan to Karthik and then to Kat, who stood at one side of the room next to a gurney with Janus lying on it. "How is he?" I was surprised at how gently I asked it.

"Not good," Kat said, running her fingers through the bobbing curls of her hair as she answered me. To her credit, she didn't fail to look me in the eye, and I didn't see any of the fear I might have assumed would be there after I'd battered her so recently. "I managed to bring him back—or more accurately, to save him in the seconds before his body gave up and let him die. The problem is," her fingers left her own hair and went to Janus's, fingering him along the back of his neck, "Weissman severed his brain stem. Even though I was able to heal the majority of the damage, that's not the sort of trauma you just get over immediately." Her fingers came back to herself, to rest on the green, low cut blouse she was wearing. "I don't know what sort of problems will come from that, and I have no idea when he'll wake up. Or ..." she let her voice trail off, very tiny and far away, "... if he'll even be himself when he wakes up."

"Dammit," I whispered. "When things start to hit the fan, you're moving him out of here, right?"

Kat nodded. "I'll move him into one of the offices right now, but I'll be back. I'm not letting Century kill me without a fight."

I shot a look to Karthik. "What about you? Are we ready?"

"We have guns," he said, gesturing to a few souls who were clustered between us and the elevators in the room. The blinds were down on all the windows that could be seen outside the offices, and it left us in a space that was lit solely by fluorescent light. "We have a few people who are trained with them, and a few others who can fight with meta abilities." He nodded to the cluster of people behind him and I counted, quickly. "Seven," he said, interrupting my count. "That makes us twelve when you account for the five of us." He gave a quick sweep of the hand to encompass those of us standing in a rough semi-circle for the conversation. "We're protecting another sixteen."

"I thought there were more," I said, eyeing the offices that had the shades drawn, where I knew the others had to be hunkered down, hiding, out of the way.

"A few decided to take their chances on their own," Karthik said. "I'm only surprised it wasn't more."

"So now we just wait?" Breandan asked, turning to look between Karthik and I.

"Unless you have any plans that will allow us to launch an offensive against an enemy that we have no current ability to track," I said.

"Not really," Breandan said glumly. "I hope they come soon. The anticipation is just killing me." He paused. "Oh, wait, it's them that's going to be killing me. The anticipation is just annoying the piss out of me."

"Save some of that piss for when they get here," Reed said seriously. "After all, you wouldn't want to get in a fight to the death without wetting your pants first."

There was a laugh that rippled through the few metas behind Karthik, and I took a moment to look at them. They were a nearly equal split, four women and three men. Two of them looked terribly young, younger than me. One of them looked to be older than Hera had been. The other four seemed grouped in their twenties and thirties. "See," I said, "we can laugh. It's not the end of the world, right?" That quieted them. "Sorry. But I find if I'm not trying to laugh death in the face, I'm thinking way too hard about what I'm up against, and that's almost never a good thing. Cracking jokes helps defuse the tension for me, and I don't do my best work when I'm so stressed that I can't think straight." I looked at each of them in turn. "Also, the people I'm fighting are usually assholes, so it's kind of nice to emasculate them while you're pounding the hell out of them."

There was another laugh that was cut off when the fluorescent lights went off with a loud pop, the hum of electricity fading with them. I drew a quick breath. "Show time. Reed, rip the blinds off the windows."

I couldn't see him in the dark but I knew he had complied with my request when I felt a tornado gust rip around the edges of the room, tearing the blinds off the few external windows that weren't protected by offices. I saw some of the others come up on their own as the metas hiding within them began to lift them to let some of London's city lights shine in on us. It cast the whole room in a dim glow, the reflected lights giving us little to see by.

"All right," I said, "I want everyone behind me. I've heard Hades himself had a hell of a range, and we don't know how far this guy has to be from a person to put the hurting on them—" I glanced back behind me but heard nothing save for a grunt that was repeated from several different sources at once. I wheeled around and saw Reed on his knees next to Karthik, Breandan on his back next to Kat. The others had collapsed as well, holding their chests as though something were being torn out of them forcibly.

"The answer is close," came a voice from behind me, near the elevator. "Your great-grandfather might have been able to draw souls from miles away, but his powers were diluted by mating with Persephone." A man stepped out of the shadows, with black hair slicked back in something that almost looked like a pompadour. He had a huge belly that hung out in front of him out from under his T-shirt. He wasn't tall, he was squat, and he walked with a little bit of a limp. "Hey."

"Um, hi," I said, a little distracted. The others were falling behind me.

"I'm Raymond," he said, his eyes still in shadow from the low light. "Or at least that's what I call myself now." I caught a whiff of a cologne. It smelled cheap.

"Raymond," I said calmly, "are you gonna release my friends from your death hold or—"

"You don't need to threaten me," Raymond said. He put his hand down for a minute and I heard the breath of life return to the people behind me. "We're related, you know? Hades was my dad. We can talk for a minute."

"You don't look like the son of a god," I said patronizingly.

"I worked in a factory in Toledo until about nine months ago," he admitted. He was cool, placid even. "Weissman came along and told me what they were planning. Asked for my help." A smile broke out across Raymond's fat face as he recounted the story. "It'd been a long time since anyone wanted anything to do with me. You know what I mean, right?"

I felt a little sizzle in the back of my head. "Not really."

"Come on," Raymond said, almost abashed. "I know how metas treat your kind. Our kind. I gave up on getting a favorable reaction to my abilities years and years ago and just started hiding it. I can't imagine what it's like for someone like you." He took a step closer to me, and I could see the light fall across his gut. "You can't control it, can you?"

"No," I said, watching the light play over him. "But you can? I'd think that someone would have tried to make you an offer like Weissman's years ago."

Raymond shrugged. "They did. I've worked for governments before, sometimes, when I needed the money. I always needed time after a job, though, to get used to the voices, to ... get them integrated in, you know? To get them to listen, and shut up when they're told. It's easy to get lost in the more forceful ones." He wore a faint smile. "Hell, I remember it was a while before I learned how to keep them from walking all over me. Talking all over me."

Kill him.

"Quiet, Wolfe," I said, and he was. "I know what you mean."

"I know you do," Raymond said, so softly, his voice just desperately quiet, like he was the gentlest soul on earth. He took another step toward me, into the light. He really was a big man, and for all the threat his power carried he looked like a teddy bear, with beetle-like eyes that stared out at me in the dark. I could almost see the thirst for approval dripping from him, and I wondered how long it had been since he had really connected with another human being before Weissman had approached him. I would have guessed decades. "No one else knows how it works but us. It's close, what you go through and what I go through. Very close. The difference is just scale."

"I can't imagine having as many voices in my head as you do."

"You get used to it," he said. "It's worse with the metas. They're different than humans; their wills are stronger. They fight back harder. Dad knew some tricks with his power, could do things I can't." His face fell. "Some things you don't really see much of anymore. He didn't want to share, you see. Not that he didn't care, he just wanted to protect himself.

"I met your mother once," Raymond said, and he extended a hand again, just for a moment, and I heard a half dozen screams behind me. "Sorry." I could hear the genuine apology in his voice. "I didn't want your friends interrupting our talk, and they were starting to get their wind back."

"You knew my mom?" I asked, apparently unconcerned with the pain of my colleagues—and friends. I was torn, this tantalizing bit of my family's history just hanging in front of me.

"Just met her the once," he said. "Long time ago, when she was just a little girl. Her mom was one of my sisters."

I blinked. "Wait, what?"

"Yeah," he said with a nod, "we grew up together."

I thought about that for a moment. "But …" My eyes widened at that. "When was that?"

He thought about it for a minute. "Oh … um … 1970s some time? Seventy-one, maybe seventy-two. I don't remember exactly. Your aunt was still a baby at the time."

"But if you were both children of Hades," I said, "and he died—"

"He died before the Year Zero," Raymond said then paused. "We're kind of old, I guess, if that's what you were getting at."

I swallowed. "I didn't know my grandmother lived that long." I watched the beetle eyes. "Is she …?"

"Died in 1989. I found her last resting place in a cemetery in Michigan."

"Huh," I said, marveling just the least little bit at what I'd heard, at connections to a family I hadn't known anything about. I watched him, and he watched me. "We don't have to do this, you know."

"No, we don't," he agreed. "You should be with us. You belong with us. What Sovereign is doing—it's something that should have been done a long time ago."

I shook my head. "Raymond … this isn't right."

"Isn't right?" A lifetime of scorn was obvious in his demeanor. "What they've done to our family isn't right. Keeping incubi and succubi under their boots, suppressed—"

"Ummm, hello?" I said, as sarcastically as possible. "Suppression? You're in the process of wiping out the whole damned species of meta-humans! Do you not possess any metrics to gauge how much irony you're spewing right now?"

"We're destroying the old order," Raymond said, "to bring about a new one, a better one, for humans and metas. Omega and all their little satellites like Alpha and the Directorate, they're just standing in the way of a better world. This one is so locked into structures of power that hand it over to people like … well, you know."

"No, I don't know," I said, feeling a chill inside. "Tell me."

"You met the Omega ministers, didn't you?" he asked, watching me. "Weissman said you helped kill them."

"Not intentionally," I said tightly, "but that was how it turned out."

"If you've met them, then you know," he said. "They were never about sharing power. They were about hoarding it for themselves while the rest of us choked to death on the noxious clouds of whatever remainder they couldn't get their hands around."

I squinted at him as I tried to work through that one. "That was … uh …"

"Yeah, I think I might have mixed a metaphor a little too hard there." He took another step toward me and he was almost fully visible in the light now. "You should be with us. Sovereign … he wants you with us. He knows you'd be great, he's seen what you can do."

"I don't think he's seen what I can do yet," I whispered, looking up at Raymond.

"It shouldn't be like this," Raymond said, almost pleading. "The sons and daughters of Hades and Persephone were a family. We shouldn't be fighting. It's not right."

"Well," I said, "it's funny you say that, because," I pointed to Kat, who was lying prostrate, gasping for breath, "she's a Persephone, and you were choking the life out of her with the rest only a couple minutes ago."

Raymond's face fell, and he looked suddenly unsure of himself. "Damn. I just … I can't just go off the list, okay? The plan says …"

"Your plan says wipe them all out," I replied. "It isn't fair, it isn't just, and I kinda think it's been crafted by an effing madman."

Raymond's face showed just the slightest hint of amusement. "'Effing'? Aren't you from Minnesota?"

"When in London, do as Londoners do."

He nodded, and I caught a whiff of sadness from him. "You're not gonna budge off this, are you?"

"Let you kill my friends?" I pointed to Reed. "My brother?" I pointed to Kat. "One of your relatives?"

He didn't blink. "She's one of your relatives, too."

"I'm not willing to admit that yet." I didn't blink away from looking at him. "You say that we should band together, but you're failing to notice that my band is going to get short shrift if I join yours. How about you join mine and we go wipe out Century together?"

He shook his head slowly. "What they're doing to upend Omega and the old order needs to be done—"

"Wake up, Raymond," I said softly. "This is all that's left of Omega. Of your old order. I'm in charge since this morning, and I was their worst enemy up until a week ago. They're done. The old order has been swept aside. You guys have already won. Alpha's finished, Omega's toast, and the Directorate was destroyed in America. There's nothing left now but Century, and they mean to do more than wipe away the old world. They mean to kill off anyone who could fight against their vision of a new one."

He looked at me with those dark eyes. "I know. But it's going to be worth it. I promise."

I gave him a slow, resigned nod. "Don't make a promise you know you can't keep. It's unseemly." I gave him a little smile. "It's time."

"I don't want to do this," he said. "We're family."

"Apparently you've never seen how my branch of the family treats each other." I cracked my knuckles one by one. "I can't let you do what they'd have you do. If you're not going to stand aside, I'm going to stop you."

"It's not supposed to be like this."

"Then don't make it that way."

He shook his big head, slowly. "I'm sorry. I know what's coming. You don't. But it's all right; you'll see it for yourself, because I won't kill you."

I let out a slow, disappointed sigh. "Well, you got one of those right."

I launched myself at him with a kick that caught him in his massive belly. All the air went out of him in one second and he hit his knees. I followed with a knee to the face that rolled him over and sent him five feet into the air before he came down again, hard, on the thin carpet.

I pursued him with the viciousness of Wolfe, kicking him in the side of the face and snapping it back. The tactical detachment of Roberto Bastian told me to hit him in the head again, to impede his cognition and analysis of the fight by knocking the crap out of his brains (that last part might have been me). I punched with the white-hot anger bubbling over from years of repressed rage that waited below the surface of Aleksandr Gavrikov, and I kept myself from laughing at the joy of a fight the way Bjorn would have. I coldly determined that another kick to the face would just about put him out, so I landed one with perfect execution the way Eve Kappler would have done it—precise, on form—and Raymond hit his back, sputtering blood. He didn't try to rise again.

"Okay," he gasped, blood trickling down his face. "Okay, I give up."

Stop.

And listening to the better angel of my nature, I heeded Zack's counsel and stopped, watching Raymond shudder in pain at my feet.

"You're tougher ..." Raymond said. "Tougher than they thought you were going to be."

"That's me," I said quietly. "One of these days you'd think they'd stop underestimating me."

"I should tell you," he whispered. "I should tell you why, why they're so afraid of you—"

"DON'T!" I shouted, but it was too late.

A spurt of blood opened from his neck and he gagged, the geyser spraying into the air around me.

"I, for one," came the voice from behind me, "am not so much underestimating you as trying to maintain a realistic picture of how big of a pain in my ass you could possibly be."

I swiveled and Weissman was there, cradling his oversized knife again, wiping the blade on a cloth in his hands. It took me a minute to realize it was a patch of shirt, from Raymond. "The prodigal jackass returns," I quipped. "Where's your little sidekick?"

"She'll be along in a minute," Weissman said, polishing the blade. "You realize, of course, that every single one of your friends here is going to die before we're through?" He was thoroughly unamused.

"Why?" I asked. "Because you've put a little distance of time between the last occasion you over-milked your powers, and your time-spinning buddy isn't going to be aggravated if you halt the flow for a few more rounds now?"

"No, mostly because you've pissed me off." His eyes were hard, and he wasn't smiling anymore. "I thought about just leaving London for last, going and clearing out North and South America first. Maybe hit those last Pacific islands we've skipped over." He pointed the knife at me. "But, no. I bring our best damned resource here to London to finish the job, the last Hades-type on the planet. Do you know how long it took me to find him?" Little flecks of spittle flew out of Weissman's mouth in rage. "Forever. Just about forever. He's not quite the linchpin of our plan, but he was close. He made my life easier. Now," he waved the knife in sharp gestures around me, "I have to do this annihilation the hard way. I have to take all our people into the field and kill these last metas with overwhelming force. Because somehow you talk Raymond the mass murderer into growing a conscience." He waved the knife at Raymond's corpse. "I mean, do you believe that? He almost told you everything."

I smiled sadly, looking at the body of the man who was related to me. "I'm persuasive."

"You're a pain in my ass," Weissman said, and he pulled himself off the wall he had been leaning on. "You're a pain in my ass is what you are. And if you weren't Sienna Nealon, I would kill you over the course of several days and spread your body parts over a five-mile radius out of pure spite."

"You're not really a warm person, are you?"

"Oh, little girl," Weissman's voice was low, running over gravel, "I want to make you hurt so bad. I just want to bleed you for a while. I'd like to kill you, but I know how he'd frown on that. So I think I'm just gonna … cut all your tendons from the waist down, rip out your liver and shove it so far down your throat that you'll never even notice it's missing, then hang you from a meat hook and let you watch what I do to your friends."

I didn't smile as I looked back at Weissman. "How do I beat you to death?"

Weissman's expression of fury turned to amused disdain. "You can't. You'd be a fool to try."

He's afraid to push his powers because Akiyama will kill him if he stops time for too long, Wolfe whispered. *Make him move, make him keep using them, and he'll get irate, get sloppy. He can't freeze time for more than a few seconds at a stretch, so if the Doll forces him into a situation where he can't save himself but by using his powers for longer, the Doll wins.*

"But you just said you were going to make me suffer," I said, smiling at him. "That makes it seem like I don't have anything to lose."

He rolled his eyes. "I'm gonna make you—"

I sprang to the side, away from him, and the blast of wind that came in my wake swept him up and slammed him into the ceiling. "I'm guessing that being flung in the air isn't the sort of thing you can just 'time freeze' your way out of. Gravity and all that, am I right?"

Weissman hit the ground firmly and squarely on his ass, and I heard the crack of something. "You …"

"Me," I said, still whirling in motion as another tornado started his way from Reed, who was now on his knees. I bounded toward him, changing direction mid-move, angling toward Reed. I saw Weissman disappear in the second before the tornado hit him and he reappeared just behind Reed, his knife raised.

"Ah, ah, ah," I said and collided with him just before he could deliver the killing strike. "Shouldn't shortcut these things," I said as I cranked his arm back and heard it crack, just before he disappeared again. The only thing that had saved Reed was Weissman's desire to freeze time as little as possible. I hoped I had broken his wrist. I thought I had. It would pull some joy out of his day.

I saw a flash of movement behind me and I realized that there was a second me, dressed exactly the same, rolling off her feet in the opposite direction I was. Weissman reappeared next to her, and I saw his left hand with the knife in it this time, and he thrust the blade into my doppelganger's belly. It passed through as easily as if he'd swept it through air, and his face burned with scarlet rage.

"Rakshasa," Karthik said as he punched Weissman in the back of the head. "Did you enjoy my illusion?"

Weissman rolled to his feet and I saw him twirl the knife in his left hand. He kept his right at an off angle, curled toward him, cradled a little. I knew if I could get hold of it I could hurt him more.

Hurt him, Little Doll. His power requires intense concentration. Without focus, he cannot use it as easily. Give him something else to think about ... make him angrier. Make it personal.

Something flashed behind Weissman, and for a second I thought it was him, shifting in time. It took me a second to realize it was Karthik again, another illusion. Weissman sensed it, twitched, turned on pure instinct and flashed as he lashed out—

He missed the tornado that vaulted him into the air from behind, flinging him into the high ceilings of Omega's bullpen. He came down again with a scream as he was forced to catch himself on his right arm. I nearly winced for him. Instead, I rushed him and slammed my foot into his knee with all the momentum I'd built running toward him. I heard the snap of bone and saw the top of his shin break through skin, giving his pants a bloody stain at the knee.

"Ouch. Pretty sure that's gonna take time to heal," I quipped. "So, Weissman, how much time do you have?"

"More than you," he grunted, and the crackle of electricity filled the air.

"Oh?" I turned as Eleanor Madigan lashed out at me with a bolt of lightning that hit me in the midsection and sent me into the wall. Other flashes lit the room and I heard others flung as well; Reed landed beside me.

"Shit," he whispered, grunting in pain. "We forgot about the one that craps thunder."

"I didn't forget her," I said, "I just had to delay dealing with her. I thought the guy who could move faster than lightning was more important than the lady who threw it, at least at the time."

Eleanor Madigan's eyes were lit with the glow of electricity running through her hands in the dark room. She stood before us, and I wondered if any of the other metas who were on the floor had any ability to hit her at range with anything. Almost as though she could sense my impending order, I saw her hand rise at me, and I knew that I wasn't going to get a chance to shout for them to do something.

The blast of gunfire next to her head caught me by surprise. Not as much as it caught her by surprise, since it sent her brains out the side of her head, but it was still a little stunning. The muzzle flash lit the face of Breandan Duffy, a pistol in his hands at point blank range next to her head. Silence filled the air in the room as Madigan's body slumped, lifeless, to the ground.

"Shouldn't you have said something like, 'Your luck's just run out'?" I asked Breandan as I struggled back to my feet, muscles burning in pain.

He shrugged. "I'm a bit new to this whole fighting thing. I was too busy burning all the luck I had to keep her from noticing me. Didn't have time or thought to make a quip." He held up the pistol and then blanched at it and aimed the barrel back down. "But … I did learn to shoot someone in the head the other day, so I figured if I could do it once by accident, I could probably pull it off a second time on purpose."

"Good call," I said, striding over to him. I held my hand out and he gave me the pistol a little reluctantly. I forced a smile. "You did good. Really good. Saved our bacon. And I don't mean your crappy English quasi-ham bacon, either. I mean the really tasty American kind."

He flushed and feigned irritation. "You're just lucky you took the gun away before leveling that insult."

"Or you'd shoot me in the head?" I asked, amused.

"Actually, in the Irish tradition, I probably would have just done you the courtesy of a kneecapping."

"A kneecapping, huh?" I hefted the gun and snapped it around so fast it made Breandan step back in fear. I fired off two rounds before anyone in the room had a chance to react.

A soft moan filled the air in the shocked silence after, and Reed was the first to speak over it. "Uh, Sienna … you missed."

"I didn't miss," I said, looking down at Weissman. He had bloody spots on his belly now, and he was holding them in with his hands, clutching at his stomach. "I hit him just where I wanted to." I looked down at him. "How does it feel being gutted, Weissman?"

"Screw … you …" he said, breathing agony.

"You wish," I said coolly. "I don't think you're going to be screwing much of anything for the near future. Though I bet you'd be the world's fastest man, wouldn't you?"

He ignored my goad and took a long, seething breath. "You can't kill me—"

"I can't?"

"No," he said, grunting. "You win for now, though. But what do you think you really bought here? Time?" Little flecks of bloody spittle washed down his chin. "This is temporary. This is a poke to the eye. It's annoying. It slows us down, that's all. We're in the Americas now, and it'll only be a matter of time before we're done there—"

"A matter of a longer period of time, if I'm not mistaken," I said. "Since your mass killer is no longer available to make it easy and painless for you."

"Doesn't matter," he said, gritting his teeth. "We have other ways. We'll bring overwhelming force to every encounter. We'll crush them, break them to pieces, leave them for the crows. And eventually, we'll be back here for the rest of you."

"Listen," I said, and stood over him, almost exactly as I had James Fries only a week—and a lifetime—ago. "I don't think you understand where we're at now, so let me explain something to you." I leveled the gun at him and he watched me over the barrel. "You are my enemy now. I know who I am because I know who you are, and what you stand for is everything I will oppose to my last breath."

He licked the blood from his lips. "I'll give you credit. You're tougher than I thought. After everything you've been through, you shouldn't even be standing right now."

"The only reason I'm still standing," I said, glaring down at him over the sights, "is so I can keep myself between you and the people you want to kill. *My* people." I kept the gun barrel fixed on him.

"Between us and them is a dangerous place to be," Weissman said, and I saw his hand twitch as he tried to hold his guts in.

I grinned. "What are you going to do, Weissman? Kill me? Like I said, you're my enemy now. Maybe you can scamper away before I pull the trigger again, maybe not. But next time I see you,

I will kill you."

"That remains to be seen," Weissman said, and he tried to drag himself upright and failed. He looked back at me. "I'm done with you. *He'll* be coming for you next, you know."

"Who?" I asked, but I already knew the answer. "Sovereign?" He nodded slowly. "If you see him before I do, tell him I'll be waiting," I said, and I gave Reed a sidelong glance. "In Minneapolis."

Weissman looked back at me, eyes filled with fury as his face split into a smile. "I don't need to tell him. He already knows. And he'll find you—when he's ready."

"Oh," I said, and raised the pistol at his face. "In that case—"

I fired three times in rapid succession then stopped. I waited until the muzzle flash cleared from my eyes to confirm what I already knew when the third shot went off.

Weissman was gone.

Chapter 36

"Maybe you could have killed him sooner?" Breandan suggested.

"Maybe," I said. "Probably."

"I actually thought you were going to let him get away unchallenged," Reed said. "I thought a little bit of the old Sienna was peeking out there for a minute." His voice held just a hint of melancholy.

"Sorry," I said softly, "but no. Every instinct I had told me it was a bad idea, because that bastard is too damned hard to kill." I felt a bleak disappointment in myself. "I should have tried to take the shot sooner."

Reed gave a disappointed nod. "You really aren't the same."

I shook my head. "I'm really not. But I meant what I said. I've got a job to do, a purpose to fulfill, whatever you want to call it. I don't know if you can trust Weissman, exactly, but I think there's some truth to what he said. I don't think they're going to pull all their resources out of the Americas until they're done over there. Which means London is probably the safest city in the world for metas right now, at least in the near term."

"What would you suggest?" Karthik asked me, in near disbelief. "Bunker down and hope the storm passes?"

"Kind of," I said, and started toward the doors of the Primus's office. I could sense them all following, and I heard the soft steps of their shoes on the carpet. I threw open the doors with both hands in a very dramatic fashion and flipped the lights as I came in. I walked to the bookshelf and looked for Dickens's *Hard Times*. When I found it, I pulled on it, and it slid out only with effort.

"This is hardly the time to read the classics," Reed said.

"Is there ever a good time for that, really?" Breandan added.

The wall slid open, revealing a hidden passage. I felt a rush of air as it opened, and lights began to flicker on along the sides of the hallway. "There's always time for a classic tale," I said as I entered the passage.

"Who are you?" Breandan asked, almost mocking. "A James Bond villain?"

"No, but I think the Primus of Omega kind of was." I let my feet carry me down the concrete hallway to a staircase at the end. I glanced back to see Kat, Breandan, Karthik and Reed following behind me.

"Well," Karthik said with a little smile, "you kind of are the Primus of Omega, now."

We descended the concrete stairs into the moldy air. It was thick, and once we'd passed the first landing, there wasn't much circulating, as though the whole area was cut off from the main air conditioning system. It retained the look of an unfinished space, the walls probably dating back to the original construction of the building.

I went down, down, down. I counted six stories, even though the building was only four plus a parking garage. I figured we were down in the depths now, below the garage, and I wondered what we'd find as the stairs came to an end under a lamp that buzzed and hummed, flickering on and off.

"Wait," Reed said, cautioning me. "This could be something dangerous."

"Could be," I agreed, then grabbed the door handle and flung it open.

"And she doesn't even give a thought or care to that notion," Breandan said, peering into the darkened door ahead of me. "Very posh."

I walked through without waiting for caution to overwhelm

me, and lights began to come on throughout the cavernous room in front of me. It was furnished with height-of-the-1700s furniture, like a private apartment from the American Revolution. A gold-plated throne lay in the far corner, shimmering in the light, along with other treasures that I saw cause Breandan to just about drool on the floor.

Spread in the warehouse-sized space between us and the treasure trove were living quarters, complete with a kitchenette, floor to ceiling cabinets with some doors that led into another room, and even a set of six cots in the corner opposite the treasure. Along the wall to our left was a lab area, filled with scientific-looking equipment. In the middle of it all was an empty space where something had been, something big, and I wondered about it even as my eyes slid over six rows of filing cabinets that lay just feet away from us.

Karthik made a noise behind me. "The Primus's emergency apartments," he said, looking over the space. "I must confess, I thought they were a rumor only."

"Where did he live the rest of the time?" I asked.

"He had quite a few palatial estates," Karthik said, looking over the dim, dank space before us. "Nothing like this, of course. Places that were presentable, that allowed him to mingle with society. This space … this is …"

"It's like a little slice of heaven come to earth," Breandan said, his eyes still fixed on the gold in the corner.

"It's like the last refuge of a man who knew things were going to get really bad," Reed said.

"And who loved to … what? Experiment on people?" Kat waved a hand at the equipment along the wall. "You need your own personal science lab in your post-apocalyptic apartment?"

"Maybe," I said, turning my attention toward the filing cabinets. "Let's see what we have here." I made my way over to them, brown metal with silver trim on the handles and doors. They looked like they were from the seventies—the 1970s, in this case, rather than the 1770s like the rest of the furniture. I came to a drawer marked with a large red S in the filing label. I pulled it open, and it was empty, all the way to the back.

I frowned, then shook my head, and walked over to the drawer marked N and slid it open. Nothing.

"Looks like the Primus cleaned things out at some point," Reed said, looking over my shoulder. "Maybe he joined the twenty-first century and went digital?"

"I guess so," I said, feeling a tug of disappointment.

"You don't mind if I clean him out, do you?" Breandan said, pointing toward the gold and baubles in the corner. "I mean, they are just sitting there, and he and his whole bloody family are dead, after all—"

"Go," I said, "but be careful."

"I am the soul of caution," he said, already running with meta speed across the room.

"If he doesn't trip all over himself laying hands on that gold, it'll only be because of his meta dexterity," Reed muttered.

"Heard that!"

"Help me look through these filing cabinets," I said, pulling out the next drawer, the one marked M. It, too, was empty.

Reed and Karthik each took a side, and we started to work our way through. Karthik made a noise at the first drawer he opened, and I paused to look at him.

"Found one," he said, pulling out a thick file.

"What does it say?" I asked, standing up and leaving the drawer for L open behind me.

"Quite a bit, I'd guess, based on the thickness," he said with the trace of a smirk. "Here." He offered it to me and I took it, turning it over to look at the top leaf. It was marked with a carefully typed label, in a font that made me think it had been done by a real typewriter or a very early printer, and it bore one word to indicate what it contained.

Agency.

I stared at it for only a second before I opened it, scanning the first page, which was a letter detailing commencement of surveillance activities centered on the old Agency, the place where my mom had worked. The file was an inch thick, filled with neatly typed reports and the occasional glossy photograph attached with a paperclip. My eyes skimmed over the text but one of the glossies caught my attention immediately: a photo of a young woman with dark hair, pale skin, and freckles. Her expression was alight with a smile, and she was caught in a tender moment, with a man on her arm. He was taller than she was, handsome, rugged, and yet looked a hell of a lot like the man standing only feet to my right.

"Mom and Dad," I whispered, and I felt the tug of emotions as I glanced at Reed, who nodded. I flipped the photo over and read the caption.

Subjects S. Nealon and J. Traeger, October 1992.

"Well before you came along," Reed said to my right.

"Yeah," I said absently. The file was thick and whispered of secrets that I hungered to dive into.

"You look a lot like her," Karthik said. "Is she still …?" He let his words trail off.

"As far as I know," I said and tried to keep the regret out of it.

It took us a few more minutes to search the rest of the cabinets, but they were empty. Not another scrap of paper was in them, nothing. Kat rejoined us after looking over the laboratory area, her face locked into a look of puzzlement. "Kind of weird," she said.

I waited for a minute to see if anyone else would bite before I did. "What?" I asked finally.

"Just equipment I've never seen before." She gestured to the room around us. "The furniture is hundreds of years old, the treasure is probably from thousands of years of collecting," she nodded at Breandan as he rejoined us, sporting three solid gold necklaces and with his pants weighed down from heavy pockets, "the filing cabinets are from the seventies, but this equipment is … I dunno. Nineties, I think.

"The former Primus was a real Renaissance man," I said. "And I mean that in the sense that he should have stayed there. Look at this place. It's like a mausoleum, a crypt dedicated to a man who didn't know where the hell he belonged. For all we know, that equipment was there so he could preserve his own life, extend it. I see a man with so much ego that he couldn't see past his own nose, couldn't see the point of leaving any kind of legacy for those he was leaving behind." I looked up at the concrete ceiling. "I mean, look at the kid he left. Some punk that got dragged in from Los Angeles based on name recognition alone by the ministers, just hoping he wouldn't make waves, I guess. Did he even seem like the kind of guy who knew his father?"

I let that thought sink in with them even as it crept up on me, and I thumbed the folder in my hands open to the photograph again.

Chapter 37

"So you're really going to go back to Minneapolis, huh?" Reed's voice was calm, smooth, talking to me almost as if we were both rational people. I could see in his face that he didn't think it was okay, though.

We were back upstairs in the office, just the two of us now, me sitting on the desk of the Primus and him on the couch against the wall by the door. "I'm really going back to Minneapolis," I said.

"Have you thought this through?" he asked, trying to gauge my reaction. "I mean, this … all this, I know it wasn't what you came to London for."

I let out a faint chuckle at the irony of what he said. "I came to London for a three-month tour of duty with Omega so they'd help me track down Old Man Winter so I could kill him."

"Really?" Reed looked at me, perplexed. "So none of this thought of higher duty was around then, this faint idea that you should help other people?"

"The ghost of it, yeah," I said. "I drove through the parking lot of Southdale Mall just before I hunted down Fries. Saw the place where Wolfe killed all those people while he was trying to smoke me out. It had been rattling in my head for a while, those people who died, the two hundred and fifty-four, but I didn't know what to do with it." I rested my palm on my chest, over my heart. "I didn't know what good I could do with Omega, especially since they were the ones who sent Wolfe after me to begin with."

We sat in silence for a moment, until Reed spoke. "You're not pregnant, are you?"

I let him wait for a beat. "No," I said, my voice hoarse. "No, I'm not." I let a grim smile cross my face. "But it's okay. It's not like that would have been all I have left of him. He's still in here, after all," I said, tapping my head. "Besides, right now I feel like I'm the mother of the whole damned meta race," I said. "Like it's my job to protect them, because no one else will."

"But not to lock them in a box, right?" Reed said with a smirk.

"I think I'd like to avoid that particular parenting pitfall," I said ruefully. "Though I do hope you and the rest stay in the underground apartments for a few days." Breandan had found an emergency pantry with enough food to last for years. "Or at least until we figure out where you're going."

"The informal poll we took suggests everyone wants to follow you," Reed said, looking somewhat puckish. "Something about seeing someone beat down all your enemies, I guess. Puts the inspiration in you."

"They're all pretty much British citizens, right?" I asked.

"Right," he said. "They'll need a few days to get passports. Karthik says Omega has some connections he's familiar with, so we should be able to get them issued soon. Hopefully, we can all head to Minneapolis in the next few days."

I thought about it after he said it. "I guess Minneapolis is as good a place as any to make a stand."

He shrugged. "Beats the underground bunker, if I had to pick. Though I'm a little unclear on why you chose it."

"It's home," I said. "We'll have to find a way to start gathering metas to us without drawing Century down on our heads."

"That could be tough," Reed said, "considering you pretty much called out this Sovereign guy and slapped the hell out of his bestie. If Weissman isn't full of crap, it sounds like you're coming up on Sovereign's list."

"I'll deal with it—and him—when the time comes," I said with a wellspring of confidence that originated ... hell if I knew where. Somewhere inside. "It's not like there's anything I can do to prepare." Reed stared at me with smoky eyes, and I knew there was something he was holding back. "Come on. Out with it," I said.

I saw his tongue move within his closed mouth, as if he were licking the inside of his lips, causing them to bulge. "What if I told you ... I know where Old Man Winter is going to be in three days?"

I felt the slow tension run through my body. "Where?"

"Rome," he said. "He was supposed to meet with Hera. Obviously, she's not going to make it, but I know the time, the place ... everything. She was holding it back as a bargaining chip." He gave me that same rueful smile. "If you want to know, I'll tell you everything."

I thought about it for almost a minute, weighing everything, before I answered. "No," I said. "No. Winter's in the past. I don't have time to deal with him now. There are people who need my help."

He smiled as he looked in my eyes. "There she is. Or just a little bit of her, at least."

"Really? You think so?" I ran my fingernails gently over my face and stared over my shoulder at my own reflection in the lit window behind me. The basics were all still there but different. Somehow I looked more like ... my mom. "I guess I just don't see it anymore."

Chapter 38

"Thank you," I told Breandan as the whole of Heathrow terminal buzzed around us. Karthik had driven the five of us to the airport; they'd insisted on sending me off in style, and I didn't argue persuasively enough to convince them. Besides, Reed had argued it was smart for my safety, and I hadn't minded. It was nice not to be alone for once.

Breandan's face wore a look of measured surprise, one eye opened wider than the other as we stood just inside the ticketing area. "You thanking me? Whatever for?"

"For reminding me that not every stranger you meet is out to destroy you," I said, tugging on his hand with my left. "For letting me believe again that people are mostly good and that they need help to keep the bad away from them."

"It's funny that a thief whose face you bloodied the day you met him would be the one to teach you that," he said with a wry smile.

"I'm appreciating the irony," I said as I clutched my ticket within my right hand. "And thank you, too," I said to Karthik, "you and Janus, for showing me that not everyone from Omega is as horrible as I believed."

He gave me a pained wince. "Based on the experiences you had, I'm rather surprised you didn't kill us all or leave us to our just desserts."

"They wouldn't have been just," I said quietly, the crowd melting around me. I could sense them, the pulse of them, as they flowed around us. They were all on Century's list too, eventually. "It would have been vengeful." I looked to Kat. "And on that note

… I don't hate you anymore." I did struggle a little to get the words out, though.

Her careful concern, her bare skepticism, dissolved and she leapt forward and enfolded me in a tight hug before I had a chance to do much more than stiffen in surprise. "Oh, I'm so glad to hear it, Sienna! You know, I never forgot you, never, and I always remembered—"

"I didn't say I *liked* you," I said, shrugging off her embrace. "I just said I didn't hate you anymore." I watched her face fall and I felt a pang of guilt. "Give it time, Kat," I said, and she perked just a little. "It's … still a lot to take in."

"I followed you back then," she said, serious, her age showing once more. "If you'd been in charge of the Directorate, I would have still been following you. I only left for Omega because I knew that Winter wasn't prepared, wasn't even thinking in the right direction."

"You could have shared that with the rest of us," I said, and I knew the traces of sadness on her face were evident on my own.

I stepped back from them, my new inner circle, I supposed, and took my first step toward the security checkpoint off in the distance. "I'll see you all in a few days. Just hurry, okay?"

"We will," Reed said and stepped forward to wrap his arms around me. His embrace I didn't try and shrug off. I might even have leaned into it a little. "Just watch your back until we get there to do it for you, okay?"

"Will do," I said, blinking the little droplets of water out of the corner of my eyes.

"You're not gonna start the party without us, are you?" Breandan asked with a grin.

"I'm not in control of the party," I said, giving him a smile of my own, this one heartfelt, for once. "But when it starts, I sure could use a little luck." I gave them all a smile and a nod and got a few in return, before I turned my back and walked through the surging crowd, heading for the plane that would carry me home. "And a little help from my friends," I whispered.

Chapter 39

"Hey," I said to the figure in my dream. He was a little blurry, but the sandy blond hair was curly, like I remembered, and all around us was the barroom I had been in less than a week earlier.

"Holy crap," Scott Byerly said, looking around like he was in shock. "Is this ... are you dreamwalking to me?"

"I am," I said and the atmosphere around us rippled like the surface of water.

Scott frowned. "Am I drunk?"

I shrugged, a little mystified. "I assume so, given the last state I saw you in, but hey, maybe you'll surprise me."

"Huh," he said, looking around, clearly impressed. "Zack told me about this once, about what you guys—" He stopped and flushed, obvious even in the dream world. "Sorry."

"Told you what he and I did in dreams?" I felt the barest hint of amusement layered with wistfulness.

"Yeah," he said with a little more blush. "And I can confirm, I am definitely drunk. I think I passed out, actually."

"I need you to pick me up at the airport," I said.

His face registered surprise again, then a moment of thinking things through before he spoke. "Wait. You used your power to dreamwalk to me so you could save yourself cab fare?"

I paused. "When you put it that way, it sounds kind of bad."

"Whatever," he said. "Give me the flight number and arrival time. " I did, and he eyed me cautiously. "I can't promise I'll be awake at that time of morning, but if I am, I'll be there to pick you up."

I smiled faintly at him. "You better. Remember the last time we talked, how you said you'd fight with Reed and me if it came down to it?"

He shrugged. "I don't know, I was drunk. That sounds like something I would have said, yeah."

"Well, we're doing it. We're putting together something to stop this extinction." I looked at him with all the strength I had in me. "I could sure use your help."

"Who, me?" He pointed at himself and spoke in a voice laced with irony. "I am become Moist, the wetter of envelopes and henchman to greater powers than myself." He was subdued for a moment then I saw a little twinge at the corner of his eye, a little emotion. "But whatever help I can offer, you'll damned sure have it."

"Thank you, Scott," I said and ran a hand along his cheek before I snapped back to wakefulness. It occurred to me in the moment I awoke what effect my touch would have given him, and I felt a hint of flaming embarrassment for just a moment. But only a moment. I looked around me, around the plane. Once more I was in a middle seat, surrounded by people. This time, though, the armrests were mine. I hadn't even been nice about it. I just took them.

I stared down at the folders in front of me. One of them held a single printout from Karthik, only a paragraph long, the only record of a man named Simon Nealon that they could find in their entire database—which, Karthik privately confided in me, probably meant that there were other things in there that he was simply unable to access. Things that no one could probably access, save for Janus, who had still not woken up even as I left. I had visited him on the day I took off, but he looked so small, so shriveled, just a shell of the man I'd known. It didn't even look like him. He had been a titan of the old world, a god who had lived for thousands of years. Century had destroyed him—him and nearly all of his kind. And they were just warming up.

It'll be okay, babe, I heard Zack's voice in my head.

"I know it will," I said, just a whisper, as I opened the second folder I had brought with me, the one with the file marked *Agency*.

I could almost see his smile. *Because I'm with you?* he asked, hopeful.

"No," I replied, with just a tinge of regret at disappointing him but with hope of my own because of the true answer. "Because *I* am."

Chapter 40

I stepped to the front of the customs line hours later in the Minneapolis airport. The direct flight was a pleasant bonus, even if the reading material hadn't quite been what I had expected. I fingered the strap of my bag as I thought about the folder within it, the one marked "Agency." I hadn't quite known how to process what I'd read from it, and it had been all I could do to keep from expressing my surprise in a way that would disturb my fellow passengers.

The synthetic smell of airport air and travelers who had been cooped up in a plane for far too long hit my nose as I broke away from the strangled mass of humanity that had snaked its way through metal posts bound together by straps to form the line. The man behind the customs desk waved me forward and I walked up to him, handing him my passport.

"Anything to declare?" he asked as he took it from me and scanned it like it was a can of beans at the supermarket. It even made a little beep.

"England is a lovely country filled with lovely people," I said.

He gave me a half nod, a grudging concession as he stared down at the computer screen he had just below my eye level. "Any fruits or vegetables?"

"No."

"Did you stay in England during your entire trip?" His voice was almost mechanical, as if he'd asked these questions a time or two before. He looked up at me on this one, and I thought I sensed just the faintest amount of stress in his expression as he looked back at me expectantly.

"Yes."

With a final nod, he handed my passport back to me. "You'll need to submit to luggage inspection to make sure you're not bringing any fruits and vegetables in—"

"My word's not good enough?" I asked with faint amusement.

He smiled tightly. "Random inspections, you understand. Just the luck of the draw that your number came up." He pointed to a door beyond the luggage carousels, just to the left of the Customs exit. "Go through there, they'll be expecting you, Ms. Clarke."

"Thanks," I said, remembering Clarke was the name on my passport. I gave him a phony smile in return and headed off across the customs area. At least I knew I wasn't going to have to worry about getting caught with any fruits or vegetables.

The air was stale and the lines had stopped moving. I glanced back at the kiosks set up for travelers, but every single one of them was on a kind of hold, shuffling papers, not calling anyone else forward. I wondered if they were in the process of doing some sort of shift change but didn't give it another thought as I approached the men standing next to the door beneath the sign that declared, "INSPECTIONS," in bold letters.

They were shuffling quietly, having something that almost seemed like a casual conversation but wasn't. I could read the tension in their bodies, as if they weren't quite comfortable with each other. I wondered which of them had slept with the other's wife, but I realized that wouldn't account for the tension in both. I took a breath and smelled the same cologne on both of them, then wondered if maybe they'd slept with each other and were embarrassed by it. I chucked that distraction aside as I passed between the two of them with a weak smile at each that wasn't returned.

I entered the customs inspection room to find one man waiting for me about twenty feet away, dressed singularly unlike the rest of the customs employees. He was waiting behind a table, in a suit that was far cheaper than most of the ones I'd seen in my life, and had his shoes sticking out beyond the edge of the table in front of me. His hands were back behind his head, and he watched me with almond eyes, his Asian heritage obvious as he stared me down.

The sound of a door slamming behind me was the signal that finally drove home to me that I had landed in some form of trouble. As I turned from the man at the table to the door at his left, that route evaporated as well as eight men in tactical vests with submachine guns stormed through and lined up behind him, their weapons trained on me.

They had me. There was no way I could take them all out before they riddled me with bullets. I gave them the once-over, looking for weaknesses but seeing none that were obvious. When enough time had passed that it had been made plain to me exactly what my situation was, the Asian man finally spoke, sliding his chair back and standing, straightening his suit.

"Sienna Nealon," he said, in a deep, smooth, serious timbre, "my name is Special Agent Li. I'm with the Federal Bureau of Investigation. I'm going to ask you to lie flat on your stomach and place your hands behind you. If you do not comply with my command, I will order my men to open fire and put you down." There was a subtle shift in his demeanor. "I'm telling you this because I don't want to have to give that order. Do you understand me?"

I watched him without blinking, my head reeling as I realized he'd used my real name, not the one on my passport. "I understand." My mind raced, and I tried to find a way out of the situation. I had taken a whole line of the old gods, beaten a man who was one of the strongest warriors on the planet only a day earlier. Now I was staring down a firing line, and I realized that something Old Man Winter had told me when I'd first entered the meta world was true—the new world had changed. One man with a well-aimed gun could end me. Eight of them was almost overkill.

Also, they were cops—really, government guys—probably honest citizens trying to do their job. Almost certainly not with Century. Even if I could cross the distance between us, I had a hard time imagining myself killing them. They were innocent, in my view.

"All right, then," Li said, and extended an open palm, face down, and pushed it toward the floor. "Get down, and put your hands behind your back."

I realized it might be technically possible for me to escape. I could roll forward, and if I was lucky, only one or two of the guys would have reacquired me as a target before I was in grabbing distance of Li. As long as none of their bullets hit me in the head, I could use him as a human shield to beat the holy hell out of them one by one. It was a long roll, though, and as fast as I was, I had my doubts that I could make it.

Even if I did, people would die. These agents would die. I was used to fighting metas, people who could take a fractured skull and walk away from it no worse for the wear within a day or two. These were men, and some of them would get killed in my escape attempt. I thought back to Rick's office, of beating him down with the chair, and all the tension fled from my body. Never again. Not like that. I unclenched my fists.

The sterile air of the airport closed in on me, felt stagnant, trapped. Like me. I gave Li one last tense look and dropped my bag off to my side, then went down on my knees, then to my belly. I folded my hands behind my back and extended them, palms up.

I felt heavy cuffs click on my wrists, heavier than any standard handcuff. A moment later, Agent Li placed a leather glove on each of my hands without any resistance from me. I looked back at him with my cheek buried in the carpet, and he watched me. He was unflinching, unexpressive, totally focused on what he was doing. He slapped another pair of heavy duty cuffs around my ankles, then another. I was trussed like a hog. "All right, stand up," he said.

I felt his hand on my shoulder as I got to my feet, a little unsteadily. I tugged at the handcuffs behind my back and then the ones on my ankles and found them strong, far stronger than standard police issue. They were some other metal and extra thick. I didn't know if I could break them but if I could, it sure as hell wouldn't be easy. Damn.

"Care to tell me what this is all about?" I asked. "Because I don't remember packing any tomatoes in my carry-on. And if I did, I hope this isn't how you'd handle it."

"Funny," he said, but he didn't show even a trace of amusement.

"Seriously," I said, tugging at the chains around my ankles. "Is this really necessary?"

He put a hand on my shoulder and aimed me toward the door that his SWAT team had entered through. "For a succubus? I think we can afford to be a little overcautious." I felt my stomach sink when I heard him say it, heard him acknowledge who I was—what I was.

"Sienna Nealon," he continued, "you are under arrest for the murders of Glen Parks, Clyde Clary, Eve Kappler, Roberto Bastian and Zachary Davis."

"I …" I felt my mouth go dry, wondering what kind of trouble I was into. "I … want a lawyer."

It seemed like the room was smaller now, like the walls had closed in, like things paused. I looked at the men surrounding me, all clad in black, their faces covered by ski masks to hide their identities. My mind rocketed at a thousand miles per second with fear, with frustration. I had a duty. I had a purpose. They bunched in tighter, ready to walk me along, but my hands and legs were bound so close that I couldn't move them more than inches in any direction. I was at their mercy.

"I wouldn't worry about that," Li said as the world resumed its steady march. He took a firm hold of my upper arm and guided me toward the exit, the men in tactical vests lined up on either side of us like a formation. "Where you're going, a lawyer is going to be the least of your concerns."

I felt my head spin, and I didn't resist as he and the SWAT Team led me on a slow walk out the door into a long, dark corridor—and whatever fate they had planned for me.

Author's Note

So, I promised a longer book this time, and BAM! I deliver. I appreciate the faith of all of you who (how do I put this delicately?) didn't automatically assume I was trying to rip the hard-earned money out of your hands by selling you progressively smaller books for the same prices after Broken. Book Eight should be longer still (preview in the next couple pages).

If you want to know as soon as the next volumes are released (because I don't do release dates – there's a good reason, I swear), sign up for my mailing list. I promise I won't spam you (I only send an email when I have a new book released) and I'll never sell your info. You can also unsubscribe at any time. You might want to sign up, because in case you haven't noticed, these books keep showing up unexpectedly early. You just never know when the next will get here...

Thanks for your support and thanks for reading!

Robert J. Crane

About the Author

Robert J. Crane was born and raised on Florida's Space Coast before moving to the upper midwest in search of cooler climates and more palatable beer. He graduated from the University of Central Florida with a degree in English Creative Writing. He worked for a year as a substitute teacher and worked in the financial services field for seven years while writing in his spare time. He makes his home in the Twin Cities area of Minnesota.

He can be **contacted** in several ways:
Via email at cyrusdavidon@gmail.com
Follow him on Twitter – @robertJcrane
Connect on Facebook – robertJcrane (Author)
Website – http://www.robertJcrane.com
Blog – http://robertJcrane.blogspot.com
Become a fan on Goodreads –
http://www.goodreads.com/RobertJCrane

Sienna Nealon will return in

LEGACY
THE GIRL IN THE BOX
BOOK EIGHT

Time is running out for Sienna Nealon. The mysterious organization Century is only weeks from wiping out the entire metahuman race, but just as Sienna has made the decision to fight them, her past catches up to her and she finds herself in the hands of the U.S. Government. Secrets long buried begin to rise, though, about the destruction of the Agency, the government's metahuman policing arm, putting Sienna and everyone she cares about directly in the path of Century's plans – and in a desperate search for the two people who can help her solve the mystery of the Agency's destruction before time runs out.

Erich Winter...and the woman she calls Mother.

Coming Late 2013

Other Works by Robert J. Crane

The Sanctuary Series
Epic Fantasy
Defender: The Sanctuary Series, Volume One
Avenger: The Sanctuary Series, Volume Two
Champion: The Sanctuary Series, Volume Three
Crusader: The Sanctuary Series, Volume Four
Master: The Sanctuary Series, Volume Five*
Thy Father's Shadow: A Sanctuary Novel*
Savages: A Sanctuary Short Story
A Familiar Face: A Sanctuary Short Story

The Girl in the Box
Contemporary Urban Fantasy
Alone: The Girl in the Box, Book 1
Untouched: The Girl in the Box, Book 2
Soulless: The Girl in the Box, Book 3
Family: The Girl in the Box, Book 4
Omega: The Girl in the Box, Book 5
Broken: The Girl in the Box, Book 6
Enemies: The Girl in the Box, Book 7
Legacy: The Girl in the Box, Book 8*

Southern Watch
Contemporary Urban Fantasy
Depths: Southern Watch, Book 1*
Called: Southern Watch, Book 2*

*Forthcoming

Made in the USA
Coppell, TX
23 March 2020